A DETECTIVE CHIEF INSPE

PRETEND TO BE DEAD

NEW YORK TIMES #1 BESTSELLER **TONY LEE** WRITING AS

JACK GATLAND

Hooded Man
MEDIA
INSPIRATION • PRODUCTION • PUBLICATION

Published by Hooded Man Media.
Cover photo by Paul Thomas Gooney

First Edition: December 2023

Before LETTER FROM THE DEAD...
There was

LIQUIDATE
THE PROFITS

Learn the story of what *really* happened to DI Declan Walsh,
while at Mile End!

An EXCLUSIVE PREQUEL, completely free to anyone who
joins the Declan Walsh Reader's Club!

Join at https://bit.ly/jackgatlandVIP

COVERT ACTION

COUNTER ATTACK

STEALTH STRIKE

DAMIAN LUCAS BOOKS

THE LIONHEART CURSE

STANDALONE BOOKS

THE BOARDROOM

For Mum, who inspired me to write.

For Tracy, who inspires me to write.

CONTENTS

PROLOGUE

'You're late,' the bald man in the anorak and baker's boy cap said irritably, as Brandon Sanders arrived at Moorgate Tube Station.

In fact, it was the entrance to Finsbury Circus Gardens, a few yards down from the station entrance where the group of fifteen tourists met Brandon, their tour guide. Usually he'd meet them outside a local bar, but the building work in the area had made many of the back streets uninhabitable these days.

'I'm very sorry,' he apologised, looking around the group. 'I was detained at a previous event. But I'm here now; we're only five minutes behind schedule. And I guarantee you'll enjoy every minute of this walk.'

The man in the anorak folded his arms, watching Brandon as he pulled out a notepaper and started jotting down people's names, comparing them to a printout he had of the people who had pre-booked. There were still two people to wait for, so, at the end of the day, Brandon knew the group would still have been here, even if he'd turned up early.

The man in the anorak was annoyed again about this too.

'Hey, I know, while we wait, why don't I tell you about the area we're waiting in?' Brandon suggested. 'Welcome to Finsbury Circus, a hidden gem in the heart of London's financial district! The elegant circular garden down the road to our left was established in the early 19th century and has a fascinating history.'

'How fascinating?' the man in the anorak asked, mockingly. Brandon was disliking the man already.

'Designed by the prominent architect Charles Dance Junior in 1812, Finsbury Circus Gardens was originally intended as a private garden for the residents of the surrounding mansions.'

'Fascinating,' the man in the anorak sighed.

'What makes this place truly unique is that it was once the site of a bustling railway station,' Brandon tried to keep the conversation going, wondering where the hell the latecomers were. 'In 1865, the world's first underground railway, the Metropolitan Railway, opened its Finsbury Circus Station here, marking the birth of London's iconic Tube network. And, although the station was later moved, the circular layout of the garden still echoes the design of the railway's underground tunnels.'

There was a small murmur, but not enough to save the moment. Brandon looked at his watch, and saw that it was now ten minutes past, and the two people who had last-minute booked still hadn't arrived. Brandon decided to call it a day, and start the tour. It wasn't the first time that people had missed his tour's start. Sometimes the trains were late. Sometimes they came out at the wrong entrance. Normally, they would find him by the time he went to the first location.

'Okay, let's start. So, as part of the History of London Festival, this is a tour of the Roman parts of London,' Brandon said magnanimously, settling with ease into his tour guide role. 'Let me take you on a journey back in time, to when the Romans first set foot in London, or as they called it, Londinium. It all went down in AD 43, when Emperor Claudius sent his Roman legions to this spot. They didn't just stroll in; they built a bridge over the River Thames, and that's essentially how London started!'

Now the group smiled as Brandon nodded to the gardens.

'If you're here over the next few days, the gardens are also doubling as a gladiator arena and a jousting area, twice a day,' he said. 'I hear it's quite good.'

'It's more than quite good, it's excellent,' Anorak man said, and Brandon just smiled back in response as they started down the street, away from the park entrance and towards The Globe Pub on the left.

Of course he's seen it, he thought. *Scary bugger probably tried to leap over the barrier and fight them.*

Throwing the thought out of his head, Brandon nodded at the pub as they passed.

'The Globe Pub here is more than just your average watering hole,' he said. 'This place has been around since the 18th century when it was called "The Globe and Bull", a pit stop for travellers and traders, where they'd grab a pint and give their horses a breather along the Great North Road. But here's the cool part; Charles Dickens, the literary legend, used to hang out here in the 19th century.'

That hit the spot, especially with the Americans, who stared up at the building, as if expecting Dickens himself to appear in a window. Brandon lowered his voice conspiratorially.

'Word has it that The Globe might've inspired "The Bull Inn" in his classic novel "Great Expectations",' he whispered. 'When you step inside, you'll feel like you've entered a time machine with its old-school vibes. So, if you're into history or just want to soak up some literary vibes, make sure to pop in at the end of the tour – it's got stories to tell!'

'Were there Romans in it?' Anorak man asked. 'I thought we were learning about Romans.'

Brandon bit back a reply and smiled.

'This area of Moorgate is steeped in Roman history,' he replied coolly. 'The "Moorgate" we say so casually now, actually refers to the gate that once stood here in the city's defensive wall during the Roman period.'

He pointed at the crossroads facing them.

'This gate was a key entry point through the wall, allowing access to the open fields behind us, which were known as the Moorfields. Over time, the gate and its surroundings developed into the bustling district we know today. So, as you pass through Moorgate, remember that you're following in the footsteps of Roman travellers who walked these very streets over fifteen hundred years ago.'

On a roll now, he looked at the others.

'Imagine London surrounded by a massive protective wall, around AD 200. That was the London Wall, and parts of it are still standing today. It was like their ancient version of city defence and was what we eventually called the "Square Mile". When we turn right—'

He stopped as he looked at the man in the anorak, now yawning.

'I know that you probably know this,' he said, 'but many of the others might not.'

The man in the anorak shrugged, bored, and Brandon ignored him as they started heading down the street, the street that not only followed the Roman boundary but was also called London Wall.

'How many of you here have been involved in the festivities?' he asked conversationally. The festivities he was talking about were a three-week-long festival of London's history. The story of Roman Britain, the London Stone, and the life that Romans in London had, all the way through Tudor times and Shakespeare, the Great Fire of London and the various plagues, and ending with World War Two had been a creation of somebody in the City of London's marketing department; probably someone who realised one day that the Guildhall was based on the top of an amphitheatre.

Over the last couple of days, they'd had chariot racing down the Strand, re-enactors performing Civil War battles and even a battleground of some kind had been built on the cricket pitch of the Honourable Artillery Company in Shoreditch for some kind of Roman and Iceni battle on Sunday, which had apparently caused major issues with the grounds people.

Obviously, this wasn't as authentic as it could be, there wasn't anyone being put to death, and there were no Christians being eaten by lions. But it was a good enough event to show how things were done back in Roman times, and it gave tour guides like Brandon a little extra money.

He couldn't wait until Wednesday when he could do a talk on Jack the Ripper. Those were always popular walks.

As they started up the London Road, Brandon paid more attention to one tourist in his group, a very pretty young blonde woman who, from her occasional accent, seemed to be from Sweden or some other Scandinavian country. She was with a female friend, and this gave Brandon hope she might be on holiday without a man and, more importantly, looking for *another* man to fill that vacancy.

Christ, I hope she's not gay.

'Is this part of the wall?' she said, pointing to a piece of ruined architecture on their right.

'No,' Brandon shook his head. 'This is Elsing Spiral, which was originally a hospital beside St Alphage's Church, next to the wall, built in the thirteen hundreds by a merchant named William Elsing, mainly for blind beggars and paralysed priests. Henry the Eighth closed it down, though.'

'Was it destroyed in the bombing?' Sexy Swedish girl asked.

'What, World War Two? No, this burnt down one Christmas in the sixteen hundreds, and was left like this ever since,' Brandon smiled. 'What we're looking for is actually up here on the right, close to a car park, believe it or not.'

There was a laugh at the thought of Romans and modern-day cars, causing a juxtaposition for the tourists.

As they continued, Brandon pointed across the road.

'Down there is Silver Street. William Shakespeare once lived there. Obviously, we're not talking about that today,' he added, giving a pointed look to the man in the anorak. 'But if you come along on Thursday, I'll be doing a talk about Shakespeare, Tudor times, and one of the great plagues of London.'

There was a moment of interest in this, and Brandon smiled. He wasn't averse to advertising his other talks while doing this. After a few more yards, the chrome and steel buildings surrounding them and the bridges above faded away as they headed towards the onetime Museum of London. Now, it was nothing more than an empty space, likely to be bulldozed down for more houses or apartments.

At this point, a couple ran across the road, joining them; a woman and a man. The woman was short, with a biker's jacket and a pink beanie, the man almost a foot taller, with long black hair, bearded and wearing a battered olive army jacket.

'Sorry we're late,' the woman said. 'Rolf and Susan. We're on the list? It was booked by someone else though, so I'm not sure if you need the email.'

Brandon pulled the sheet out, ticked them off, and nodded.

'You're just in time,' he smiled, waving everyone on.

He didn't notice the two arrivals glance at Anorak man, as if surprised he was there.

To the right, after the covered and modern 140 London Wall, there was a little pathway, a small roadway that led down to the left, and an underground car park.

'Come with me,' Brandon said. 'Let me show you a part of the Great Roman Wall of London.'

Walking down the roadway, ignoring the concrete barrier and garden on the right, Brandon pointed to a sizeable chunk of ancient stone ahead of them. It was a tall, broken structure, a couple of storeys high and the remains of the tower, with its patchwork of stone and brickwork dating from between the 13th and 19th centuries, looked strangely out of place here.

'This was one gate of London,' Brandon started his patter. 'Soldiers would walk the perimeter of the wall every day, checking for attacks. Now, I know it looks a tad weathered, but consider its age and you'll appreciate how well it's holding up, eh? It's made from Kentish ragstone, and trust me, the Romans didn't mess about when they built things. It's like the olden days meeting the modern era.'

'How many gates were there?' Sexy Swedish Girl asked.

'Well, technically there are seven,' Brandon replied with a tap of his nose. 'Seven openings in the Roman wall which controlled what entered and exited the medieval city. Moving clockwise, they're Ludgate, Newgate, Aldersgate, Cripplegate, Moorgate, Bishopsgate and Aldgate. But ...'

He lowered his voice, as if this was a massive conspiracy.

'There are actually two others which open onto the River Thames: Billingsgate, which was the old market where fish were landed, and the infamous Traitors' Gate in the Tower of London, both built into the Roman wall, and both technically gates.'

He waved off to the south.

'In fact, we'll be visiting Cripplegate next,' he said. 'As you're taking selfies with this tower gate, just think of all the stories it could tell if it could talk. Between skyscrapers and busy streets, this relic's a neat reminder that London's always been a hotspot, even when folks wore togas and sandals.'

'What's that over to the right?' Anorak man asked, glancing over the wall, and looking into the dark area of grass behind the ruin.

'Oh, that's the gardens of the Barber-Surgeons' Hall,' he said. 'In fact, there's an interesting story here—'

'No, no,' the man interrupted, getting a little irritated with Brandon's responses. 'I mean ...'

He pointed to the side of the multi-century brick wall.

'On the grass, there, lying face down.'

Brandon followed Anorak man's finger and saw that on the grass was a figure, lying face down as described and with something jutting out of his back – making him look in the darkness like some kind of weird shark, going through the grass.

Brandon walked closer, pulling out his hand torch and turning it on.

It was a Roman soldier; a young man in what seemed to be full Legionnaire's uniform, with what looked like a battered old Gladius blade sticking out of his back.

'Oh, for God's sake,' Anorak man snapped. 'If I knew we were going to have actors on this walk, I would have done something else.'

Brandon looked back at him.

'What?' he asked, uncomprehending.

Anorak man pointed back at the body on the floor.

'That. "Oh, look, I was a Roman soldier, and I was killed in some battle." Come on, mate. Get up and tell us your story then, so we can move on to something more interesting.'

Nothing happened, and Brandon stared back at the Roman soldier lying on the floor.

'Buddy, I don't have actors on my walk,' he said. 'I've got no idea what this is.'

He looked around quizzically. Could this be some *other* event happening and no one had told him? Was the Barber-Surgeons' Company doing something on their grounds and this was simply bad timing? There didn't seem to be any other re-enactors around. The man in the Roman uniform was obviously an actor, after all. There was no way an actual Roman had travelled through time to appear.

Sexy Swedish Girl walked over and stared down at the body.

'He's dead,' she said matter-of-factly.

'How would you know?' Brandon asked.

'Because he has a great big sword sticking out of his back,' she replied, looking back at him. 'I think we should call the police.'

Brandon nodded, staring back at the Roman soldier. The costume looked nothing more than something you would buy in a fancy-dress store, but the sword was different. The sword looked genuine ... and old.

Brandon felt a shudder of fear slide down his spine. Looking at the pink-haired lady's horrified expression as she stared silently at the body, Rolf's arm around her protectively, he knew he wasn't the only one.

'I think that's the end of today's talk,' he said. 'Thank you for coming. I need to call the police right now. Maybe you should return to The Globe and wait. It's warm there, and I'm sure the police will want to take statements.'

'Bloody marvellous,' Anorak man muttered as he turned and stormed off. 'I hope we get a refund for this.'

Brandon didn't have an answer. For the first time in a very long while, he couldn't think of anything to say.

He looked back at the body as he pulled his phone out, but then smiled.

It was sad, but one thing it meant was that the next talk he did here would be *packed*.

1

STAG FRIGHT

As far as stag nights went, Alex Monroe's was quite tame, if Declan was being honest. However, this wasn't actually what one would call a stag night. It was more like a gathering of people to "wish the old man luck on his oncoming wedding that weekend."

Amusingly, the Temple Inn Detective Superintendent had used his connections to old cases to provide the location for the event. A city restaurant named *Essence* had been closed for the day, and its owner and head chef, Harnish Patel, had allowed Monroe and his friends the place for the night – which, considering Temple Inn had helped him avoid a very nasty Tetrodotoxin charge, and had even assisted him in taking over the business after the Houses of Parliament attack a year or so earlier, was a very small price to pay.

Declan hadn't been here since the case, but Monroe had apparently found it quite relaxing and had dined here frequently.

There was no three-star Michelin food that evening,

however; it was more of a buffet situation. Monroe hadn't been sure how many people would turn up and didn't want to pay out for a bunch of meals that no one was going to eat, so had planned something simple. Harnish had said "hello" at the start and then disappeared, allowing the congregation of mainly police to deal with what they needed to do.

They liked that.

Declan was there, as was Billy, De'Geer sitting in a corner chatting to DCI Freeman, his onetime superior, while DCI Farrow – recently married to Declan's ex-wife – was doing his best to be cordial, but keeping a small distance.

Declan understood this; the last time he had seen Farrow, the man had been kidnapped and almost killed.

There were a few more people from the unit: Commander David Bradbury was there, chatting away to DCI Hendrick, down from Edinburgh, and to Declan's amusement, the MP for Bethnal and Bow, Johnny Lucas, was there with some friends. If this had been a year earlier, it would have been the "Eastern Crime Lord Johnny Lucas," but now he was respectable, and this meant he could attend police events like this.

DCI Esposito, SFO Andrews and several other people had also appeared throughout the evening, some staying, some arriving and leaving. And in general, it had been a fine event.

Monroe had expressed nerves about marrying someone like Rosanna Marcos; after all, this was a woman who, if she was angry at you, could kill you and hide your body in a dozen different ways. But the things they had gone through together already, meant there was a strong chance the pair were ready.

Declan's phone buzzed; he looked down and saw it was

from Anjli Kapoor. She was annoyed that she couldn't attend the stag night, instead being forced to attend Doctor Marcos's hen night, which apparently seemed to be some kind of lecture series at Bart's Hospital. Declan smiled and typed a reply, suggesting that instead she escaped the event, placed a fake moustache on her face, and came to the restaurant. But this suggestion, when mentioned to the others before sending, had been met with a cacophony of boos and cries of "men only", many of these from Derek Sutton, who had come down specifically from Scotland for this event – although pointedly not with Hendricks – and strangely, for nothing else. Declan didn't trust Derek and knew that he'd now be in London for the week leading up to the wedding, and a week in London for Derek Sutton was something very dangerous.

There'd even been a message from Charles Baker, something along the lines of *'sorry I can't be there, but you get why I can't, right?'*

Nobody had really expected him if Declan was being blunt.

There was one more guest, an unexpected one, who turned up about two hours into the event.

Tom Marlowe was Alex Monroe's de facto nephew, having been the son of an MI5 operative who had worked with Monroe several years earlier. Who, when she died in the Seven-Seven attacks, Monroe's then-wife, DS Emilia Wintergreen, had replaced in the top-secret *Section D*, in the process erasing her existence from all official channels in 2011, and leaving Monroe with nothing but photos; no proof that they were even married – or that she'd ever existed.

It had been tough, and Declan had learned over the years that Monroe and Wintergreen had been on the verge of breaking up, anyway. Other issues had happened, and she'd been having an affair at the same time. But it'd still been hard, and one reason why Monroe was so hesitant to marry again.

However, Marlowe, being a kind of adopted nephew, had been around a few times and had even assisted Temple Inn on a few cases, most importantly, the "Red Reaper" case where Karl Schnitter had been placed in an MI5 black site on Declan's request. This had, however, backfired when Schnitter had been freed by Trisha Hawkins and a team of Phoenix mercenaries, the attack leaving Tom Marlowe critically injured, something that had affected his career ever since.

Marlowe smiled when he embraced his uncle, and gave Monroe a bottle of very expensive brandy, claiming it was a "gift from the CIA." Which, knowing Marlowe, it probably could've been. He passed apologies for not spending more time with Monroe recently, explaining that there'd been a bereavement in his own family; an estranged father he hadn't really known much about. Then he'd wandered over to Declan, grabbed a drink and sat down beside him.

'Good to see you, Declan,' he said. 'How're you doing?'

'Okay, as can be,' Declan smiled. 'You look a bit distracted.'

'I'm waiting for confirmation of something,' Marlowe said, checking his phone again. 'If it comes the way I think it will, I don't think Uncle Alex is going to be happy.'

Declan wanted to know more, but also knew that Tom Marlowe was very good with secrets – and if there was something that was about to happen, he wouldn't be told until the moment it was about to happen.

Declan leant back in his chair.

'I understand you screwed over Trisha Hawkins?' he said.

'Yes,' Marlowe replied with a smile. 'I screwed up Phoenix from it as well. Hawkins... well, I don't think she'll be holding any important jobs for a while.'

Declan raised a glass.

'That's appreciated,' he said. 'So, we need to talk about Karl Schnitter.'

'This is connected to the favour you asked, right?' Marlowe lowered his voice. 'I'm sorry I couldn't help at the time. I was saving a Presidential candidate from assassination.'

'I saved the Queen once,' Declan shrugged. 'And the Prime Minister. All the Cabinet, too.'

'It's not a contest,' Marlowe laughed. 'Tell me about the "old friend" you mentioned.'

Declan leant closer.

'I had a message given to me a couple of weeks back,' he said. 'A German Kriminalkommissar we'd worked with on the Schnitter case. She told me that in Germany, a friend of hers who was connected to what had been going on at the time had been given information. Schnitter was provided a new life in the USA. A car mechanic in Lombard, near Chicago. She said about a month ago there was an accident, a car crash. His tow truck exploded, and he was burnt to death.'

Tom narrowed his eyes.

'Body?'

'Apparently the DNA matched,' Declan replied. 'But you know how that goes.'

Sipping at his drink, Marlowe considered this.

'Two options. One, the CIA has decided to take him somewhere else. It's common enough. Or two, he got bored with his life and planned his own escape,' he said as he looked around the restaurant, as if expecting Schnitter to appear. 'The question, of course, is why. The second question is whether he's in America still.'

'You don't think the car explosion killed him?'

Marlowe glanced at Declan with a chuckle.

'We both think he's still alive,' he said. 'And if he is, you need to be careful.'

Declan shook his head.

'The last time I spoke to Schnitter, he was clearing out some loose ends before giving himself up. He said he believed in justice.'

'Yes,' Marlowe nodded. 'But he paid his dues, as far as he's concerned. He did his witness relocation and there's a very strong chance that he might believe he's paid all his debts. If that's the case, then the Red Reaper might return – and if he returns to England, he might come back to finish anything else he needs to do.'

Declan felt ice slide down his spine, but kept quiet as Marlowe continued.

'I'll keep an eye out for you. But you really need to do the same for yourself. If Schnitter is alive, then he's likely created himself a new identity, something that can get him out of America. We need to work out what it is.'

He went to carry on, but then his phone beeped.

'Sorry,' he said. 'I've been waiting for this. It's from Trix.'

'How's she doing?'

'She's on sabbatical. She's deciding her future.'

'And you? I hadn't asked if you are happy with where you are.'

'Well, I'm no longer in MI5,' Marlowe shared. 'I mean, I probably could still enter the building, but I'm on a kind of suspended sabbatical of my own. Apparently, I'm part of an organisation that MI5 wants to destroy.'

'How did you manage that?'

'Family gift,' Marlowe shot back distractedly, reading the message.

'Not going back to Section D? Wintergreen will be annoyed—'

'She doesn't want it anymore.' Marlowe was still reading; the text was lengthy. 'She's been given a slightly bigger role at the moment at MI5, Whitehall head of station; a little more public and it's …'

His face darkened.

'Shit,' he muttered. 'I'd really hoped this wasn't the case.'

'What?'

Tom didn't reply, instead just showing Declan the message.

'Yeah, that's not great,' Declan nodded after reading it in its entirety. 'Do you want to be the one to tell him, or shall I?'

'I'll let you,' Marlowe replied, tapping on his phone. 'I don't really want to be here when he hears this.'

He finished his drink, tapped Declan on the shoulder and left out the back entrance, doing what was known as an "Irish goodbye". A second later, the message Tom Marlowe had received, now forwarded on to Declan, appeared on his phone.

Declan sighed, got to his feet and approached Monroe, who was currently telling some tall tale to a group of officers.

'Might I have a word?' he mumbled.

Monroe turned to face him, visibly irritated that his story

had been interrupted, but said nothing the moment he saw Declan's expression.

'What's happened?'

Declan looked around. He decided there was no point waiting or trying anything else. This was something that was going to affect Monroe no matter what.

'Tom was waiting for a response from Trix, a message about a concern he had. He left before telling you, but he's asked me to pass it on.'

'Well, that doesn't sound ominous in any way,' Monroe said. 'Super spy Tom Marlowe running from telling me something.'

'It's about Emilia Wintergreen,' Declan said. 'You know when she took over Section D she had to go dark, and she had the government remove all of her data – schooling, university, the police, even her marriage to you. Everything was removed and disappeared.'

'I am aware,' Monroe said tersely. 'I lived through it.'

'Tom had a message,' Declan said, showing his phone. 'He'd already told me Wintergreen no longer ran Section D, and in fact was now running something a little more important in MI5. Apparently, she's now head of station in Whitehall, so she goes to COBRA meetings and speaks to the Prime Minister personally.'

'She did that anyway when she ran Section D.'

'Yes, but this is a little more public friendly,' Declan said. 'Because of that, you can't have a ghost in the role. The text confirmed it; the moment she accepted the job, they unlocked her files.'

'What do you mean *they unlocked her files?*' Derek Sutton asked, eyes wide.

'He means when they wanted her to have no existence,

they didn't exactly *wipe* her existence,' Billy responded, taking the phone from Declan and reading the forwarded message from Trix. 'It looks like they placed everything in a box and stuck it in a vault. And now it's been removed. Emilia Wintergreen exists again in the public domain. Her police record is back ... and so is her marriage certificate.'

At this Monroe rose, facing Declan.

'Are you telling me, laddie,' he asked bitterly, 'that because Wintergreen has got a bloody promotion, I'm now *married* to her again? I can see why Tom didn't want to be the one to tell me. What am I supposed to tell Rosanna?'

'That the wedding's postponed?' Declan suggested. 'I'll be honest, there's no way you can get married this weekend if you're still married. I'm sure you can find a way of getting some kind of annulment ...'

He let the message drift off. He didn't need to continue; Monroe knew exactly what he was talking about.

'Bloody hellfire,' Monroe muttered. 'She's going to be livid about this. I need to ...'

He stopped as his phone beeped.

At the same time, Declan's and Billy's phones beeped, and a scream, some kind of battle cry, came out of De'Geer's phone.

De'Geer looked up apologetically.

'Sorry. It's my message tone,' he said.

Declan checked the message. It was from Anjli.

> Hen and stag over, murder called in. Roman soldier found on London Wall.

Declan wondered whether this was a joke, but that everybody else had received it meant it was deathly serious.

'Laddies, you're welcome to stay here this evening, but I'm

afraid I must go to work,' Monroe said to the others. 'That said, if any of you high-ranking officers want to come with us, you can scare the shite out of the local plod.'

DCIs Freeman, Esposito, and Farrow smiled.

'Sure,' Esposito said. 'We've got nothing else to do. Let's take this stag party to a crime scene.'

2

CRIME SCENES

IF THE MURDER SCENE BY LONDON WALL WASN'T A CARNIVAL before, the comprehensive collection of police detectives that turned up certainly made it one. Doctor Marcos already had a tent around the body, positioned next to the Barber-Surgeons' Hall. Anjli, in her more official capacity as DI Kapoor, was managing crowd control, with PC Esme Cooper beside her.

'Tell us what we have, Detective Inspector,' Monroe said as he approached.

'Detective Superintendent, Detective Chief Inspector,' Anjli said to Monroe and Declan, strangely more official than she usually would be. Declan realised it was because she was now surrounded by an absolute convention of Detective Chief Inspectors, and probably felt a little intimidated.

'The body was found an hour ago by a tour guide and his group,' Anjli explained, leading them towards the tent. 'They were doing a Roman London walk because of the festivities.'

'Festivities?' DCI Freeman asked.

'Someone in the city decided that we should have a three-week-long festival of the history of London,' Declan explained. 'Starting all the way from the Romans up to World War Two. We have days based on Shakespeare, we have Romans, we have Civil War re-enactors … there's a whole tonne of events going on. There are even gladiators fighting every day of the week for our amusement.'

'Sounds wonderful,' Freeman deadpanned. 'I can't work out why people would want to kill each other over it.'

'Well, I don't think this is that—' Declan started, but then paused as he saw Anjli shake her head.

'No, DCI Freeman's right,' she said. 'We think he was killed exactly because of that.'

She nodded at the tent.

'Inside there is Adam Harris, thirty-five years old, Chartered Accountant by day, re-enactor by night. We think he was part of some Roman re-enacting group, an offshoot of the Brittania re-enactors, and he was part of the festival.'

'As what?' Declan asked.

'He was one of the gladiators in the arena, over at Finsbury Circus Gardens,' Anjli nodded back up the roadway, back along the London Wall road. 'It's a ten-minute walk from here, so not that far. Obviously, we weren't expecting to find him actually dead after his bout.'

'I'd hope not,' Declan said. 'I know it's a gladiator ring, but I thought it was more "showing how the gladiators worked" and things like that than actual murders.'

'Do we have any clue what's going on?' Monroe asked.

'I reached out to the organisers to find out what the situation was,' Anjli shrugged. 'All I can think is maybe the person he fought with today wasn't happy about the outcome, and made it a more personal vendetta.'

She stopped as Doctor Marcos emerged from the tent, pulling off a pair of blue latex gloves.

'Ah, so your group of miscreants finally made it then, I see,' she said with a smile. 'Bloody hell, you brought the lot! Hello, Henry,'

DCI Farrow nodded in return.

'Sorry to break the stag night up,' Doctor Marcos continued. 'I know you're probably in the midst of some japes and frivolity.'

Monroe weakly smiled, and Declan wisely kept his mouth shut as Doctor Marcos continued.

'The body was stabbed in the back, and from the looks of things he fell forward, died almost instantly. There are defensive wounds, but we don't know if that's from the attack, or his day being a gladiator.'

'He'd have defensive wounds from the make-believe fight?'

'Well, you know, bruises and scratches. They might be mucking around, but most of them actually use blunted metal swords. I'm not too sure what level the re-enactment was here,' Doctor Marcos pursed her lips. 'He could have caught the occasional smack across the temple or on the arm. The Roman uniform was bare-armed and bare-legged, so could have been that. And an attack from behind usually demotes surprise, so I wouldn't have expected wounds.'

'Unless he fought, turned to run and then was stabbed?' Anjli suggested.

'True, that's possible,' Doctor Marcos admitted. 'The problem we have, though, is the uniform he's wearing, that of a Roman legionnaire, wasn't the one he was wearing in the gladiator pit. Apparently, he was looking a bit more like Spartacus back then.'

She looked back at the tent.

'I suppose it's horses for courses, really,' she said. 'It's the blade I'm interested in.'

'How come?' Declan asked.

Doctor Marcos nodded over at Sergeant Morten De'Geer, who had emerged from the tent with the Gladius in his hands – or, rather, the Gladius in an evidence baggie big enough to hold it.

For a second, Declan found himself having a flash-back at the sight of a tall blond Viking man with a sword in his hand, bringing some kind of primeval ancestral memory, but he shook it away quickly as De'Geer approached.

'I need to get an expert to look at this,' Doctor Marcos said. 'Although it's a Roman Gladius and from the looks of things, I don't think it's recently made, or a re-enactor's weapon.'

'What do you mean?' Anjli frowned. 'You think it's the real deal?'

Doctor Marcos looked at Monroe.

'No, because then it'd be nothing more than rust, but it's definitely a few hundred years old. If that's the case, then it's worth thousands in the state it is in, and to leave it in someone's back ... well ...'

'It's a pretty personal message,' Monroe finished. 'Do we know somebody who could look into this?'

'I can ask around,' Doctor Marcos said. 'But I was hoping Billy might be able to help with that.'

'Why me?' Billy asked, keeping to the back of the group, and then slowly sighed as realisation crossed his expression.

'Uncle Chivalry.'

'Could you call him?' Doctor Marcos asked. 'I seem to

recall from a conversation we had the last time he was saving your arse, that he dealt with a lot of old antiquities?'

'Occult antiquities, sure,' Billy replied. 'This is more of a historical "British Museum" level of enquiry.'

He paused, sighed, and continued.

'But he's worked for them as well.'

'Chivalry Fitzwarren worked for the British Museum?'

'Well, I say worked, but I mean more infiltrated and stole from them. So it's kind of a mixture,' Billy sighed. 'I'll give him a call. He's probably already waiting, with his network of spies telling him what's going on.'

Declan looked around, once more taking in the scene.

'I'm guessing there weren't any witnesses?' he asked.

'Only the people that found the body, actually,' Anjli replied. 'And they were on a tour, had only just arrived.'

'Barber-Surgeons' Hall was having an event, but they weren't going out onto the gardens, and so they wouldn't have seen either,' Cooper added, reddening as she realised all the DCIs were now staring at her.

Declan glanced behind, looking back at the carpark.

'How about CCTV?'

'I'll look into that,' Billy was already noting this down.

'I don't have a time of death yet,' Doctor Marcos was staring back at the tent now 'Davey's having a look.'

'DC Davey's here?' Declan frowned at this. 'I thought she quit the force and now works with Ellie Reckless?'

'She does, but she was at my hen night, and I decided I'd take whatever help I could get,' Doctor Marcos squared up against Declan, but then relaxed as she realised he wasn't starting a fight. 'Sorry, long night. But a rough estimation is probably an hour or two before they found him. He was still quite recent, but the blood spatter from the blade doesn't match the ground.'

'So, he wasn't murdered here?'

'No,' De'Geer replied. 'In fact, from the looks of things, they stabbed him with that blade in the back and then brought him here to be left.'

'Carried with the blade in his back? That has to have been difficult,' Monroe mused.

Doctor Marcos shook her head.

'It looks like there are multiple wounds in the back,' she replied. 'At least two, most likely from the actual attack itself. My current working hypothesis is they rammed it in, pulled the sword out, drove him to where he needed to be left, and then stuck the sword back into the necrotic tissue. A kind of stabby Hokey-Cokey.'

'If that's the case, he could easily have been driven to the car park in a van or in a car's boot, taking him out once they got here,' DCI Freeman said, looking around. 'There's no reason anyone would suspect a car driving down to the car park was anything more than just a car driving down to the car park.'

'The ramp and the wall beside it hides anything from the cars outside,' DCI Farrow added, as he looked around. 'Maybe you could get something from the surrounding buildings, but I'm genuinely not sure what you're going to do here.'

Declan straightened. As much as he appreciated the input from his onetime boss and others, there were definitely too many cooks here right now.

'I think we're going to have to wait for forensics to give us more to this,' he said. 'We also need to speak to the person who organised the gladiator games, see if there was any bad blood between combatants.'

'You think this could be revenge?' Monroe asked.

'It's pretty bloody specific, you have to admit,' Declan shrugged. 'It's the best we have right now, boss.'

'I suppose we ought to go back to the restaurant then,' DCI Farrow shrugged. 'There's nothing else to do here until Doctor Marcos has worked her magic.'

'That's a polite way of saying "before Doctor Marcos kicks us out", isn't it, Henry?' Doctor Marcos smiled.

DCI Farrow didn't reply, looking innocent.

'We should check around while we're here,' Monroe shook his head. 'This is fairly recent.'

'Oh, absolutely, Alex,' DCI Freeman said. 'You guys can do that. We're going back to our stag night, as too many feet on the ground trample everything down. There's good food there and free drink.'

Declan chuckled at Monroe's expression. It was almost as if Farrow's words had cut to the quick of his soul.

'You would go to my stag night without me?' he asked.

'Well, it's not really a stag night anymore, is it—' Farrow started, before stopping himself.

But it was too late.

Doctor Marcos, hearing this, glanced over.

'And why would that be?' she asked sweetly.

Monroe gave a daggers glare at Farrow, who gave an apologetic look back at Monroe, now taking Doctor Marcos by the arm.

'I think we need to have a chat,' he said. 'Let's go for a stroll towards the river.'

'There's no river here.'

'Well, whatever that water is over there.'

Doctor Marcos, suspicious, sighed and followed him off from the others, stopping about twenty yards from everyone.

Anjli looked at Declan.

'Problems?'

'Oh, you can definitely say problems,' Declan replied. 'I'll explain more when we get back to the hotel. I don't really want to say anything here.'

He looked back at Monroe and Doctor Marcos, now deep in discussion.

'I think they'll try to keep this a little secret at the moment,' he continued. 'It's not something that everybody ...'

'She *bloody did what?*' Doctor Marcos yelled at Monroe, standing there patiently as she looked around the garden, as if looking for something to throw. 'I'm going to *kill* Emilia Wintergreen. How dare she screw up my wedding!'

'Or,' Declan smiled, looking back at Anjli, 'I can just tell you right now, it seems.'

3

OLD FOES

DECLAN AND ANJLI HAD BOTH STAYED IN LONDON THAT NIGHT, rather than return to Hurley. Both had believed that their nights would be rather drunken and filled with debauchery – or, more likely, just too drunk to drive back. The trains would also have stopped by the time they ended, and a cab to Berkshire was unthinkable. The following day was a Saturday, and as planned, neither of them were intending to go to work, so they'd drink, meet up at the hotel, pass out and snore, and then drive back the Saturday morning.

This, obviously, had now changed, but the hotel they'd booked in the City of London was still a place they could go back to and ruminate on the night's events.

Anjli had given Declan an update on the hen night, pretending in the process that she'd enjoyed it, but Declan could see that an evening of pathology discussions and lectures wasn't quite her cup of tea. Whereas when Declan had informed her of everything that he'd been told, including the conversation with Tom Marlowe about Karl Schnitter, she pouted, and complained that the moustache option was a good idea, and his event sounded way more fun than hers.

'Well, we thought he might be back,' she eventually said, after sitting on the bed and eating the fries from their hastily gathered dinner. 'After all, Margaret Li told us that. Do you think we're in trouble?'

'I don't know,' Declan said. 'I felt we had some kind of truce at the end, an "enemy of my enemy" kind of thing.'

He looked out of the window across the skyline of London from their high-storey hotel room.

'But this is still the man who caused the death of my parents.'

'He killed your mum because she asked him to,' Anjli paused eating. 'And it was his daughter who effectively killed your father. But, he had a hand in both, I'll agree.'

'You're defending him?'

'No, just adding context. He was a murdering, psychotic bastard, but he had his moments.'

She sat back on the bed, considering the situation as she fed another handful of fries into her mouth.

'If he's back, we need to take him in,' Declan said.

'You tried your way, and it didn't work. The moment we arrest him, if he even *is* alive, the CIA will just take him back again.'

'Maybe not. He'd have been seen to have faked his death to get away from them,' Declan shook his head. 'But if he's dead, he's dead. And these things can happen. We haven't mentioned the other option, though. What if he's dead, but it was deliberate?'

'How do you mean?' Anjli replied. 'Why would he deliberately kill himself?'

'I'm not saying he deliberately killed himself,' Declan said. 'I'm saying what if *someone else* killed him?'

Nodding at this, Anjli started counting off her fingers.

'Trisha Hawkins has an axe to grind with him. Frankie Pierce, wherever she is, also has an axe to grind with him. Phoenix Industries was almost destroyed because of him. He blew up the cottage in St David's, so the village is probably after him too.'

'I get what you're saying,' Declan nodded. 'But with Pierce, he thought he was righting a wrong. I don't know if he even realises she's still alive. Tom reckons he removed the bite from Phoenix Industries and Trisha Hawkins, though.'

'You can remove the bite from a snake, but it's still a snake,' Anjli replied.

Declan gave out a groan, slumping in the chair facing the bed.

'I've asked Tom to see if he can find any information on this,' he said, leaning over and grabbing his own burger, half eaten, taking a mouthful. 'I've also reached out to a couple of people I know who might be able to check into the DNA. It matched, but DNA tests can be faked.'

'If he's back, Declan, there's a reason. Are we in his crosshairs?'

'I hope not. But I don't know,' Declan said, staring back out of the window, wondering if somewhere else in London, Karl Schnitter, aka the Red Reaper, was staring back at him. 'We need to keep our ear to the ground. If Karl is out there, he won't be able to stop himself; he'll start killing.'

'And when he does, we'll find him and we'll stop him,' Anjli said, sitting up. 'Now hurry up and finish your food, because you're getting it all over the bedclothes.'

Declan went to reply, to point out *she* was the one eating

on the bed, but then realised he was dripping ketchup over the covers.

'Sorry,' he said, wiping it; but that just made it worse.

'No, please, make this room look like a crime scene,' Anjli laughed. 'Because that's exactly what we want here.'

THE FOLLOWING MORNING, DECLAN AND ANJLI MET UP WITH the others who had stayed at the hotel. There were only a couple left, however; DCI Freeman, for example, was going back to Maidenhead that morning and had a booked a room in case he was worse for wear, but DCI Farrow had returned home, living in North London, and Derek Sutton had his own plans. Declan hadn't wanted to know what they were.

Nobody wanted to talk about the case. It was a Saturday, and for many of the officers there, they were having a day off. So, with breakfast finished, and the suitcases packed, Declan and Anjli said their farewells, checked out and headed up to Temple Inn to see the others.

Billy was already at his monitor desk when they arrived.

'Good morning,' he said cheerfully, optimistic and chirpy as they arrived.

'I see Billy was on the soda pops last night,' Anjli mocked. 'Because there's no way in hell he would be this happy with a hangover.'

'Of course he would,' Declan replied. 'He's twelve.'

Billy smiled and leant back in his monitor chair.

'I've checked the CCTV,' he said. 'There's three or four vans that could have brought the body, but we're still checking into them.'

'Anything from the organisers?'

'Monroe's talking to them at the moment,' Billy said, nodding over at Monroe's office. 'But each part of the event seems to have a dozen different people running it, all members of multiple societies that cross over into every event.'

Declan, patting Billy on the shoulder, walked over to his own office – which still felt weird, considering the fact that several months earlier it had been Monroe's office before the upward jump that everybody had seemed to make, with Declan the last to do so.

Moving into the office, he closed the door and changed from his T-shirt into a collared shirt and tie. All officers in the Temple Inn unit had changes of clothes there; nine times out of ten it was because something would have stained the previous set of clothing, like blood, or engine oil, or a dozen other things. Often they'd spend the night upstairs in a cot, staying over when the case was time-dependent, and because of this, Declan was well used to having showers downstairs and changing into a spare set of clothing when he could.

The hotel had provided the shower this time, but the spare set of clothing he had for his Saturday trip back to Hurley was a more relaxed jeans and T-shirt situation, so he just simply opted to wear the same suit he'd worn the previous day, but at least change the shirt and tie.

Exiting out of his office, he saw that Anjli and Monroe had effectively done the same.

'Morning boss,' he said. 'Good night?'

'And why would you think for the slightest wee second it would be a good bloody night, after the bombshell bloody Tom Marlowe dropped on me?' Monroe snapped back.

'Yeah, sorry,' Declan fought the urge to return to his

office, shut the door and hide from the irritated Scotsman. 'I take it you've contacted Wintergreen?'

'I didn't need to,' Monroe muttered. 'Rosanna had done that before she left the crime scene. I don't know what she said, either, but I'd bet my salary it wasn't polite and flowery.'

'So, we're working on the case instead, to ignore our personal woes?' Anjli asked innocently.

'Aye, and you can be replaced too,' Monroe growled. 'Let's just start working out what the merry hell happened last night.'

He nodded over at the briefing room.

'Is it worth that?' Declan asked. 'I mean, De'Geer and Marcos are likely still with the body, Cooper's not in yet, it's just the four of us and we're here.'

'Bloody DCIs, no penchant for tradition,' Monroe sighed, looking up to the ceiling as he spoke, as if apologising for Declan's words. 'Fine. We'll do it here. What do we have?'

Billy shrugged.

'To be honest, not a great amount,' he said. 'He's a re-enactor, does a lot of events for a group called the Ninth Legion.'

'Isn't that a film?' Anjli asked.

Billy nodded.

'Yes, it's some lost Legion from the end of the Roman Empire, disappeared in Britain. I don't know the full story, but I think Channing Tatum was in it, which means it was obviously a very action-packed time for them all, with probably some dancing and some comedy.'

'And the re-enactors?'

'They're an offshoot of another organisation. Spend a lot of time doing weekend history events and charity drives. He used to be in a Dark Ages group too, according to his social media, but over the last couple of years he'd bounced between the two.'

'Is that common?'

'Apparently so.'

'I've seen them,' Declan nodded. 'Or at least people who do this sort of re-enactment. They usually do stately homes and things like that, show how Romans performed in squares and how they marched. Usually there's a battle related to the area. I seem to recall there was a lot of marching.'

'Is there much call for this kind of thing?' Monroe asked, frowning. 'You know, dressing up and playing soldiers?'

'I don't think it's really a case of playing soldiers,' Anjli replied. 'Many of the people I've met who do this find it educational. They want to show people how the Roman world was. It's kind of why this entire festival is happening, I suppose.'

'Either way, he liked to role-play a Roman, and died in a Roman uniform, complete with sword stuck in his back,' Declan muttered. 'Seems like he was living the life he wanted to do.'

'Well, I don't think being killed in the back with a sword was probably on his list of things to do this week,' Monroe replied. 'What do we know about this?'

'I spoke to Matt Butcher, the guy who runs the gladiator arena event at Finsbury Circus Gardens, and he said Adam Harris had been involved in several of the events during the day, including the gladiator games, where he was dressed like Spartacus or something,' Billy leant back on the chair looking around. 'He did two of the fights in the arena, both times dressed in different costumes, one time wearing a full head helmet – probably so people couldn't wonder how the guy who died in the previous fight came back in a second –

but they also didn't have that many people to do the fights, it being a Friday. Apparently, the weekend is easier to get re-enactors because of work.'

'Harris took time off?'

'Harris was apparently a self-employed chartered accountant, so probably did whatever he wanted.'

He tapped on the screen, showing some images.

'This is from the Instagram page,' he said. 'You can see here that they had a good old gathering—'

'And a few of them got a pretty good punch in the face by the looks of things,' Declan said, pointing at one scene where a gladiator was staggering back after a blow to the head. 'That looks pretty painful. I thought re-enactment was supposed to be fake, you know, like pro wrestling?'

'I wouldn't let anybody hear you say pro wrestling was fake,' Anjli smiled. 'Those guys get the shit kicked out of them sometimes. It's a sport, sure, and it's entertainment, but they suffer broken limbs regularly.'

'And from the sounds of things, so do these guys. This isn't like live role play,' Billy added.

'Hold on,' Monroe held a hand up. 'What the hell is *live role play?*'

'Live action role play, or LARP, as it's called,' Anjli explained, 'is a gathering of people who want to play make-believe. It's very fantasy based, like *Dungeons and Dragons*.'

'Oh, I know *Dungeons and Dragons*,' Monroe smiled. 'It's the thing where you roll your dice and you attack the dragons and the wee beasties.'

'Yes, the wee beasties,' Anjli mocked. 'That's exactly what it is. But in this case, instead of rolling dice to see what happens, you're hitting them with a bloody great big foam hammer, or some kind of sword.'

'It sounds like Nerf weapons,' Declan replied.

'They're more foam core with a solid base,' Anjli explained. 'My cousin does it, goes into a field once a year and has battles with three to four thousand other people. It's quite therapeutic, really.'

'You sound like you've done this,' Declan raised an eyebrow as he glanced back at Monroe, folding his arms to prepare for the inevitable backtracking, as Anjli realised she'd overshared.

'Well, I've sparred with her with the weapons,' Anjli said, reddening a little. 'I mean, I'm good with a bastard sword, but—'

'A what sword?'

'A bastard sword, a one-handed weapon, like a saber,' Anjli realised quickly she was digging herself a hole. 'Anyway, as I was saying, with live roleplay, you play the part free-form, and your actions decide what happens. If you piss somebody off, instead of rolling dice to see if you survive or not, you have to literally defeat them in a fight. People pull their blows and move at two-thirds speed, so it's not as dangerous as it could be, but she's had a couple of concussions when something's gone wrong, or there's been a fight. This is probably the same way with re-enactors, except they're not using rubber swords. All their weapons are metal.'

'I've heard horror stories of re-enactors losing eyes in fights,' Billy said ominously. 'Most of the time it's cuts and bruises though, broken legs, arms ...'

'Those gladiators are going in there effectively with live ammunition—'

'Apart from the fact that they don't actually have any ammunition,' Monroe replied.

Anjli gave him a scathing look.

'They're still walking in there with bloody swords and maces and nets, and all they've got on is a couple of pieces of leather straps to stop those things cutting into them,' she said. 'They're not performing theatre, this isn't some kind of choreographed show. They would literally be trying to batter the living shit out of each other. The only difference is they're better at it than we are, and they understand what they're doing. They probably pull their blows and things like that, but I reckon when Doctor Marcos comes back to us, she'll tell us that body's got welts and bruises all over it.'

'So, what about the sword then?'

'The sword is a different story,' Doctor Marcos said as she entered the office through the main doors, and for a moment Declan wondered if Anjli stating her name had summoned her somehow. 'Is there a reason we're not in the briefing room?'

'Declan wanted a change of scenery,' Monroe replied.

'Of course he does,' Doctor Marcos glared at Monroe. 'It's all about the change of scenery in this department these days, isn't it? New office, new briefing, but same old *wife.*'

Monroe winced and Declan saw that although it was a joking comment, there was still a little bit of a barb behind it.

'What have you got?' he asked.

'A wound to the back definitely killed Harris, with what looks to be a Roman Gladius,' Doctor Marcos said. 'It was done while he was alive, but when he fell, the sword was removed – as was Harris. When they arrived at their new location, the sword was re-inserted for dramatic effect and left. The blood spatter shows that by the time he arrived, he'd been dead probably a good hour or so, and with this being a Friday evening I'd say wherever he was brought from wasn't too far out of the City of London, which makes sense if he was performing Roman things during the day.'

'The Legionnaire's uniform?' Anjli asked, noting that Billy had received a message and was reading it, ignoring the conversation for the moment.

'The uniform he's wearing isn't anything from a costume store,' Doctor Marcos replied, checking her notes. 'Nor is it something that he would have worn in his Ninth Legion duties. I asked around, and it's custom made, with a solid breastplate hidden under the leather.'

'So what,' Declan asked. 'Harris did his gladiator stuff, then put on a custom-made Roman tunic and went for a stroll?'

'Either that or he went for another fight,' Doctor Marcos replied.

'First rule of Roman Fight Club is not to talk about Roman Fight Club,' Monroe shrugged as he looked back at the crime photo on Billy's monitor screen. 'So what else do we know about this guy?'

'He's a work from home accountant, which means he doesn't really spend much time in an office, doesn't talk to his clients that much, he's in and out, a bit of a loner, no significant other, or pets. We're still getting into whether he's a lone wolf in other ways,' Billy replied, looking back from the screen. 'From what Matt Butcher said, he's a nice enough guy. They spent time together, and he's always been good when performing in live events.'

'But at some point, somebody killed him with a sword,' Anjli countered. 'Do we have anything from your uncle yet?'

'Chivalry takes his time with these things,' Billy sighed. 'He finds it better to look good that way.'

He turned his attention back to his screen as his

computer beeped a second time. Leaning in, he examined the email that he'd been given.

'Of the four vans that turned up, we've got information on three of them. One of them, however, doesn't match the registration documents.'

'How do you mean?' Declan asked.

'I mean that we have a grey Ford Transit in front of us on the CCTV screen, but the car registration is that of a Mini Cooper.'

'Well, that's not suspicious at all,' Declan replied. 'Do we know anything about the Mini Cooper?'

'Just that it was marked as having its plates stolen two days ago.'

'Well then,' Declan replied, looking at the others, 'I think that's where we need to look first, don't you?'

'Actually, hold on that,' Billy held a hand up. 'I had another email. There's a new dead body.'

'Roman?'

'No, I think it's 18th century this time,' Billy looked back to the others. 'Someone called the police early this morning saying they'd heard a gunshot in Pickering Place, in Mayfair. When the police investigated, they found a dead man in Regency gear, a duelling pistol in his hand.'

'What time was the call?'

'About two minutes after sunrise,' Billy checked the email.

'Pistols at dawn,' Monroe muttered. 'What the bloody hell is going on?'

4

BOUDICCA

THE CRICKET GROUND AT SHOREDITCH LOOKED MORE LIKE A building site than a sports ground as Georgia Wingate stared across it. In her early forties at best, slim with long, curly red hair, she wore a green Barbour jacket over a white jumper, jeans and Hunter boots. She looked for all intents and purposes as if she'd walked out of a farm in Chipping Norton and found herself in London.

Unlike many other locations used in the festival, parkland or streets, private gardens and suchlike, the cricket club had raised seating around, which meant they didn't have to worry about crowd control or similar, and it gave them more space in the middle for what they needed to do.

The groundskeeper, a miserable old bastard by the name of Kaleem, had wandered over the ground, adjusting his cap as he did so.

'You're going to destroy the ground,' he said.

Georgia understood why he was annoyed. He wasn't wrong. The battle itself was going to involve a couple of chariots, several horses, and about two hundred people running around, screaming at each other, throwing weapons. It was going to be a wonderful spectacle, but the price was the ground they fought on, which was going to get incredibly chewed up.

'I don't know why you're complaining,' she said, looking at him, deciding that she wasn't going to apologise. 'The council have said they're going to cover the costs of a completely new pitch, and you've got months before you play again here.'

'It's not the point,' the groundskeeper said. 'I've spent years making sure this works.'

At this, Georgia laughed.

'Come on, chap,' she replied. 'I know for a fact you had to redo half of it last year, and you've had a problem with the clay underneath the pitch for the last ten. This is your opportunity to get all that fixed.'

She could see that Kaleem wanted to complain more, that he wanted to argue the toss about this, but her point was valid. One reason the City of London had gained the cricket ground for such a small outlay was because they'd guaranteed to fix the grass, something that had needed to be fixed for a while.

Kaleem grumbled under his breath and stomped off, probably to shout at another grounds person or complain about something else. Georgia sighed and shifted her backpack, watching as the setting for Sunday's battle was being made in front of her eyes.

The fight would be the same as it always was. Two armies facing each other; one side Iceni, the other side Roman, and the commentator would give a lot of the story behind it. He would give the story of why Boudicca, leader of the Iceni had such problems with the Romans, what the stakes here were and, as the fight started, there would be no need for intricate land works or buildings on the pitch to help tell the story. All you needed was a Roman army, an Iceni army, and some chariots.

However, the one thing they weren't allowing here were the *spikes* on the wheels of the chariot.

Whenever people talked about the legend of Boudicca, they always talked about her famous war chariot, with spikes jutting out of the side, which took Romans down at the shins as it went around, cutting off legs as it did so. When they did this at larger places like Tewksbury, she could have fake 3D printed-and-painted-up spikes placed on the wheels where she could ride around before the battle, showing this. Then, of course, during the battle they'd be removed, because the last thing that they wanted was a lawsuit from pissed off re-enactors who'd had their legs taken out at the knees.

Here, however, there was no such possibility because of the size. She had a smaller than usual war chariot which looked to have been built at a three-quarter scale, while the Romans only had three or four horses, one of which was to be used by Gaius Suetonius Paulinus, the rival Roman general, played, she believed by Aaron Forden, the weaselly skinless prick.

No, be nice. He's been useful recently.

There was movement from the left, and Georgia turned to find Susan Cowell walking towards her. Like Georgia, she was in her late thirties, possibly even her forties now, Georgia wasn't sure, but her short pixie-cut hair, dyed pink for the occasion, was an incredibly vain attempt to make her look younger.

It didn't really work, but Georgia found herself not caring;

they were all getting on in age. Georgia herself had been playing the re-enactment game for almost twenty years, had been playing Boudicca events for the last three – but had been a shield maiden, a bodyguard to the previous Boudicca, as well as other things, for five years before that. Susan had been around just as long—

But then Susan had *other* reasons for hanging around the re-enactment group at the time.

'Come to see the rehearsals?' she asked.

'I didn't think there were any,' Susan replied, glaring at Georgia as she stood there. 'I thought they were just working out the areas, as it's not until tomorrow evening.'

Georgia shrugged, turning around, taking in the spectacle of it all.

'I like to be here,' she said. 'You know, scope the land out.'

Susan didn't laugh at the line, even though it was a mocking tribute to leaders of battles, scoping their battlefield out before the battle happened, envisioning what would happen on that land. She knew many re-enactors did this, purely as you never quite knew what would happen on the day.

Georgia waited for Susan to speak, but Susan just carried on staring at her as if she was waiting for *Georgia* to say something.

'Go on and spit it out,' she said. 'You've got a problem with me. I'm guessing it's a new one or you would have just started—'

'Was it you?' Susan snapped, interrupting.

'Was it me *what?*' Georgia replied.

' Did you kill him, Georgia?'

' You're going to have to be a little more specific,' Georgia frowned. 'I do a lot of battles.'

'Don't give me that shit!' Susan was half-shouting now. 'Did you kill Adam? We all know you offered the duel. You told me outside it was a joke and you were just doing it to make him back down.'

'It *was* a joke, and I *was* making him back down,' Georgia glanced around. Something felt off, and she didn't mean whatever Susan was going on about with Adam sodding Harris. She saw at the entrance Susan's brother Rolf was standing there. He looked angry as well, his face scowling across the field.

'What's his bloody problem?'

'Adam Harris,' Susan snapped back. 'You sent us to him. Last night, the walk. Are you telling me you didn't?'

Georgia turned back to face the smaller pink-haired woman now.

'Susan, we've never been friends,' she said. 'We've got along with each other because of what we do, and I'd like to feel that we respect each other to an extent. I'm aware I took the job you thought you should have, and I'm sorry about that. But I haven't got a bloody clue what you're talking about and you're pissing me off!'

Susan went to speak and then stopped, watching Georgia.

'You really don't know, do you?' she muttered.

'Explain to me what I don't bloody know!' Georgia was shouting now, and she saw out of the corner of her eye Rolf walk towards them.

'Stay back, Fido,' she snapped, pointing at him. 'Or I give it to you as well. Don't you dare think I can't beat the shit out of you if I tried.'

Surprisingly Rolf stopped, as Susan turned and held her hand up to pause him.

'Last night,' she started, 'we were planning out the battle

and got an email from you saying you'd gained a couple of tickets for the Roman walk, and did we want them. You said it would be worth our time, and there was going to be a surprise.'

'I don't know any of this,' Georgia replied.

Susan wasn't listening, just carried on talking.

'We were running late,' she said. 'The directions you gave said we'd be meeting near Silver Street, and we ran across to join them on the London Road, but learned we'd missed the starting point. Or, rather, were given the wrong one. We joined the tour, walked over to where Barber-Surgeons' Hall was and that's where we found him.'

She paused.

'Rather, that's where Aaron Forden found him.'

'What was Aaron Forden doing there?'

'You tell me! We spoke to him afterwards, and he seemed as confused as we were. He'd also received an email from you to turn up saying you had something for him to see.'

'And what did you see?' Georgia reckoned she knew the answer, but had to ask anyway.

'Bloody Adam Harris, dead, face down with a sword in his back,' Susan snapped. 'Someone had left him by Barber-Surgeons' Hall, by the Roman fort.'

Georgia didn't answer. She glanced around.

'Adam Harris is dead?'

'Did I stutter?' Susan snapped. 'The police turned up and everything. They took the names of everybody on the walk. Me, Rolf, Aaron, we're all on there.'

'I don't understand,' Georgia was shaking her head. 'Are you telling me that somebody emailed you, claiming they were me, and had booked you on a walk that meant that you would find his body and become suspects?'

'Bingo,' Susan said. 'And you bloody well know, the moment they look into it, they're going to realise that we had a history. They're going to see that Aaron knew him – and there we are, standing there. We're the bloody idiots that found him. Aaron saw the body, Georgia. They'll speak to him first.'

'Do you still have the emails?'

'Yes,' Susan opened her phone, showing it. 'See, look, Georgia dot Wingate at Hotmail—'

'I don't use Hotmail,' Georgia interrupted. 'I use Gmail. Whoever sent this, it wasn't from my address. You've been phished.'

She looked back at Rolf.

'I didn't do this,' she said.

'You challenged Adam to a duel,' Rolf said from the edge of the cricket pitch, 'and he was killed with his weapon.'

'What? Re-enactment weapon?'

'His sword,' Rolf said.

Georgina nodded at this. She knew what he meant.

'Maybe he stole it from someone. And then maybe the person who owned it wanted it back.'

'If they wanted it back, they would have taken it,' Rolf shook his head, ignoring the accusation of theft. 'They wouldn't have left it in his spine as a message.'

'Depends on what the message was,' Georgina sighed. 'Look, I get you're pissed off, but I didn't do this.'

Sighing, she turned and started back towards Rolf.

'We find this was you,' he said, 'or if we get into any trouble because of this, I'm telling them everything.'

'Go for it,' Georgia said. 'You don't know anything.'

Susan looked back.

'I know where the money came from,' she said. 'Adam told me.'

Susan wasn't expecting it, but Georgia's speed for her age was faster than you would have thought, and she hurried towards her, grabbing her by the throat.

'Listen here, you little bitch,' Georgia hissed. 'I was given that money. You stole for yours. Yeah, I know the truth. A little birdie's working it all out and is singing to anyone who's listening. So if you want to be a bitch at me, feel free to. It's a habit of a lifetime. Don't for one second think that I won't destroy you.'

She let her hand go, and Susan stepped back, rubbing at her throat.

Rolf, wisely, hadn't moved closer.

'Do you know why they didn't pick you to be Boudicca?' Georgia asked. 'You don't have the guts. You don't have the killer instinct, and you couldn't hack it in a fight.'

'And you could?' Susan asked, still rubbing at her throat, grimacing as she glared at the woman in front of her.

Georgia smiled, and it was a warm, friendly one, an amused expression.

'You're damn right I could,' she said. 'And, for all you know, I might have shown it to Adam Harris last night, when I stabbed him with a Gladius, and left him behind a Roman fort. Or maybe not. Who knows? You'll never know, so I suggest you piss off back to the organisational area, and I'll see you tomorrow.'

With that said, Georgia Wingate stormed off.

Susan swallowed, shook herself, turned back to Rolf, who was watching quietly.

'Come on,' she said. 'I'm sick of this bloody place.'

She stared after Georgia, and the slightest hint of a smile appeared.

Georgia claimed she knew what had happened, but then she also said Susan didn't have the killer instinct.

Which, in a way, meant she *didn't* know what had happened – to *either* of them.

5

ONE ON ONE

'I UNDERSTAND THIS IS THE SORT OF THING YOU GUYS ARE looking for,' DCI Cohen said as Declan arrived with Anjli and De'Geer.

De'Geer had offered to bring Declan on his motorbike to go through the Saturday morning traffic, but Anjli had brought her own motorcycle the day before and, as Declan wanted her beside him here, she would have to have made her own way, anyhow. Besides, a squad car hurtling through the centre of the West End seemed to be quite fun on a Saturday morning.

Declan shook Cohen's hand warmly. He was slim like a stick, with closely cropped grey hair and chunky black glasses that seemed too big for his head. The last time they had met was during the "Justice" case, when the body of Darryl Marr, the Durham Ripper, had been found in four separate parts, placed in boxes on a junction beside Marble Arch, on what was once Tyburn Gallows.

A Paddington and Mayfair Met Police DCI, Cohen had been given the case – and had happily passed it over to

Monroe and Declan. It seemed from the smile on his face, he was happy to do the same with this.

Declan looked around the passageway.

'I didn't even know this place existed,' he said as he stepped into it.

It was a small narrow passageway between buildings, with black-painted, wooden side-panels, leading into a small and somewhat hidden square, known for being the smallest public square in Britain, and accessible through a narrow passage next to the Berry Bros & Rudd wine shop on St. James's Street.

The alley leading to it was tight, and opened up into a small courtyard with a cobbled surface, with tables to the left pushed to the side wall of a restaurant that likely used it for outside dining. Despite being in a busy area, and currently filled with forensic officers, Declan felt it had a quiet, almost secretive feel to it.

The square was lined with traditional Georgian townhouses, their red and brown brick facades giving off a sense of history. These buildings, with their white-framed sash windows, with a focus on symmetry and simplicity, added to the old-world charm of the place.

Declan looked down at the other end of the small courtyard, where a blue forensics tent had been placed over what he assumed was the body.

'What do we know?' he asked.

'Still waiting for an ID on the body here,' Cohen replied. 'From what we can work out, someone had a dawn duel. Chappy under the tent obviously lost.'

He looked back at Anjli.

'It was weird, though,' he said. 'I mean, turning up on a Saturday morning to find a body in full Regency gear, lying dead on the floor, a bullet wound to his head and with a duelling pistol in his hand. Not the kind of thing I expect.'

'Weirdly, it's not our first time,' Anjli grinned, and Declan remembered that duelling pistols had been used when he'd been checking the death of his onetime partner, Eddie Moses up in Castleton, in the Peak District. Then it had been a black-powder duelling club using 19th-century pistols to shoot at each other.

This, however, seemed a little more *traditional*.

'Strange thing about the pistol, though,' Cohen carried on. 'It's old. It looks like it could actually have been a real one, rather than one of these re-enactor things.'

'Well, I'm guessing it was real,' Anjli said, 'if he was shot with another one in a duel.'

'Yeah, but we don't know if this was a duel,' Declan replied. 'I mean, it sounds like one, but we were told there was only one gunshot?'

Cohen nodded at this.

'Yeah, only one, which means he either didn't have time to fire, or was killed early. If it *was* a duel, that is.'

'First thoughts?'

'My thought is that he was killed, and then they placed the gun in his hand,' Cohen pushed up at his glasses, repositioning them on his nose. 'Maybe the single gunshot is them shooting him, but there was only one shot heard, and his pistol is empty.'

One forensic officer was talking to De'Geer, and he walked over, a small evidence baggie, passed to him by the officer, in his hand.

'Name of the victim is Benedict Dee,' he said.

'Ben Dee?' Declan frowned. 'Surely not.'

'I think that's why he preferred the full name, and probably killed his parents when he was young for naming him so,' De'Geer shrugged. 'His wallet had a credit card with his name. We're checking into him now.'

He showed the baggie. In it was a handwritten, folded note.

'This was in his pocket,' he said, allowing Declan to read it.

Pistols at Dawn. Practice for the real thing. Be there for five.

'Five am, perhaps? So he was invited here?' Cohen said as Declan showed it to him.

'Or ordered to come here, maybe even blackmailed,' Declan looked around the courtyard. 'And if it's a practice, why is he dead?'

'Accident, maybe?' Anjli glanced up at the windows. 'Arriving at five in the morning is a little earlier than dawn, though. Perhaps they practiced, and then had the duel when dawn rose?'

'Why here though?' Declan pursed his lips.

'Pickering Place is said to be the last place in London where a duel was fought,' De'Geer replied. 'I checked it on the way here. In the 18th century, its secluded location allowed a notoriety for gambling dens and bear-baiting, as well as its shady reputation as a popular location for duels. It was also the home of the Embassy of the Republic of Texas, when Texas was nominally an independent country before it joined the United States in 1845 ...'

He paused.

'Although that probably means nothing here,' he admitted.

'Was Dee involved in any of the festival?'

'Haven't looked into it yet,' De'Geer replied.

Cohen, looking around at his officers, shrugged.

'Look, I'll leave these guys with you, but as far as I'm concerned, this is your job,' he said. 'I don't know what's going on here, but it sounds very similar to what yours is.'

'What you're *really* saying is you don't want this on a Saturday morning,' Declan replied with the slightest of smiles.

At this, Cohen grinned.

'You see, this is why they promoted you to DCI,' he said. 'You're really quick on the uptake.'

This stated, he nodded to Anjli and Declan and then walked back out of the passageway onto St. James's Street.

Declan glanced around the walls of the courtyard.

'There are windows looking out,' he said. 'But I'm not sure how many of these are residential. Saturday morning at dawn, probably not that busy here.'

'That might be why they picked it,' Anjli suggested. 'Feels weird, though. Two people killed in two completely separate yet traditional ways.'

She glanced down at her phone as it beeped.

'Message from Billy,' she replied. 'Dee was part of the festival.'

She paused as she carried on reading.

'Apparently he was performing, or whatever they do, in Malet Street Gardens, just north of the British Museum, showing people how duels were used and telling the story of the Field of the Forty Footsteps.'

'Field of the Forty Footsteps?' Declan frowned. 'Don't know that story.'

Anjli looked up from the text.

'What, and I'm supposed to?' she asked. 'I'm just telling

you what Billy said. He reckons there's a duelling area on Southampton Fields, which were meadow lands somewhere north of the British Museum and Malet Street Gardens is the only green area left. So, he was there explaining the story and talking about the duelling history of the area.'

'Then he's found early the next day shot in the head, in a place known for duelling,' Declan said. 'Shortly after a man who had been performing as a fake gladiator in a fake arena was found stabbed with a Gladius.'

'Yeah, they're probably connected,' Anjli replied. 'But I have no idea how.'

THE FIRST THOUGHT THAT WENT THROUGH NICHOLAS Stephens' mind when he heard about the rumoured death of Benedict Dee was that Georgia Wingate's deal had been fatal.

The second thought was one of fear, as he realised this was all because of *him*.

Walking into Finsbury Circus Gardens, he paused as he wandered over to Matt Butcher, who was ordering some Marshalls to clear the arena up, following the previous day's "fights." As he approached, Butcher nodded at him, moving away from the others.

'Hey man,' Nicholas said, lowering his voice. 'Did you hear about the body?'

'Of course I heard about him,' Butcher looked around the makeshift arena. 'It's all over the bloody place. What was he even doing by the wall?'

'What wall?' Nicholas asked.

'The bloody Roman wall,' Butcher replied. 'What are *you* talking about?'

'I'm talking about Benny Dee being found in Mayfair,' Nicholas replied. 'What are *you* talking about?'

At this, Matt Butcher paled.

'Benedict Dee was the duellist? Oh my God!'

He pulled Nicholas to the side, away from the others.

'I was on about Adam Harris,' he said. 'He was found by the Roman wall. He'd got a bloody sword stabbed into his back.'

Nicholas shuddered and felt more than several strands of ice slide down his spine at the news.

Harris had been at the pub too. Harris had probably spoken to Georgia as well.

'Dude, we need to tell the police,' he said.

'About what?' Butcher glanced around nervously the moment the word *police* was spoken. 'That Georgia bloody Wingate came and complained to us about the fact that she was excluded from this? That she offered us money to take her up on one-on-ones?'

'Yes!' Nicholas nodded vigorously. 'Dude, she's killed two people.'

'We don't know she killed them.'

'Oh, I'm sorry. Did you not get the challenge? Ten grand to have a fight with her?' Nicholas snapped. 'Because Benny Dee did.'

At this, Butcher straightened, staring at Nicholas in horror.

'He took her *up on it?*'

'Of course he took her up on it!' Nicholas shook his head. 'She was bitching about not being allowed to duel because girls weren't duelling back then. Made a comment about the Pennington gig, hinted you stopped the women duelling because of me.'

'I didn't say that.'

'But it's true, isn't it?' Nicholas snapped. 'Didn't make your life worse either, did it? Women being banned due to safety rules meant you didn't have to face her friends.'

He looked away.

'Neither did I,' he muttered.

'Get a hold of yourself,' Matt snapped. 'You're spotlighting. Georgia made the deal because she was aiming us away from the other thing.'

Nicholas shook his head, his expression changing.

'I don't know about anything like that,' he said, rather unconvincingly.

At this, Matt Butcher leant closer.

'Someone spoke to the police,' he hissed. 'Claimed it wasn't an accident, opened up the case again. Was it you?'

Nicholas straightened up.

'I'll admit, I looked back into it recently, Matt. I saw a video filmed on the day.'

'How—'

'I was given the details by DCI Warren,' Nicholas replied. 'And someone else, someone who wanted the truth out. I watched it, Matt. Never had before. There's no way, even with Adam's jostle, that I hit her. No way.'

Butcher looked around, some of the other re-enactors were watching them, Nicholas's raised voice gaining their interest.

'Look, Georgia's just trying to get in your head,' he said. 'Walk away.'

'I did, but the others didn't,' Nicholas shook his head. 'Benny Dee took the bet. And, after talking to Forden, I'm assuming Adam Harris did as well.'

'Forden took the bet?'

'No idea. But the other two probably did, and now they're both dead.'

'Harris was a blowhard,' Butcher said. 'But he wasn't stupid.'

He glanced around.

'Look, do me a favour, yeah? Don't tell anybody this yet.'

'Don't tell anybody what? That we pretty much know who killed these two people?'

'We don't know it was this,' Butcher snapped. 'And the moment it comes out that the people involved in the history festival are killing each other in their own time, how long do you think it will be before this gets closed?'

'Good!' Nicholas snapped. 'I don't want to be here if I'm going to die.'

He shifted his bag on his shoulder.

'You know what,' he said, thinking about it, 'I quit. I don't want to be here today. If this mad bitch is taking us out one by one, then I do not want to be here. I didn't kill her, it wasn't me, and no threats are going to change my mind.'

He turned around, shouting loudly.

'Do you hear this? *It wasn't me!*'

Butcher frantically grabbed at him to shut him up, but Nicholas pulled away.

'I'm leaving,' he said. 'I'm going to the police – I'm going to tell them everything. Open up the case again if I have to. I've spent three years believing I killed her, and now I'm realising it was all lies.'

Nicholas saw Aaron Forden walk over, curious as to the raised voices.

'It's up to you if you want to corroborate my story or deny it,' he said. 'But I tell you now, I know exactly who gained from her death, and they're the ones I'll aim the bloody coppers at.'

With this, Nicholas Stephens turned and walked back out of Finsbury Circus Gardens.

'What the hell was that all about?' Aaron asked as he arrived.

'Nicholas Stephens just signed his own death warrant,' Butcher sighed.

———

HIS HEART WAS BEATING SO FAST IT WAS THREATENING TO BURST out of his chest as Nicholas walked back out onto Moorgate. He didn't know what to say; he was scared, couldn't think of what to do. People were dying, and finally he had the truth of what happened three years ago.

Nicholas shifted his bag. He didn't have his armour in there, that was kept in the storage unit at Finsbury Circus Gardens, beside the pagoda bandstand thing. It was a full set of plate armour, and nobody in their right mind lugged it around without a wheelbarrow or something. Besides, it wasn't his; he was the "Black Knight" during the festivities, and this was pretty much because he knew how to joust and could fit in the bloody armour.

They could find another sodding Black Knight.

He wouldn't have been wearing it until they brought the horses in anyway, and the jousting wasn't until three pm.

He needed to get home, lock the doors, and hide. The last thing he wanted to do was joust when people were dying.

Turning around in slow circles outside Moorgate Station, unsure what direction to take right now, he tried to work out what to do.

Reaching into his phone, he scrolled to the last text he'd received.

> Don't be hasty. We can make a deal. Let me send you a goodwill gesture.

This had been from the day before a courier had arrived at his house with a package to sign for, a USB stick apparently, according to the text file within, holding ten grand's worth of cryptocurrency. He'd held on to it ever since. He hadn't even checked more into it, in case it was all a massive catfish, aimed only at gaining his bank details.

He laughed; currently, losing everything in his bank account seemed the better solution here.

Quickly, he typed a message back.

> I don't want this. I don't want your money. I want the truth. I know you're the only person who could have swapped my weapon. I will find out the truth. And then I'll go to the police.

He sent it, and stood beside the station's entrance, nervously watching the screen, as if by watching it, the message would come through quicker.

Whether it was quicker or not, the reply came through a moment later.

> The police don't need to be involved.

Nicholas started sweating, glancing around and hurrying down the steps into Moorgate Station. He felt that if he could get away from the surface, maybe he could get away from what was going on, as he tapped out a hastily texted reply.

> Were the others involved in this?

He reached a platform, waiting for the train. And a moment later, another reply appeared.

> Yes.

> Were they killed because of this?

> They were killed because of Pennington Hall, yes. If you want the truth, meet me in fifteen minutes, in Regent's Park. I'll tell you everything, and you can make your own decision.

Nicholas paused as a chill ran through the platform.

> So it was you.

There was a pause. And then

> You know that. We know that. But the police won't. And they won't believe you. Regent's Park. We'll make it worth your while.

Nicholas quickly clambered onto the train as it arrived, sitting back as it started towards Baker Street; he could get off there and grab a bike into the Park. He didn't know what would happen when they spoke, but he knew he had to give it a go. Rummaging through his emails, he found another number, dialling it once a signal appeared.

'Hello? DCI Warren?' he said eventually, as the phone went to voicemail. 'It's Nick Stephens. I was the chap you talked to in the Pennington Hall ... well ... debacle. Could you call me back? I have new information about the accident. I think they're on to me.'

He gave his number and then disconnected, sitting back.

For three years, he'd believed he killed her.

Three.

Whole.

Years.

There was the ding of a new message.

> You'll get what you deserve.

He looked at the text. *Could he use this to his advantage? Could he convince them to give up everything while thinking he was on their side?*

> I don't know, I deserve a lot for this. Especially if I keep my mouth shut. I expect more than a "goodwill gesture."

He sat back, shutting his eyes for a few minutes. There were no more texts; however, as he exited the train and returned to the surface of Baker Street Station, his phone buzzed again.

> Bring the USB stick. We'll triple what you had on it.

It had been ten minutes since the meeting text; there was every chance they were there already.

No, I don't want that. I need to be there faster. I can't let them have the high ground.

Walking to the side, a minor road between Baker Street Station and Madame Tussauds, he used his credit card to contactlessly open the lock on one of the Santander Cycles, sponsored pedestrian bicycles usually known as "Boris Bikes," in London. Taking it and riding it northwards away from the Euston Road, he headed towards Regent's Park, turning right into York Terrace West. It was a resident-only road, with ornate brown and white bricked Georgian terraced buildings on either side, but it was only about a hundred yards until the other end, and it was an effective shortcut for him. In fact, he was through the barrier on the other side before anyone could say anything. Then, turning left onto York Gate and on to Ulster Terrace, he paused beside the pavement. They'd said to meet in Regent's Park, but he didn't actually know where.

They also said to bring the USB device. That they'd give Nicholas more money.

Quickly, he rummaged in his pockets, looking for the USB crypto ledger device. He knew he'd kept it on him. He hadn't known what to do with it after he signed for it. Ten grand worth of bitcoin was quite expensive, and he didn't want to leave it anywhere where someone could steal it. But he also wanted to make sure he had it, because if he didn't, this whole meeting was pointless, especially after he used his phone to record the conversation and clear his name forever.

He eventually found it, pulling it out as he glanced along the road. It was strangely quiet at this time of the day, but then that was probably because of the congestion charge.

It was flashing, however. He didn't understand why it was flashing; maybe it was low on power or something. Or, maybe they were transferring more funds onto it. But now, with it in his hand, he felt a little more secure as he opened his phone.

I have your device. Where do you want to meet?

A moment waiting, and then.

> Don't worry. I'll come to you. Just keep
> heading anti-clockwise along Ulster Terrace
> and the Outer Terrace.

Relaxing a little, Nicholas cycled again, heading the way that the message had told him to. But it was only about twenty yards further down the road that he realised there was a problem with the message.

He hadn't said where he was in the Park.

So how did they know where he was?

Was he being tracked? Was the USB ledger some kind of tracking device that told them where he was?

He didn't want to be involved in this. Screw the meet up, screw the recorded confession, he knew he had to get to the police as quickly as possible. They could look after him. He'd speak to DCI Warren, and she could tell him what was going to—

He was so caught up in this change of plan, in fact, he didn't see the motorcyclist on the other side of the road, riding clockwise towards him. He didn't see them veer into his lane, and he definitely didn't see the metre-long length of jagged tree branch they held in their right hand. He didn't see the sharpened end until the last moment when, as they went past, it slammed into his chest, puncturing through it in the same way that a rival knight in a jousting tournament would puncture their rival's breastplate with a lance, knocking them off their horse and onto the floor.

The shaft through his chest, Nicholas Stephens didn't have a horse to fall off, all he had was a bicycle, and he slid to the side of it, tumbling onto the pavement in a floundering mass of arms and legs and blood and screams from the people beside him. People who watched as the motorcyclist, now without their makeshift lance, rode off into the park along one of the many pedestrian pathways along the side.

Nicholas Stephens hadn't expected to die there and then, and as he lost consciousness, staring down at the shaft of wood protruding from his body, all he could think was one thing.

I never got the confession.

But then Nicholas stopped thinking that, as the screaming around him grew louder, and the sirens could be heard.

6

BODY COUNT

'WELL, THIS IS A FINE MESS WE'RE IN,' MONROE SAID AS HE stared at the briefing room filled with police officers. 'Less than twenty-four hours ago I was celebrating my stag night and now we have three cases, all connected to duels or fights, and no idea what the merry hell is going on.'

Declan, sitting in his usual chair, glanced around the briefing room. Anjli sat beside him, with Billy in his usual place, laptop open, ready to send images to the plasma screen behind Monroe whenever needed.

At the back, Doctor Marcos sat with De'Geer, and PC Cooper had found a seat near the door. The only other person in the room was Declan's daughter Jess, who he had forgotten was visiting that day, and had happily decided she was going to assist in the investigation while there.

Declan knew that standing in front of everyone and running the briefing was technically *his* job as the DCI, but the Temple Inn unit had always been a bit cavalier in its way of working, and even though Monroe was now a Detective

Superintendent, it felt a lot easier to have him take over rather than Declan.

After all, if Declan had bothered trying to start this, Monroe would only have interrupted, anyway.

The only person not here at the moment was Detective Chief Superintendent Bullman, but then she only came in a couple of times a week now, and Saturdays were never usually a day for her to attend. Actually, Saturdays were usually a day nobody here attended. There was often another Unit who would deal with anything that came up, Bishops-gate, or some other office along that line.

But not today. Today, they had three cases and no idea.

'Are you listening, laddie?' Monroe asked, glaring at Declan, who now looked around, realising he had drifted off into his own thoughts.

'Sorry,' he said. 'What were you saying?'

'Jesus,' Monroe looked around at everybody. 'I'm supposed to be the one drifting off into morose melancholy pits of shame, not you.'

There was a small chuckle to this. After all, Monroe was the one who had reason to be pissed off that day, following his news he could no longer marry Doctor Marcos.

Declan pulled out his notebook and read from it.

'Adam Harris, thirty-five, re-enactor, part of the London Festival of History, performing as a Roman gladiator. His speciality is Roman era re-enacting, and he's been at Finsbury Circus Gardens for the last few days, performing twice a day as a gladiator in their arena.'

'For "arena," read "area of the park fenced off with the small barriers we place along the pavement during the London Marathon",' Monroe muttered.

Another photo came up, that of a man in his late thirties,

with small gold-rimmed glasses and an already receding hairline, wearing a suit.

'This is Benedict Dee,' Declan said, pointing at the image. 'He's a Regency re-enactor, specialising in the 1700s.'

'Is there much call for that?' Anjli asked.

'He usually does open-house tours and things like that for places like Hampton Court,' Declan answered, checking his notes as he did so. 'But he's also a specialist in the art of duelling and does talks about the history of it. He was part of the History Festival as well, discussing duelling, and the Field of the Forty Footsteps, which is an urban story about a duel happening behind Montagu House.'

'And Montagu House is?' Monroe asked inquisitively.

'Sorry, sir, it's what we now call the British Museum,' Declan replied. 'Apparently Montagu House was a large stately estate with lands north of it, which were called Montagu Fields, or London Fields or even Southampton Fields, before becoming, well, buildings, I suppose. When the Duke of Montagu owned the house, he would allow people in to perform duels or whatever. Many times in those days duels weren't purely to kill, it was more of a blustering of bravado.'

'Aye, we know all about duels in this unit,' Monroe nodded. 'And the Forty Footsteps?'

'An area on his land bore the print of forty irregular footsteps, which gave it its name,' Declan explained. 'The traditional story was that two brothers engaged each other in fight. Both were killed, and forty impressions of their feet remained on the field for many years, where no grass would grow.'

'And he told this story to people, did he?'

'Yes, boss. He told stories, gave the history of duels and

also performed a couple of fake ones, with blank-shot duelling pistols.'

'Until he was found dead at dawn in Pickering Place,' Billy added.

'Aye, why there, exactly?'

Declan went to reply, but Billy got there first.

'Apparently, this was where the last duel was ever held, and where Beau Brummel apparently duelled.'

'Who the hell's Beau Brummel?' Anjli asked.

'Beau Brummell was very important in Regency England, celebrated for his wit and refined taste in fashion,' Billy quickly added. 'He transformed it by introducing the tailored suit and emphasising simplicity over the styles of the time. He also invented the cravat.'

'Ah, the patron saint of tailored suits, that would explain why you know about him,' Declan smiled.

Billy didn't reply immediately; instead, he sighed, returning to his laptop.

'Bloody philistines, I work with bloody philistines.'

'Okay, so he was killed in a notorious duelling area,' Monroe nodded. 'What about our Roman guy? Where was he found again?'

'Barber-Surgeons' Hall,' Declan shrugged. 'And all we know about that section of the wall is it was near Cripplegate, which was an entrance to the city. I don't know why he was there, apart from the fact that maybe it was a location that they could place the body with nobody knowing.'

'He also wasn't killed there,' Doctor Marcos said. 'In fact, we can guarantee he *wasn't* killed there because of the distinct lack of blood on the grass.'

'Anything on the van yet?'

'Still waiting,' Billy admitted. 'With Jess here though, we should get things done quicker.'

'Oh aye? Why's that?'

At the question, Billy reddened.

'I might have pissed off the guy looking into it for me,' he said. 'Purely a casual comment, nothing more.'

'Which said?'

'I might have said a trained monkey could work faster than he was,' Billy answered sheepishly. 'So Jess asking instead of me is likely to get a better response.'

Monroe sighed as Anjli looked at the notes.

'Benedict Dee was believed to be killed in Pickering Place,' she said. 'We have witnesses who heard the gunshot shortly beforehand.'

'And this new one,' Monroe asked, as Billy tapped on the laptop, the image of Nicholas Stephens appearing. The image was from a festival page and showed him in full plate armour, holding his helmet under his arm, his black curly hair flattened with sweat. 'Tell me more.'

'Nicholas Stephens, thirty-one,' Anjli opened her own book now. 'Stephens was a jouster, spent a lot of time doing things like festivals in Warwick Castle, or local fairs and stuff. He's a mainstay of medieval banquets and parties. His re-enacting group was to perform full-plate battles, duels, jousts, you name it, they did it. He was apparently an expert at the javelin throw, where you threw a spear at a hay bale with a shield on it. He got it every time.'

'He was here jousting, I suppose?'

'He'd been working at Finsbury Circus, as they had a section where there was a jousting line put in, and they would bring in horses and armour and show how it was done,' Anjli replied. 'Apparently next week it was moving to a different location, but Nicholas won't be joining them now.'

'Do we know anything else about this one?' Monroe asked.

At this, Doctor Marcos rose.

'It was only a few hours ago,' she said. 'So we're still looking into it. At first, people thought it was some kind of accident just south of Regent's Park, but checking further, the moment we arrived we could see that it was far from that.'

She nodded to De'Geer to continue, and he also rose, reading from his notes.

'Witnesses say he was riding a pay-as-you-ride bicycle anti-clockwise around Regent's Park itself, on the roads that surrounded it, and a motorcyclist came at him from the other direction,' he said. 'There was a collision, but the motorcyclist rode off unscathed, and he fell to the floor. It was only after he fell they found he had a bloody great big lump of wood stuck in his chest.'

At this, Billy pressed the button, and the screen once more changed. Now it was an image of what looked to be some kind of violently torn off tree branch – slightly crooked and tapering off at a narrow, sharpened point.

'What is it?' Declan asked. 'I mean, apart from the obvious?'

'It's a branch, sure, but in this case, it was used as the equivalent of a lance,' Doctor Marcos said. 'It's got a knot in the haft that makes it an almost-shaped handle to rest against, as you can see here. You can lean it over the edge of the motorcycle, and the other end, where it was torn from the tree, gives a rather jagged and sharp pointy end. Perfect for vampires. Or, in this case, jousting champions.'

'This is the only duel we have witnesses seeing in real-time,' Declan said. 'But the cyclist didn't have a weapon. So, was this a duel, or was this an attack?'

'The impression we're getting from witnesses is that the cyclist wasn't aware it was even happening,' Doctor Marcos replied. 'He was cycling along, the motorcyclist veered into his path and stabbed him, leaving the tree branch, or rather the *lance* in his chest before mounting the pavement and riding off into the park. It went into his chest with such force that a good foot of it continued through him as well.'

'Dear God,' Declan looked at the others. 'And he *survived* this?'

'Well, I wouldn't say "survive" is the correct term. He's in a coma, and he's in intensive care. They don't think he's going to make it through the night, but technically, yes,' Doctor Marcos shrugged.

'The end was sharpened, unlike a lance,' De'Geer added. 'A traditional jousting lance is blunt at the end or at best fluted-out wood. If the lance had been broken with wood fluting, it probably would have shattered his ribcage and destroyed him. But with it being effectively a narrow spear, it pierced through cleanly and somehow missed every vital organ in the area.'

'Like a javelin,' Declan mused.

'It did enough trauma to screw him over big time though,' Doctor Marcos added. 'But currently, he's our only proper witness on this.'

'You must really hate someone to do this to them,' Monroe muttered. 'Did he have any enemies?'

'Possibly,' Billy said. 'There was something in Newbury, a place called Pennington Hall about three years ago. Stephens accidentally killed another re-enactor when his spear went wide.'

'That's motive right there,' Monroe leapt up. 'Details, laddie!'

'Waiting for the DCI who dealt with it to come back to us,' Billy looked back at Monroe. 'A DCI Warren.'

'Lenette Warren?' Monroe rolled his eyes. 'My day can't get better.'

Declan recognised the name; she'd been a DCI he'd met with Monroe while on the Victoria Davies case. She hadn't liked Monroe.

Declan felt the feeling was mutual.

'Do we at least have the victim's name?'

'Bridget Farnsworth,' Billy read. 'Looking into it more.'

'Well, that's a definite start,' Monroe nodded as he looked back at the room. 'Do we have anything else?'

'Cyber are going through the phone at the moment, but we're still checking into that,' Billy replied. 'We think we might have some text messages, but we need permission to check, so we're waiting on his family.'

'Keep on it,' Monroe nodded. 'Okay, so, wrapping up, we have a genuine Roman sword killing a Roman cosplayer—'

'A re-enactor, sir.'

'Oh, I thought *cosplay* was the term for people dressing up like other people?'

'That's more comics than film and TV, boss,' Jess raised a hand and said. 'I think this is more of a historical re-enactment.'

'Okay, so it's not the fancy-dress-up brigade or anything like that?'

'I don't think they like that, sir.'

'Good to know. But, as we said, we have an antique sword that's killed a Roman soldier—'

'It's not really a sword,' Doctor Marcos added. 'We're

looking into it, but currently it looks like a 17th-century copy. Still old and very fragile, but not the murder weapon. Or, at least, not the weapon that killed him.'

'Great. Fake swords. I'm guessing the gun was fake too?'

Monroe looked back at Billy, who grimaced a little as he looked at his boss.

'I'm waiting for my uncle to come back to me right now,' he said. 'We should know some time in the next half an hour.'

'Oh aye? And why half an hour?'

'Because that's when he said he's arriving,' Billy said.

'Chivalry Fitzwarren is coming to the station,' Monroe chuckled. 'Oh, you'll be having a great day with your family today.'

He looked back at the others.

'So, we have an antique duelling pistol found on a 17th-century duellist, a sword that's a fake sword but used as a sword, and then we have a tree branch that doesn't even really look like a proper lance, that's almost killed a third re-enactor. Why the change from the real thing, do you think?'

'You can hide a sword and a duelling pistol,' Declan suggested. 'Lances are bloody long things, easily six or seven feet in height. You can't really walk around with it.'

'I spoke to Matt Butcher, the guy who ran the event, and he said that the lances and the horses were brought in separately purely for the jousting and sent home afterwards,' Cooper added. 'It could have been a case of the killer wanting to have something that fitted the murder, but was working with whatever they had to hand? I mean, they were south of Regent's Park. It might have been a crime of opportunity, and the only thing they could find on short notice was a tree branch.'

'There is that,' Declan said.

'There was something else, boss,' Cooper said. 'Butcher said he hadn't seen Nicholas today, but I spoke to a couple of the other re-enactors and they said that Nicholas arrived, spoke to Butcher briefly and then left.'

'I'll pop by and speak to him later on and see if he's changing his story,' Anjli suggested. 'He might open up if he realises we're on to him more.'

Monroe sat back on the desk as he considered what had been said so far.

'So, we have three people attacked in the space of twenty-four hours. Two dead, one on life support. At the moment, we still have no bloody clues about what's going on, and the only thing they have in common is they're all part of this bloody festival.'

'I think we need to have a chat with the organisers and see if there's something we're missing,' Declan said, but stopped as there was a movement at the main door, seen through the briefing room's windows. Declan noticed Doctor Marcos's face tighten, her eyes narrowing and her lips thinning in anger.

He understood why; the familiar figure of Emilia Winter-green was now standing in the main office.

'Oh, she has some nerve,' Doctor Marcos said, rising from her chair.

'I called her in, Rosanna,' Monroe said. 'I need to speak to her if I want to arrange a divorce. How else can I marry you?'

Doctor Marcos gave a slight sighing acknowledgement and sat back down on the seat.

'We'll deal with her in a minute,' Monroe looked back at the others. 'In the meantime, let's find out what we can about these three men. Let's see if they ever met each other, and if they have a connection other than this event. Find out more about this Bridget Farnsworth, and see if we can get any more information on where our first chap, Harris, was murdered, because he seems to be the only one who wasn't left at the scene. There has to be a reason. Let's work out what it is.'

7

FAMILY

DECLAN HAD RETURNED TO HIS OFFICE BY THE TIME JESS nervously knocked on his door. Looking up as she entered, he gave a smile.

'Sorry it's not quite the same as spending the day at Madame Tussauds, or whatever we were going to do,' he said.

Jess sat in a seat and shrugged.

'You know I like this better, Dad,' she said. 'Anything I can do that helps me when I apply to Hendon is always good.'

'You do your A-levels first,' Declan waggled a finger. 'And I still think you should be doing a degree.'

'I've spoken to Detective Chief Superintendent Bullman about that,' Jess grinned. 'She reckons she can get me through a fast track because of the amount of work I've done already.'

'Well then, maybe you shouldn't be here,' Declan said. 'Because you're still my little girl and you shouldn't be seeing bad things.'

'On the subject of that,' Jess replied nervously now, and Declan realised that *this* was the reason for her visit. 'I was thinking, with Anjli going out to see some of the witnesses, perhaps I could go with her?'

Declan shook his head.

'I'm sorry, Jess, you're here with Billy. He needs your help right now.'

'Oh, come on, Dad,' Jess glowered at him now. 'You know damn well Billy doesn't need anybody's help. He can do everything himself. I sit there and I get the grunt work. Script kiddie stuff a teenager could do.'

'You *are* a teenager.'

Jess stayed silent, glaring at her father.

'I know you feel it's grunt work,' Declan pretended to shuffle some papers, so he didn't have to look her in the eye. 'But it's important, Jess, and I'd like to keep you here under my supervision, if you don't mind.'

Jess rose from the chair, but then paused, watching him.

'What's the real problem here, Dad?' she asked.

'I don't know what you mean.'

'I mean, I know you'd spoken to Henry about me,' Jess continued. 'Mum's been keeping a closer eye on me than she usually would, as well. What aren't you telling me?'

Declan went to deny this, to say this was nothing but foolish thoughts, but then sighed, slumping back into his chair.

'I've got something to tell you,' he said. 'Karl Schnitter, the Red Reaper. You know how we believe the CIA had taken him and given him a new life?'

Jess didn't reply, she simply nodded, waiting for the next part of the conversation.

'Well, I had information telling me he'd died in a truck explosion in America,' Declan continued.

'When did you hear this?'

'Margaret Li, the German detective, told me when we finished the "lipstick" case.'

Jess leant against the chair, her hands gripping the top of it tightly, staring at Declan in a mixture of anger and surprise.

'That was weeks ago, Dad,' she replied coldly. 'You haven't bothered telling me until now?'

'I was waiting for the right moment,' Declan replied awkwardly. 'Also, I needed to check a few things.'

Jess straightened now, working through what Declan was saying, realising the unspoken statement.

'You needed to check if he was dead or not,' she stated. 'You don't think he is?'

'This is why you'll make a good detective,' Declan smiled weakly. 'We don't know. I was told there was an explosion and the body was badly damaged, beyond visual identification, but the DNA confirmed it was definitely him.'

'You don't trust the DNA.'

'I don't trust the DNA,' Declan nodded. 'We all know DNA can be altered, and there's every chance he found a way to fake his death. And if he's faked his death and has a new identity ready, well, Tom—'

'You spoke to Tom Marlowe about this?' Jess chuckled, but more in disbelief than humour. 'God, Dad, it sounds like everybody knows about this except for me.'

'Of course everybody knows except for you,' Declan snapped back. 'I'm trying to keep you safe.'

'And why would I need to be kept safe?'

'Because you're the one who *put his daughter in jail*.'

The statement was brief and to the point. Jess stopped, her mouth opening and shutting twice as she tried to think of the words to say and realising she had none.

'If the Red Reaper is back in this country, he'll be looking for his own brand of justice,' Declan said. 'When I last spoke with him, he said that you were off the list, but who knows what's going on now in his head? If he's back, I have to take him down again. If I do that, he's going to go for you, to stop me.'

Jess nodded.

'This is why you want to keep me here,' she said. 'This is why you've got Mum and Henry Farrow keeping an eye on me.'

'It's for your own safety,' Declan replied, leaning back against his chair now. 'I felt—'

'Did you think for a second that maybe I *don't* need your constant guardianship?' Jess growled, her anger visibly building. 'I mean, let's be honest here. I go to college. I go and see my girlfriend. At no point do you have anybody there with me.'

She watched Declan for a moment.

'Tell me you don't have somebody watching over me, Dad,'

Declan smiled weakly again.

'Tom got a friend to monitor you,' he said. 'A guy called Marshall Kirk. And I may have had a couple of other people watch over you, here and there.'

'Christ, Dad,' Jess started walking to the door. 'Just because some killer might be alive and might have a problem with you, doesn't mean that *I* have to be watched 24-7.'

She stopped at the door, looking back at him.

'Every time I had a problem, Dad, it's been because of you,' she added. 'When the Seven Sisters were having their fight with everybody, I was the one being held at gunpoint. Remember? That wasn't a serial killer, but I don't see you hiding me from gangsters.'

'It's the reason I want you to stay with Billy,' Declan observed his daughter as he spoke. 'It's the safest place, really.'

'Yes, *Boss*,' Jess said icily, leaving Declan alone in his office. 'Whatever you say, *Guv*.'

Declan waited until Jess had returned to her seat beside Billy before he let out his breath. He wanted more than anything to get up, walk over to the wall and punch it hard, but he knew that if he did so, all he'd do was break his fingers.

He was angry at himself more than anything else. He knew Jess was right. He was knee-jerking over this. But at the same time, he couldn't explain how he knew, but out there somewhere was Karl Schnitter. And Declan was definitely in his sights.

The question was whether he was still being classed as an ally ... or an enemy now.

'HELLO EMILIA, I UNDERSTAND WE'RE MARRIED AGAIN,' Monroe said as he faced his believed ex-wife across the office. 'Come into my room, let's have a chat.'

As he started towards his office, however, he noticed Doctor Marcos following. He paused, stopping, glancing back at her.

'Rosanna, I've got this,' he said. 'I need you to be looking into the case.'

'And I need to make sure that she's not playing us,' Doctor Marcos replied, glaring at Emilia Wintergreen.

'This might come as a surprise to you, Rosanna, but I'm just as annoyed by this as you are,' Wintergreen said, looking back at Monroe. 'What I did was harsh all those years back, but it was required. I never thought I'd have an identity again. I was a grey man, as they say, and now I've been promoted up past where I ever thought I'd be I'm public again. Apparently you can't have nameless people helping the Prime Minister in a COBRA meeting.'

Monroe shrugged.

'Congratulations, I suppose?' he said, his tone questioning. 'As much as it's great to hear you're doing so well in your new role as "spooky ghost person," I was very much looking forward to marrying my beloved on Saturday, and now it seems I can't.'

Wintergreen nodded, looking back at Doctor Marcos, still standing in the doorway.

'He used to call me his beloved once,' she said with a smile. 'I suppose emotions change when you're betrayed in the way he was.'

'Damn right they do,' Monroe snapped angrily. 'Now, unless you have some documents for me to sign that effectively annuls our marriage, I've got nothing to say to you right now.'

Wintergreen reached into her inside jacket pocket, pulling out a folded wad of documents.

'Actually, I have one better,' she said. 'If you sign these documents, I can have it annulled by tomorrow, and your marriage can carry on just as it is.'

'Fine, pass them here,' Monroe said, grabbing them.

'Wait,' Doctor Marcos said, stepping forward. 'This seems a bit too easy. What else do these documents say?'

She took them from Monroe, quickly flicking through them.

'This isn't a marriage annulment,' she said. 'This is a death certificate.'

Wintergreen nodded.

'When they created my promotion, they had to bring me in under a new identity, until they could open the file,' she said. 'I had a complete legend designed for me, and it's that legend I'll now accept as my full-time role.'

She turned back to Monroe now.

'And this document is a confirmation that Emilia Wintergreen, for all intents and purposes, is now dead. People will still call me by the name in MI5, but I will now officially be somebody else.'

'No, wait.' Monroe shook his head. 'I can't let you do that.'

'She's had no identity for years,' Doctor Marcos looked at him. 'Why stop her from changing it?'

'Because it was still her name, Rosanna,' Monroe replied. 'She was still Emilia. We just couldn't see her resume. But with this, everything she did is removed. All her citations, all her personal details, she not only loses them again, she can never claim them back. And no matter how bad I want this, I can't do that to her.'

He looked back at Wintergreen.

'We do this the official way,' he said. 'Keep your name, keep your identity. If it takes longer to annul our marriage, it takes longer.'

Wintergreen thought about this, nodded and then left the office, walking out of the Unit without a second word.

Doctor Marcos looked down at the paperwork, still on the desk, and then returned her gaze to Monroe.

'You stubborn bloody goat,' she said, but then the slightest hint of a smile hit her lips. 'But I wouldn't have it any other way.'

'You're okay with a delay?'

Doctor Marcos clicked her tongue against the top of her mouth as she thought for a moment.

'Not really,' she said. 'But if it means we don't owe Wintergreen, or she doesn't get to play the martyr, I can deal with it.'

She turned to leave, but then looked back with a wider smile.

'Besides, it means we can have another hen night,' she continued. 'And there's a superb lecture series coming up at Barts soon. I can wait.'

She left the office, and Monroe stared down at the paperwork.

It would be so easy to sign it now, move everything on.

'No, Alex, you're better than that,' he spoke aloud, taking the paperwork and dumping it in a drawer. 'Maybe only just, but it's still enough.'

BILLY WAS ON HIS MONITOR, TRYING UNSUCCESSFULLY TO GET out of Jess why she was in such a bad mood when the email from Cybercrime arrived with the text message history of Nicholas Stephens. He scrolled through it, but paused as he read the last messages.

'Get the guv,' he whispered.

Jess, working on a laptop beside him, frowned.

'Which one?' she asked.

'Bloody all of them,' he said, looking back at her. 'We've got something. Is Cooper still around?'

'I think she was going to the hospital to check on Mister Stephens.'

'Good,' Billy reached for his phone. 'I need her to check his belongings.'

As Jess rose from her desk, however, she paused, glancing over to the door where a new arrival now stood, his arms outstretched, his face beaming.

He was wearing a brown Harris tweed blazer over a khaki waistcoat, with deep-blue corduroy trousers and a white collarless shirt; all of it looked bespoke. He had a large, brown, bushy beard that matched his wild, curly hair, both now peppering with more white than brown, and his eyes sparkled as he spoke.

'Rejoice,' Chivalry Fitzwarren boomed to the office. 'I have returned to save the day.'

'Christ,' Billy muttered, looking away. 'Here we go again.'

———

8

PAID HELP

'What do we have here?' Declan asked, as he emerged out of the office, walking over to Chivalry and warmly shaking his hand. 'Is it the great Chivalry Fitzwarren, here to save the day?'

Although he was a rogue and probably involved in half a dozen illegal items, Declan found he enjoyed Chivalry's company these days, mainly because he annoyed the hell out of Monroe and Billy, and anything that did that was good in Declan's books.

Chivalry Fitzwarren turned and pierced Declan with an intense gaze.

'Your Gladius isn't a real Gladius,' he said. 'But it's a damn excellent copy for the time it was made, that being the time of the War of Independence.'

'It was used in the War of Independence?' Declan asked.

Chivalry wandered over to a chair and sat down in it, not even checking to see whose chair it was.

'God no. I mean, dear fellow, that if it was a real Gladius, it'd be almost two thousand years old and probably collapse the moment you hit somebody with it. This is a fine replica of a Gladius, but in itself was made in the late seventeen hundreds.'

Declan glanced at Billy at this.

'Why use an old replica, if any replica would do?' he asked.

'I think we should ask them that when we find them,' Billy shrugged.

'Okay, Chivalry,' Declan nodded. 'What about the gun?'

'Ah, now we're talking.' Chivalry smiled. 'This is a duelling pistol manufactured in England by the celebrated gunsmith Robert Wogdon, of Wogdon & Barton fame, an 18th-century firm of gunsmiths based in London. The name Wogdon became synonymous with duelling to the extent that they sometimes referred to duels in England as "a Wogdon affair".'

'And you're sure it's—'

'The name is on the side,' Chivalry smiled. 'It's almost worn away, but there. And from the looks of it, I believe it has a set, or "hair" trigger, which reduces the pressure needed to fire. Wogdon's duelling pistols were fitted with set triggers as a standard feature, although I'd need to see the genuine item to confirm this.'

'Are these common?' Declan asked.

'If you're in the right circles, they can be,' Chivalry replied. 'But I'll be honest, I've only ever seen a couple of these in all my years of searching. These are almost the exact same pistols used in the infamous Burr–Hamilton duel in 1804, although possibly an earlier model. It's most likely some kind of family heirloom—'

'That was just left with the body?' Declan frowned at this.

'Well, I think it was part of a duelling set, and whoever

did this decided it was better to lose the heirloom and keep their freedom, than find themselves arrested with a dead body beside them,' Chivalry shrugged. 'It is, after all, illegal to duel, and they would have been arrested for murder, even if it was a self-defence situation.'

'How on earth can you have a self-defence situation in a duel?' Billy asked.

Chivalry turned and sighed as he looked at his great nephew.

'If you're challenged to a duel, the first attack has been given,' he explained. 'A slap around the face with a glove or a note sent via your second – whatever it is, the first action has been started. Any reaction you give is just that, a reaction. It is a defensive manoeuvre. And as such, if you are held to a duel and you kill someone in that duel, you are only performing your civic duties as self-defence. If you did not agree, the chances are they have murdered you, shot by your opponent. As the great Alexander Hamilton said, "I'm not throwin' away my shot".'

'I think he said that in a musical,' Billy replied.

Chivalry didn't reply, smiling as he turned back to Declan.

'Either way, this is a very expensive duelling pistol that you have in your hands, and a replica of a Gladius that is, again, probably incredibly expensive and well made. From the looks of things, it was created in exactly the same style that the original Gladiuses were forged and is, for all intents and purposes, as exact as you could have to one of the Roman swords. And the lance, well, it's just a branch, isn't it, really?'

Declan frowned.

'How did you know about the lance?' he said. 'We hadn't mentioned that to you.'

'Yes, Declan, I forgot you still believe that I don't have contacts everywhere,' Chivalry chuckled.

'Do you know who could have owned these things?'

'A dozen families come to mind immediately: anyone with money, a curator of a museum who has a key to the cabinet, anybody, really. I'd need to have a better look at the duelling pistol,' Chivalry said. 'All I've had is photographs. Perhaps there is some kind of identifying feature or carved initial that I can look at?'

'I'll let you have a chat with Doctor Marcos with that one,' Declan said. 'She'll know better.'

'Wonderful,' Chivalry nodded and rose from his chair. 'I'll visit her now. I understand she's probably in her forensic lab of death?'

The way he stated it was so over the top and rambunctious that Declan couldn't help but laugh.

'You know the way,' he said.

At this, Chivalry gave a bow and left the office, heading downstairs.

'Chivalry by name and Chivalry by nature,' Declan said, knowing it would annoy Billy.

'It's not his name,' Billy snapped. 'His name's Steven. People just call him Chivalry because he tells them that's his bloody name.'

'I know,' Declan smiled. 'But it annoys you, and that's good enough for me.'

'If you're going to be like that, I won't tell you the amazing thing I've just discovered,' Billy said.

Declan walked over to the computer.

'No, Billy, you'll tell me anyway, because you hate having a secret you can't tell people,' he replied. 'What have you got?'

'It's an interesting series of messages,' Billy said. 'On

Nicholas Stephens' phone. Going through them, it seems he'd recently learnt he wasn't guilty of Bridget Farnsworth's death, and that someone else was. He was trying to get them to admit it. They were trying to pay him off.'

He pointed at a text on the screen.

> I don't want this. I don't want your money. I want the truth. I know you're the only person who could have swapped my weapon. I will find out the truth. And then I'll go to the police.

'He had a back and forth, and then a meeting for later that day was planned.'

'Let me guess, south of Regent's Park, or north of the Euston Road?'

'The former,' Billy said, pointing at another of the texts. 'We've examined the phone's contactless payment records, and it seems Nicholas Stephens did arrive at Finsbury Circus, even though Butcher claims he didn't. Shortly after that, he left, walked to Moorgate Station and caught a train to Baker Street. At Baker Street, he grabbed a rental cycle and carried on up Ulster Terrace and the Outer Terrace—'

'Where he died,' Declan finished, pointing at the screen and a line of text. 'Wait, what's that?'

> Don't worry. I'll come to you. Just keep heading anti-clockwise along Ulster Terrace and the Outer Terrace.

Billy tapped the message.

'It's the last message he was given,' he said. 'And, as you can see, it's a little concerning.'

Declan nodded.

'There's no message saying where he is or what he's doing. How did the killer know he was there?'

'I think he was being tracked,' Billy replied. 'I've asked Cooper to check through his items to see if there's any kind of tracker on them. As yet, I haven't heard back.'

'What about this cryptocurrency?' Declan asked and then paused. 'No, we've had this before. It's pretty untraceable, isn't it?'

'Depends on where it was placed,' Billy replied. 'There's a chance we could find it, but I wouldn't hold my breath.'

'Okay, so we know Nicholas was involved in something that paid him money he didn't want any part of.'

He pointed at two lines of text.

> I don't know; I deserve a lot for this. Especially if I keep my mouth shut. I expect more than a "goodwill gesture."

> Bring the USB stick. We'll triple what you had on it.

'Although he seems to want a part of that. I'm guessing this is a burner number he's texting?'

Billy nodded.

'Looks like it, I'm checking into that right now,' he said. 'And yes. I think Stephens changed his mind, but his killer wasn't happy about it. Arranged to meet him near the park, purely so they could fashion a makeshift lance and finish the job.'

'Killing a man by sword, by gun, and by lance,' Declan replied. 'Someone's really out to prove they're the best.'

'True, guv, but they didn't best Harris though, did they?' Billy asked as his phone rang. 'They stabbed him in the back.

Harris was either running, or he wasn't even aware he was in a fight.'

As Billy answered his phone, Declan considered the statement. *Billy was right. Harris had turned his back on the killer, and Stephens had tried to renege on the deal.*

This seemed less like "honourable duels" and more like murder every passing second.

'It's Esme,' Billy said. 'She has something.'

IT HADN'T TAKEN LONG FOR PC ESME COOPER TO FIND Nicholas Stephens' personal effects and clothing, and the ward sister that showed her the items was happy for Cooper to quickly flick through, looking for anything that could help them with his tracking. After all, Cooper was a police officer and Nicholas had been a victim of an attempted murder; anything they were doing was purely in his best interests.

Nicholas's pockets had held the usual things; a wallet, some change, a set of keys, a small Leatherman penknife set – but there was also a USB stick, black and unidentified, the stick itself having a USB-C end to it – which meant it was a newer model.

It also flashed with a blue light, sometimes with a red light joining in. Esme wondered if this meant there was a Bluetooth connection going on, but either way she gave Billy a call.

'I think I've found what you need,' she said after he'd answered and told someone else she was calling. 'But it's a flash drive with a USB-C end, I don't know what to do with it.'

'What phone do you have?' Billy asked down the line.

'Right now? It's an iPhone.'

'Is it the new model?'

'Yeah,' Cooper said. 'Look, no offence Billy, but I'm not really in for discussing ...'

'No, that's fine,' Billy said. 'I wasn't asking because I want one, I'm asking because it means that your phone has a USB-C connector rather than a lightning charger.'

'Yeah, that's the charging bay,' Cooper replied. 'Wait, can I plug this into my phone?'

'You should be able to,' Billy said. 'Your Files app will tell you what's on it. It does the same on an iPad, and I'm assuming the newer version iPhone does this as well.'

With Billy still on the phone, Cooper turned the USB stick around and placed it into the base of her own phone.

After a moment, her Files app opened, showing one file.

'There's a text document on it,' she said. 'Called "Click Me." What should I do?'

'Click on the document,' Billy replied.

'Is this going to give me some kind of virus?'

'I would highly doubt it,' Billy said.

Sighing, Cooper pressed the button and read the text on the screen.

'It's a text file, giving information on how to open the crypto cold wallet that's also on the USB drive,' she said. 'Gives the password, the phrases, everything.'

'That's interesting,' Billy said, and she could tell from his tone he was likely frowning as he spoke. 'Usually you don't have something like this on your USB stick, saying how to get into the wallet, in case somebody steals it. But, it looks like somebody else has given him money on a stick, with information on how to get it. Which fits in with what we know.'

'Why is it still flashing though?'

'What do you mean, flashing?' Billy asked.

'The drive, it's flashing sometimes red, but definitely blue, constantly.'

There was a pause down the line.

'That's how they knew,' Billy eventually said. 'It's tracking. Do you have something you can block the signal with?'

'I think they know it's here already if they're tracking it,' Cooper replied.

'True, but if they're still tracking it, they'll know it's at the hospital,' Billy's voice was heard over the tapping of his keyboard. 'I don't want them to know it's been brought back to Temple Inn.'

'I'll get onto it right now,' Cooper said, disconnecting the call and waving at the nurse.

'I need a favour,' she said, the drive now out of her phone and back in her hand. 'Your equipment, medical instruments or supplies – they come wrapped in metallic foil, right?'

'Yeah, but we throw it away,' the nurse said.

'Awesome,' Cooper smiled. 'I'm guessing there's some still around. I need the foil wrapping to place around this USB.'

Declan was just entering his office when the phone went. Picking it up, he saw from the screen it was from the front desk.

'Walsh,' he said. 'Problem?'

'More something that needs to be looked at personally,' the voice of Sergeant Mastakin spoke. 'We have a lady here, wants to speak to a senior detective, and Monroe's not answering his phone.'

'Monroe's talking to Doctor Marcos, I think,' Declan replied. 'I'll be down in a minute.'

Replacing the receiver, Declan walked back out of his office and past the others, all still huddled around Billy's monitor as he checked out how to build a Faraday cage – Declan didn't really want to know why right now – and headed down the stairs to reception.

There was a woman waiting for him.

'Can I help you?' he asked. 'I'm DCI Walsh.'

The woman turned and swallowed nervously as she nodded.

'My name's Georgia Wingate,' she said. 'I'm here about the murdered men.'

'Oh?' Declan waited, sure there was more coming. 'What exactly about them?'

Georgia looked around and took a deep breath.

'I think I'm the one who killed them,' she replied.

———

9

ORGANISERS

ANJLI HAD ARRIVED AT THE FINSBURY CIRCUS ... WELL, *amphitheatre*, she supposed, shortly before the late afternoon events started.

As she'd already heard, the "Gladiator Colosseum" was nothing more than a large ring of metal barriers, about four feet in height, that the visiting public could stand behind to watch. There was minimal seating at the far end, opposite the bandstand end, with tents either side for the performers, but this was a tiny part of the expanse, and likely for dignitaries, like the Mayor of London, or well-known celebrities.

There was nobody in it right now, so Anjli couldn't confirm if her hypothesis was right or not.

Currently, there was a woman in the ring doing some kind of heel work show with a dog, a Golden retriever with a fake lion's mane around its head. This was likely some kind of "thrown to the lions" act, but the few members of the audience watching seemed amused, and it passed the time. After all, the events were free to the public, so they could come and go as they wanted.

There were food vans parked outside the railings on either side, and Anjli heard her stomach rumble – she'd had a large breakfast at the hotel, and as it was a buffet she'd had seconds, but it was well past lunch now, almost teatime, in fact and she hadn't eaten since she hit Temple Inn. She had a moment's consideration of grabbing a burger or something before she spoke to anyone, but a man in gladiator's armour suddenly appeared, walking in her direction. He was slim, short and bald, but held himself with a sort of arrogance that made him seem taller.

He stopped beside her.

'You're the police detective doing the follow up, aren't you?' he asked. 'I'm sorry to interrupt. My name's Aaron Forden.'

He spoke as if Anjli was supposed to know his name. She stared at him, confused.

'You're right, I'm Detective Inspector Kapoor,' she replied. 'And you are?'

'I was the man who found him,' Aaron said. 'Adam Harris. Last night.'

'What do you mean you found him?' Anjli paused. 'Wait, were you on the walk?'

'Yes,' Aaron replied. 'I was the one who found him beside the fort, the sword sticking out of his back.'

'And you just so happened to work with him?'

Aaron nodded.

'I can see why this sounds odd,' he said. 'And this is why I wanted to speak with you. I wasn't the only one. Georgia Wingate had given us tickets. She'd emailed us and said, you know, the City of London had given us a couple of passes as a kind of thank you for what we'd been doing. She'd asked around, and obviously a few people didn't want to do it, or couldn't find time, but she knew I had an interest in Romans—'

He made a self-deprecatory motion to his armour.

'—So she gave me a ticket.'

He looked across the field.

'There were a couple of her Dark Age people she gave to as well, Susan Cowell and her brother Rolf. The three of us were there.'

Anjli nodded as she pulled out her notepad, the thought of food long gone.

'So, you weren't there by your own decision, it was a ticket someone had given you?'

'Yes,' Aaron said.

'And do you think you were expected to find it? The body?'

'I don't know,' Aaron replied. 'But I'll be honest, if we hadn't seen it, we would have walked straight past it, as it was in the darkest corners of the grass.'

He straightened, and his eyes narrowed.

'If I was a suspicious man, I'd think somebody made sure we were there, so we'd be linked to it,' he said. 'We'd become suspects. I wanted to get ahead of this, and suggest you speak to the Cowell siblings.'

'Because?'

'Because all societies have secrets.'

'I understand,' Anjli noted this down. 'Were you friends with Adam Harris?'

'I worked with him,' Aaron replied. 'In re-enactment. I didn't spend time with him afterwards. We had our own issues.'

'We'll need to speak to you properly about this,' Anjli was still writing. 'A full statement.'

'I understand. Whatever I can do to help.'

'And you said your email came from ...'

'Georgia Wingate,' Aaron replied. 'She plays Boudicca in the big battle tomorrow evening. She's been part of the scene for years.'

'Have you spoken to her about this?'

'No. But there is one other thing. Rolf and Susan? They weren't there at the start. We had to wait for them. I didn't know it was them, just that some people hadn't arrived on time,' Aaron shifted uncomfortably, as if unhappy he was "telling" on others. 'They were ten minutes late, and we started the walk without them. And then a couple of minutes before we arrived at Barber-Surgeons' Hall and the Roman Gatehouse, they turned up apologising for being late.'

He shifted his grip on his belt, looking around in case they were being overheard.

'They claimed they parked nearby and came over, but it seemed really convenient that the two of them were near where the body was, and came to visit us just as the body turned up.'

'You think they were providing an alibi?'

Aaron shrugged.

'Maybe,' he said.

Anjli frowned at this.

'Surely, if they were making an alibi, they would make sure they were as far from the body as possible.'

At this, Aaron frowned. He hadn't obviously considered this option, and he shrugged.

'Look, I'm just telling you what I know,' he said. 'Use it as you want.'

'I see,' Anjli smiled. 'Secrets.'

She looked around the arena.

'With what you just said, we might need you to come down and answer some questions.'

At this, Aaron paled a little.

'Is there any way I could do this without having to go to the station?' he asked.

'Do you have a problem with the station?' Anjli asked, keeping her expression simple.

Aaron shrugged.

'I had a misspent youth,' he said. 'I spent many nights in police station cells, and I'd rather ...'

'Did you do time?' Anjli looked at him.

'No,' Aaron said. 'But I could have. I was very lucky I had family that pulled me out of it. Stuck me on the straight and narrow. But the fact of the matter is, I was in a situation when I was a teenager where, let's just say I was very skilled in something. And it almost cost me my career. If it hadn't been for distant family, I might not be here today. I definitely wouldn't have got into re-enacting when I did.'

He smiled.

'Re-enacting, no matter what you think of it, was the thing that made me the man I am. It stopped me from being a tearaway. And gave me discipline in my life.'

'Thank you, Mr Forden,' Anjli said, noting this down. 'We'll be back in touch.'

'I don't doubt it,' Aaron replied, nodding. 'Anyway, I'd better carry on. Nice meeting you, Detective Inspector Kapoor. I hope you find out who did it.'

This stated, Aaron gave a brief nod, and Anjli frowned as he walked off.

He was strangely formal, as if taught etiquette as a child.

However, before she could consider it further, she saw the man she'd actually come to see.

Matt Butcher wasn't walking towards Anjli, it was pure chance he was even in her eyeline, but she took the moment's opportunity. She'd seen his photo on the Festival website, so knew it was the right person; he was short, maybe five feet five, stocky and with shortcut greying hair. He looked like Bob Hoskins, if drawn by AI.

'Mister Butcher?' she asked, stepping in front of him. 'I'm Detective Inspector Kapoor. I was hoping to have a word?'

Matt Butcher paled and paused his walking, and for a brief moment Anjli wondered if he was about to run from her. But then he straightened his jacket, a black "all weather" one, and nodded as he moved closer.

'Is this about the two deaths?' he asked.

'And the attack,' Anjli added. 'Nicholas Stephens. My colleague, PC Cooper, spoke to you about him?'

'Oh, yes, of course,' Butcher nodded eagerly. 'How is he?'

'Still being operated on,' Anjli replied. 'You told PC Cooper he hadn't arrived today for the jousting?'

'It was cancelled,' Butcher explained.

'Before or after the attack?'

Butcher sighed, looking around.

'After,' he admitted, lowering his voice. 'Felt a bit off doing it after the, well you know.'

'So, he would have been coming here before that, though, right?' Anjli leant in. 'After all, if he hadn't had the attack, you wouldn't have cancelled?'

'Yeah, that'd be right,' Butcher reluctantly nodded. 'But Nick didn't come today. Probably intended to, but was attacked first.'

'Yes, you told my colleague that,' Anjli nodded, opening her notebook. 'And you're still sticking to this story?'

Butcher's eyes narrowed, and Anjli could almost see the

cogs spinning around as he tried to work out if he was being entrapped into something here.

'I'm waiting,' she said. 'If it helps your decision, we spoke to several people here this morning who saw you talking to Nicholas, and his own phone records show he was in the area. So, I ask again—'

'He was here,' Butcher blurted out, and it was as if all the tension slipped out of his body as he finally admitted this. 'Turned up this morning, came straight to me. He'd heard about Harris and Dee. No, that's not quite right. He'd heard about Dee. He didn't know about Harris until I told him.'

He looked around the park.

'He quit,' he continued. 'Said he was going to go to the police. I assumed that's where he was going next. I told him not to.'

'You told him—'

'Yet,' Butcher quickly added. 'Not to call you yet. I asked him what he thought would happen the moment it came out people involved in the history festival were killing each other. I knew it would get us closed.'

Anjli went to comment on this – but Butcher hadn't finished.

'We didn't think she was serious,' he whined. 'She was drunk. We all were. And when she made the bet, we laughed at her.'

Anjli noted this down and then looked back at Butcher.

'Do you have a name?' she asked.

Declan sat in the interview room, with Monroe beside him. Opposite them, rubbing her hands like Lady Macbeth, obviously distraught, was Georgia Wingate.

'Look, lassie,' Monroe said with a smile. 'We're not putting this on record and you're not a suspect until we know what you mean by your statement. So let's have a wee chat first, aye?'

'I killed them,' Georgia said again. 'I killed them all.'

'And how did you do that?' Monroe continued. For a confession, this sounded a little suspect, and he wanted more before continuing.

'There was a party, a pub piss up, really, before it all started,' Georgia began.

'The murders?'

'The Festival. I'm part of it. I've been organising some of the other events and tomorrow I'm playing Boudicca in the re-enactment of the Iceni versus the Romans in Londinium.'

She sat back on the chair, still wringing her hands.

'I was drinking, and I was being bolshy,' she said. 'Matt Butcher was arranging a lot of the conflict-based exhi-bitions—'

'Conflict based?'

'Duels, battles, that sort of thing,' Georgia explained. 'I was angry that we weren't being included.'

'We being ...?'

'Women!' Georgia slammed her hands on the table, anger in her eyes. 'None of the women re-enactors were being allowed to fight for "safety" reasons. Which is bollocks as we've been fighting for years in the MSS scene.'

'MSS stands for ...'

'Medieval Siege Society,' Georgia relaxed, the anger gone for the moment. 'It's a group formed to promote knowledge of the Hundred Years War and the Wars of the Roses. Mainly 15th century stuff. Though not just that. The Dark Ages guys, the Vikings, we all have women fighting.'

'I can see why you were angry.'

'Matt was sorting out the gladiators and the duels, the jousts and the Knight fights – you know the "trial by combat" fights with sword and mace, all that. He said women weren't involved in those, historically. I said he was a misogynist and a prick, and it was him blaming everyone for Pennington Hall.'

Before Declan could ask what she meant, recognising the name of the hall from Billy's information about Nicholas Stephens, she counted off her fingers.

'Joane Agnes Hotot, thirteen hundreds, trial by combat, pretends to be her father who's ill, unhorses her rival. 1892, in Vaduz, we had the "Emancipation" duel between Princess Pauline Metternich, and Countess Anastasia Kielmannsegg. Isabella de Carazzi and Diambra de Pettinella in 1552 Naples—'

'I'm sure there are many examples,' Monroe held a hand up.

'There were women gladiators too,' she muttered. 'They were called gladiatrix. And they fought over here too, as twenty years ago the Museum of London said they found remains of one in Southwark. They called her the "Great Dover Street Woman," although I suppose they couldn't prove without a doubt she was one.'

Declan leant forward.

'Look, I get why you're annoyed,' he said. 'But that doesn't explain why you're confessing to the murders of two men and the attempted murder of another.'

'I didn't murder anyone!' Georgia snapped. 'But I did kill them. I killed them the moment I made the bet.'

'The bet?' Monroe looked at Declan now. 'Perhaps you could enlighten us about this bet?'

Georgia slumped as she considered the question.

'Look,' she said. 'I'm not without funds. I have a comfortable life and I can afford easily to do the things I want to do. I'm not married. I don't have children. I don't even have a dog. But I do have over two million pounds worth in Bitcoin. Maybe a little less, as I took some out.'

'Jesus,' Monroe said. 'And you just leave it in there?'

'Why not?' Georgia replied. 'I don't need the money. I took out what I needed and kept going with it. Sure, it's worth around two million, but if I was to try to sell it, the fact that I'm selling a couple of million's worth of Bitcoin would actively bring its cost down. You can be a crypto millionaire on paper, but it doesn't mean you have the money to hand.'

'How is this connected to the bet?'

'I thought it was funny, but on second thoughts, maybe not,' Georgia sighed. 'I told them I could better them in a duel. They didn't believe me, they laughed at me. I'd done an event with Benedict in the past and found him to be an arrogant little knob-end. He was very much of the belief that women couldn't do anything that men could do. I wanted to prove him wrong.'

She stopped.

'No, I didn't want to prove him wrong, I wanted to ram his nose in it and push hard down. I wanted him to know more than anything that a woman had beaten him, and there was nothing he could do about it.'

'Who was there when you made this bet?'

Georgia considered the question.

'Adam Harris was there. Benedict, he was the main instigator of the argument. Nicholas Stephens was there, the organiser Matt Butcher, Aaron Forden, but he was just lurking in the background like a creepy short Nosferatu. There were a few others, a couple of women re-enactors who had taken my side. It had become a bit of a moment, shall we say, in the corner of the bar.'

She shook her head as she remembered.

'I said to Benedict I could beat him in a duel, and I was so confident at it, I would give him ten grand if I lost,' she looked at Declan. 'I'd had a few drinks, as I'd said, and my bravado was up, and by the end of the argument I'd offered anybody who wanted to take a shot at me ten grand if they could do it. I even said I'd send them the money in advance. They could have the money in their hand when they had the duel and give it back when they lost.'

'And how were you going to work this duel out?' Monroe asked. 'Surely you couldn't have pistols at dawn without having someone shot by a pistol at dawn?'

'That was the problem,' Georgia muttered. 'With a sword fighting contest, or something like a joust, I knew that I could win by simply making them yield. Pistols, however? That caused a problem, and when I woke up the following morning, I decided I wouldn't be continuing the bet. To be honest, the only ones who had actually taken me up at the time were Benedict and Adam, and I knew as much as Adam was sensible, Benedict would take the piss out of me if I backed down. But what could I do? I offered an exhibition match, re-enactment wise, freeform fighting, him versus me. He made some big speech about how he was an 18th century dandy and such people didn't fight common garden foes. But I knew what he meant; he wouldn't fight a *woman*.'

'Surely there's an element of chivalry to that,' Monroe said.

'Spoken like someone who doesn't understand feminism,' Georgia replied.

'I didn't mean it like that,' Monroe held his hand up. 'But surely somebody who spends his time living in a world of 18th century beliefs would look at the 18th century belief of chivalry at the same time?'

Georgia nodded.

'I see that,' she said. 'And I understand what you're saying, however wrong it might be.'

Declan held his hand up to interrupt Monroe before he started into a long argument about women's rights.

'Hold on,' he said. 'You made a bet that no one took, and that you cancelled the following day – yet you've turned up here and said you killed people. How does that work?'

Georgia sat back on the chair.

'Because I made that bet publicly,' she said. 'And someone somewhere must have decided it should carry on, even after I'd stopped. I heard this morning that Adam Harris was dead – he'd stated publicly he was going to help Benedict prepare for the duel, even though there wasn't one. And then, of course, there's Benedict, killed in … well, a duel.'

Declan now understood how she felt she'd killed the men, while not actually killing the men.

'Georgia, I don't think you're the suspect you think you are,' he said. 'You might have been an instigator, but it sounds like someone else took your idea and ran with it. Do you have any ideas of who else it could have been?'

'No,' Georgia said. 'And from what I've been told, Adam was killed early yesterday evening and Benedict was killed at dawn. I can give you proof of where I was both times.'

'And the jousting incident of this morning?'

'I was planning for the Boudicca uprising,' Georgia said. 'I can give you details.'

'So,' Declan said, looking back at Monroe, 'it sounds like you're almost as innocent as the others are here. What we need to do now is work out who was listening to you at the time of the original bet being made.'

'Or,' Monroe said, 'who realised that you were a perfect excuse to kill some people.'

BUTCHER LEANT AGAINST THE BARRIERS, STARING OUT INTO THE arena.

'I didn't take it on because I knew how good she was,' he said. 'I've seen her play Boudicca before, and she's a devil. When she gets into the fight, she loses it. She goes crazy.'

'Crazy enough to kill?' Anjli asked.

Butcher shook his head.

'No, she turned around the following day and reneged on the deal,' he said. 'Backed down from the whole bet, said it was a silly thing to be doing. I heard from a couple of people that she realised there was a chance she could lose a chunk of money. People reckoned she didn't even have the money in the first place. Benny Dee was crowing around like anything. Took the piss royally, he did. Said a deal was a deal, a bet was a bet and a loss for her would be a loss for her, forfeited or not. He was laughing all the way to the grave.'

'So, if she didn't do this,' Anjli said, 'who did?'

Butcher looked back at Anjli now, narrowing his eyes.

'I didn't say she didn't do it,' he said. 'I said that Georgia came back the following day and said she was stopping the bet. But yesterday morning, Adam Harris walked up to me and told me Benny Dee was still planning on taking her up, and he was considering it too.'

He shuddered as he remembered the conversation, with the hindsight of how it ended.

'Did Nicholas take her up?'

Butcher shrugged at this.

'I don't really talk to him unless it's an event, and I avoid him on social events, but he was there when she spoke,' he said.

'Not close?'

'Me and Stephens? No, not really,' Butcher replied, deflating slightly as he continued. 'It's one reason why I lied about seeing him. Thought it might make me a suspect in his death.'

'And why would we think that?'

At the question, Butcher frowned.

'I'm sorry, I thought you knew,' he said.

'Know about what?'

'Pennington Hall?'

'The spear throwing accident? We know Nicholas Stephens accidentally struck someone there who died later if that's what you mean.'

Matt Butcher nodded.

'Bridget Farnsworth,' Butcher said. 'She kept her maiden name. Her married name was Butcher. She was my wife when Nicholas Stephens killed her.'

10

ANTIQUES AND ASHES

CHIVALRY FITZWARREN STARED AT THE DUELLIST PISTOL IN HIS hand, turning it, allowing the light to shine upon it – well, the forensics baggie it was still in, anyway, examining it carefully for any markings he could find.

'It's a beautiful piece,' he said. 'Could I borrow it?'

'No,' Doctor Marcos said with a smile. 'If you took it away from here, I'd probably never see it again.'

'You sound like you don't trust me,' Chivalry replied, almost hurt in his tone.

At this, Doctor Marcos grinned.

'And I think you'd respect me less if I did trust you,' she said.

Chivalry nodded, placing the gun down.

'It's an original,' he said. 'But I can't work out where it could be from. I can check into records and see if there're any families that had arrangements with the gun company, but ...'

'I appreciate anything you can do to help,' Doctor Marcos said as the door opened, and De'Geer walked in.

He glanced at Chivalry Fitzwarren and almost turned

around and left, pausing, aware that doing this would be visible.

'Good morning, my Viking friend,' Chivalry said with a slight bow. 'What do you have for us?'

'I have nothing for *us*,' De'Geer replied as he walked in. 'But I do have something for my boss.'

'What have you got?' Doctor Marcos asked.

De'Geer passed over a piece of paper. 'Information from the forensics labs at Lambeth,' he said. 'We knew that Adam Harris's body had been moved to the Roman wall as the van had been seen, but Lambeth reckoned that Benedict Dee's body was also moved after his death. In fact, they reckon he'd been dead a good ten to twelve hours before the body was found.'

Doctor Marcos took the paperwork and read it.

'Interesting,' she said.

She looked back at Chivalry.

'That gun,' she said. 'Is it workable?'

'I don't know what you mean,' Chivalry said.

'I mean, is it a firing pistol?'

'Oh,' Chivalry considered this as he picked the gun up again, looking at it. 'It certainly looks as if it is. You'd have to fire it to see, and I might have some gunpowder and ammunition in my car.'

'Of course you do,' Doctor Marcos decided. 'Or, more importantly, you might know somebody in the City of London who would—'

'Actually, I have an idea, Guv,' De'Geer said. 'Malet Street Gardens. Although Benedict Dee isn't around, they're still doing talks on the era there. The re-enactors are still about with their weapons. All we need is somebody from around the time of the American War of Independence, and who has a ball that fits. We've got all the prints and DNA we can from it, and if we make sure only myself and Mister Fitzwarren hold it, we can remove those from the records later if needed.'

Chivalry nodded at the suggestion.

'If I'm allowed to go with this Viking extraordinaire to the gardens with the pistol, I could tell you if it could fire,' he said. 'Why do you ask?'

'Because if Benedict Dee wasn't killed in Pickering Place,' Doctor Marcos said, looking down at the paperwork, 'then there was no need for a duel. The gunshot would have been purely that, a shot to alert the locals at a set time, to make them go find out what was happening.'

'They wanted his body to be found at dawn?' De'Geer was surprised at this.

'Especially if he was killed elsewhere and brought to the spot. This wasn't a duel, this was a message being given.'

She stopped, reading something else.

'Here,' she said. 'On the clothing report. Did you see this?'

'What is it?' De'Geer moved closer, looking at it. 'Both bodies had traces of ash on their clothing?'

'Ash on their clothing,' Doctor Marcos said. 'The same ash. But looking at it, I think it's more likely soot.'

'And what does that mean?' Chivalry asked. 'They were attending a bonfire together?'

'Actually, you could be closer than you think,' Doctor Marcos smiled. 'But what it does say is that both bodies died around the same time, in possibly the same location.'

She glanced back at Chivalry, who'd now returned to the pistol, peering intently at it.

'That's interesting,' he said, examining the base of the pistol. 'Do you have the sword to hand?'

Doctor Marcos waved over in the room's corner where, in

a second baggie, the Gladius rested on a bench. Nodding a quick thanks, Chivalry placed the duelling pistol down, walking over to the Gladius and checking it.

'Yes,' he said. 'Look.'

He pulled the two items together, motioning for Marcos and De'Geer to walk over to him. Sighing, she placed down her pen and joined De'Geer as Chivalry started his "show and tell", pointing at two markings, one on each. It was almost as if someone had punched a marking on to both in the same way that someone would place their hallmark on a ring. It was small, easily miss-able, only half a centimetre in height, but it was the same on both.

It was a circle with a vertical line going down the middle, and a small, what looked like a dash, going from left to right in the median.

Chivalry tapped at it.

'That's an ownership stamp,' he said. 'I don't know whose it is, but they're both from the same location. If they were donated to somebody, or if they were part of a museum, that's where they're from. It's effectively like a branding on a cow or a horse back in the Wild West.'

He looked up at Doctor Marcos.

'You must have watched Western movies,' he said. 'You've always struck me as a kind of cowgirl.'

'I don't know if that's an insult or a compliment,' Doctor

Marcos smiled. 'But I always saw myself as the drunk town doctor, so I'll take it for what it is.'

Chivalry was drawing it on a sheet of paper as he spoke, holding it up to show them.

'Give me a day or so, and I'll find this, as there's definitely something familiar about it. I know a few people; with luck we'll have something by the middle of the week.'

'Make it end of weekend, and I'll be more impressed,' Doctor Marcos smiled. 'We work fast around here.'

'I know,' Chivalry sighed theatrically, pausing as De'Geer's phone went off with a piercing war cry.

'Sorry,' De'Geer said, walking over and checking it. 'It's Anjli – DI Kapoor, I mean. She has news. The woman who was killed in the accident at Pennington Hall was Matt Butcher's wife.'

'Curiouser and curiouser,' Doctor Marcos replied, noting Chivalry was staring off. 'You okay?'

'Pennington Hall,' Chivalry nodded. 'Sad case of affairs. I knew him.'

'Are we still talking about the re-enactment episode, or are you off on a tangent?'

Chivalry returned his attention back to Doctor Marcos.

'Lord Henry Crawford-Dunne,' he said. 'Owner of Pennington Hall. Used to buy some exquisite pieces from him – the funds were always low there. It's why he always rented the hall out. Died of a heart attack. Unexpected, and it meant I didn't get my "mates rates" deals anymore.'

Realising he was off on a morose memory now, Chivalry straightened.

'Never mind, I'll speak to people and see what I can find,' he said, walking to the door. 'I shall be back, anon. And then we'll go to Malet Street Gardens, and fire off some good old weapons.'

With that, Chivalry Fitzwarren left Doctor Marcos and De'Geer alone.

'Right then,' Doctor Marcos returned to her desk. 'Now the circus has left town, what's next?'

BILLY HAD CREATED A MAKESHIFT FARADAY CAGE IN ONE OF THE cells as Cooper arrived with a metal foil bag around the USB drive.

'Jesus,' she muttered.

The Faraday cage had been created from thick material from the upstairs sleeping area's blackout curtains. He'd then commandeered a large roll of aluminium foil from a shop on Fleet Street, picked up by Jess, and found an assortment of unused copper mesh from the maintenance closet. With a careful, methodical approach, the two of them had lined the interior of the blackout curtains with layers of aluminium foil, creating a metallic barrier. The copper mesh was woven into the fabric, ensuring no gaps were left. They'd then erected this contraption around a small, nondescript table in the middle of the cell, using the sturdy chairs to support the impromptu structure.

Inside it Billy sat, laptop on his lap, while Jess stood outside, seemingly forcing the makeshift structure to stay intact by the power of her mind.

'I have the drive,' Cooper said. 'I don't think it's been tracked here.'

Billy nodded, waving for it to be passed over and then for Cooper to back out while Jess lowered the curtain, with a wire mesh window the only visible view of the Detective Sergeant.

This done, he started unwrapping it. The drive wasn't flashing anymore, and Billy nodded with a slight smile.

'I think it's working,' he said. 'As far as anybody who's following this knows, it's gone dead at the hospital and with the amount of things that a hospital can have that could block this, lead aprons, x-ray machines, MRIs, all that kind of magnetic imaging, there's a very strong chance they won't even consider it's been taken away.'

He plugged it into a laptop.

'This is an air-gapped laptop,' he continued. 'Not connected to any internet. It'll tell me what's going on and it won't cause any alarms, either.'

He opened up a file, reading it.

'This is the file you saw, right?' he asked, turning the screen to show Cooper through the mesh. On it was a document, a simple text list of instructions on how to open up the cold wallet.

'Yes,' Cooper nodded. 'It didn't show me anything else.'

'It wouldn't,' Billy said, scrolling down the file structure. 'Because there's nothing else on the drive. Look, it's completely empty apart from this one text file.'

'But the document says there's a file on the drive,' Cooper argued.

'Oh, I know exactly what the document says,' Billy replied. 'But I can tell you now, it's a lie.'

He sat back, taking the USB out of the drive and placing it back into the wrapped metal casing. This done, he rose, the makeshift cage collapsing around him, to Jess's dismay.

'This USB stick is worth nothing,' he said. 'There's no cryptocurrency on it, no cold ledger. Everything in that document is made purely to make somebody looking at it casually think there is. If somebody was giving him money, and they weren't giving it here, he could have had this emailed, so this was purely a tracker for someone to follow him.'

He looked back at the document.

'The question is, who?'

BY THE END OF THE DAY, THE TEAM HADN'T GOT ANY FURTHER. Although Butcher was convinced that Georgia was some kind of psychopath and they all now knew the woman accidentally killed by Stephens three years earlier had been Butcher's wife, Declan and Monroe had both felt that there was something more to the story than "crazed re-enactment woman going berserk," and there was the fact she had alibis for several of the locations, especially the joust on a motorcycle, during which she was organising an uprising against the Romans as Boudicca elsewhere – which Declan felt was one of the strangest alibis he'd ever heard.

By the time the end of the day hit, Declan and the others were already deciding to call it. Until they had anything more on the soot that was found on the bodies, CCTV footage on where the van had come from, news on Pennington Hall, in case it was relevant or even images of the motorcyclist – the fact it was a Saturday, meaning the footage was slow to come through – there wasn't much more they could do.

It was around then they heard the news that Nicholas Stephens had passed away on the operating table. Although the wound had missed many of his vital organs, the trauma had simply been too much.

Monroe walked into the main office, a bottle of Scottish

malt whisky in one hand and four glasses in the other. Gently, he placed them down and poured a small measure of whisky into each one.

'Well, it's been an interesting twenty-four hours,' he said. 'And I don't think we've ever been so in the weeds with three bodies.'

'At least by now one of us would have a clue as to who did it,' Declan admitted. 'But here we've got nothing. No DNA, no fingerprints, no witnesses.'

He took one of the passed tumblers of whisky, raising it in thanks to Monroe.

Anjli sat back with her own glass in her hand.

'Butcher was terrified,' she said. 'I'm sure there's something more going on there. He was aiming everything at Georgia, too.'

'Aye,' Monroe said. 'I'd like to know more about this drunken bet they made and who was around. Also, if someone killed my wife, I wouldn't be so relaxed about it, so I think there's more going on there than we know. Search into this Bridget woman, will you?'

Anjli nodded as she noted this on a post-it.

'What do we actually have that's workable right now?' Monroe now asked the room.

Declan shook his head.

'We're back to where we were at the start,' he said. 'It could be a rival, another re-enactor who's unhappy with what's going on. It could be Georgia, having decided after all to get revenge on the men who took her spots. It could be something completely different. If it had been Stephens on his own, then Butcher's a suspect, but Harris and Dee? I mean, Harris worked closely with him for years, from what I saw, and had nothing to do with the death. Dee doesn't even do Dark Ages stuff. At the moment, we have no clue.'

'We need to deep dive,' Monroe said. 'Go off-piste a little. Is there anything that connects these men that isn't to do with duelling or this bloody festival?'

Billy looked around from his monitor station.

'They're all roughly the same age,' he said, 'give or take a few years. Perhaps they were at university or something like that.'

'Maybe a university group,' Anjli added.

'Do we have anything on their families?'

'Nothing,' Billy looked back at his screens. 'From what we have here, all of them were single. Only one of them had a living parent, the rest were orphans. Could this be the connection?'

'What? Single orphans, laddie?'

'We've had stranger in the past,' Declan pointed out.

'Look into it, I suppose.' Monroe didn't sound too optimistic, however, and there was a long, drawn out moment of silence.

'I didn't want to ask, sir,' Declan said. 'But what happened with Wintergreen?'

'Believe it or not, she offered to go back under the radar, kill her identity again to allow me to marry Rosanna,' Monroe said. 'I couldn't let her do that. After twenty-odd years, she's finally gained her life back. I felt it was only right we wait for her to sort herself out. We can go through the divorce, annul the relationship the proper way.'

'And how does Doctor Marcos feel about this?' Anjli asked.

'Oh, she's ecstatic,' Monroe deadpanned. 'What the bloody hell do you think, lassie?'

He looked around.

'Where's Jess?' he asked. 'Has she gone home already?'

'No, she's ... sitting with ... reception at the moment,' Declan replied hesitantly. 'Learning the process of *Holmes2*.'

'I thought she already knew how to use *Holmes2*,' Billy frowned.

Declan nodded, realising he was digging a hole he couldn't get out of.

'She does,' he replied. 'But at the moment, she's looking up a particular thing and ... well, she needed a bit of uniform help.'

'What kind of thing?' Monroe asked, frowning. He could tell there was something else going on here.

Declan winced. His poker face had never been that good.

'She's looking into similarities in local murders ... with the Red Reaper case,' he finally gave up, slumping back into the chair.

At the name, Monroe almost spluttered his whisky out.

'Bloody *Red Reaper*?' he said, looking around. 'Is there something you want to tell us, laddie?'

'Not really,' Declan shook his head. 'Margaret Li told me about him.'

'That was weeks ago!' Monroe's face was reddening with anger now. 'You've waited until now to tell us he's alive?'

'I don't even know if he is alive!' Declan snapped back. 'She told me he was apparently killed in an explosion, and the DNA confirmed him, but let's be honest – with the CIA playing games or even with his ability in hiding, who knows if that's real? We're just keeping our options open, and the moment I had any confirmation, I was going to let you know.'

'You should have let me know anyway,' Monroe muttered.

'No, you were busy with other things, and the last thing

you needed was conspiracy theories,' Declan folded his arms defiantly. 'When I have something concrete, then you'll all know.'

There was a long silence. Apart from Cooper and the uniforms downstairs who turned up after the refurbishment, every other officer in the Last Chance Saloon had worked on the Red Reaper Case in some way. This was personal for all of them.

'So, let's solve these murders before we go looking for new ones, yeah?' Declan said, his anger dissipating. 'Just a thought.'

———

11

MORGUE-ING

DOCTOR PETER OSBORNE, FORENSIC PATHOLOGIST OF THE Metropolitan Police Forensic Science Laboratory in Lambeth, gave a warm smile as Doctor Marcos walked into his office. His "office," of course, was a morgue, and Osborne was currently elbows deep in the body of a young woman. Late twenties, stocky, black with premature greying hair, he looked almost too young for the position, while at the same time too old.

'Doctor Marcos,' he said with a smile. 'I would give you a hug but uh ...'

Doctor Marcos smiled back and shook her head.

'I'm fine, thanks,' she replied.

'Give me a moment,' Osborne said, rising from the body, pulling off the long latex gloves he wore and placing them in a bin beside him. 'I'm guessing you want to have a chat about the others.'

'Please,' Doctor Marcos replied, following Osborne through into another room which was his actual office, although he was barely ever here. Osborne sat down behind his desk, taking a swig of water, washing it around his mouth before swallowing.

This done, he removed the nose clip he wore over the base of his nose. It was the kind of clip that Olympic swimmers would wear to stop water going up their nose while swimming, and Doctor Marcos smiled as she saw this.

'Still don't like the smell?' she asked.

'I thought I'd get used to it once I moved on from blood-work,' Osborne smiled. 'I don't know what it is, but there's just something about a freshly murdered body that just makes me want to puke all over it. I'm guessing you don't have that problem?'

Doctor Marcos shrugged noncommittally.

'I'm sure there's a reason,' she said. 'But I'm hoping it's not that I'm some kind of psychopath or sociopath. I find it comforting to work with the dead.'

'Probably because you don't have to have a conversation with them,' Osborne replied, his face softening. 'Hey, I'm sorry to hear about your wedding being postponed.'

'How the hell did you hear that?' Doctor Marcos raised an eyebrow. 'I haven't told anybody yet.'

She paused and nodded.

'You were at Monroe's stag night?'

'No, but Raj was, and he told me what had happened when he popped by today,' Osborne grinned. 'I was only asking if De'Geer and Cooper had split up yet, and I got the entire story.'

Doctor Monroe nodded, understanding now.

'Rajesh Khanna is a bloody gossip,' she said. 'Yeah, it's a pain, but we're hoping it's a minor delay rather than something long and painful. We're both not getting any younger.'

'Well, if there's anything I can do to help ...' Osborne left the offer on the table, trailing off as Doctor Marcos slowly leant forward, malevolence in her eyes.

'Well,' she said, 'if ever the body of a woman, white hair, looks a bit like Helen Mirren turns up? Just agree it looks like accidental causes.'

She chuckled and Osborne laughed with her, but he gave the laugh of a man who wasn't sure whether the woman in front of him was serious or not.

'I must admit,' he said, quickly changing the subject, 'I was surprised to see that you'd passed us the bodies. Usually you like to do this yourself, and I'm nowhere near your league.'

'I do,' Doctor Marcos replied. 'But Temple Inn isn't that large. We don't have space for multiple bodies and it looks like we now have a third coming in as well.'

She shrugged.

'Besides, at the time I thought I was going to be getting married in a week, and I didn't really want things around that could take my time, if I could outsource it to experts like you.'

Osborne gave a mocking bow.

'You always say the right things,' he said.

'So what do you have for me?' Doctor Marcos asked. 'De'Geer came by earlier on and said you'd found stuff?'

'Yes,' Osborne started pulling up the notes on his computer screen. 'Interesting case you have, but then I don't think you guys have ever had a boring one.'

He read for a moment, nodded to himself, and then looked back at Doctor Marcos.

'Benedict Dee was definitely killed by a bullet to the head. That's not been contested. Entered through the eye socket, was still there when we found it. It matches the size and calibre of the duelling pistol you found in his hand too, so probably from its twin.'

'Okay,' Doctor Marcos replied. 'But you have more. I can see it in your eyes.'

'Well, the interesting thing was when we examined, there wasn't enough blood there to show he'd been killed on the spot. He'd obviously been moved there,' Osborne explained. 'When I examined the body, I gave an estimation that he'd been dead over twelve hours by the time we found him.'

'Twelve hours.' Doctor Marcos nodded at this. She'd already seen this in the notes, but it was good to have it spoken to her. 'So we're talking before six in the evening?'

'That's an estimate,' Osborne said. 'If I'm being honest, it could be thirteen, fourteen hours. The body changes around then. But, in my honest and professional opinion, I would say the time of death was probably somewhere between four in the afternoon and six in the evening.'

Doctor Marcos leant back on the chair at this.

'We have witnesses saying Benedict Dee was teaching duelling in a park in London until around three,' she said. 'Are you telling me he left the duel, went straight to some unknown location and got shot in the head?'

'Well, I don't know much about the location, but we know something,' Osborne replied, tapping on his keyboard a bit more. 'There was some kind of ash residue on Dee's back, on his clothing, as if he'd fallen back onto soot of some kind. Since checking into it, I can tell you it's coal.'

'Coal?' Doctor Marcos straightened at this. 'You're saying he was in some kind of coal cellar?'

'Possibly,' Osborne shrugged. 'That sort of thing's your job, not mine.'

Doctor Marcos considered the information.

'Do you have anything else that you may have found strange?' she asked.

'Well, Mister Dee had gunpowder residue on his hand, but then if he was teaching duelling and firing pistols in the afternoon, he would have,' Osborne turned back to his computer. 'However, there's something more interesting about the other body.'

At this, he tapped on his computer again, pulling up another file onto the screen.

'Adam Harris,' he said. 'This is the one that you knew had been brought to the location, right?'

'There was a van, but it had fake licence plate numbers.'

'Yes, that's what I thought. The body was brought to the location you found it in, laid on his front, and then the sword was stuck in his back,' Osborne looked up at Doctor Marcos. 'Interestingly, though, we have a slight dilemma with this chap.'

'How so?'

'Time of death comes in at roughly the same time as Benedict Dee.'

At this, Doctor Marcos half rose from her chair.

'Wait,' she said. 'He was murdered somewhere between four and six in the afternoon?'

'Pretty much, yes.'

'That can't be,' Doctor Marcos started flicking through her notebook, looking at the notes that she had made during the briefing. 'He'd been working as a gladiator in Finsbury Circus on Friday. He did two shows. The second was at four thirty, five in the afternoon. There's no way he could have performed as a gladiator, made his way to wherever this is, had a duel and died in the space of an hour.'

'I'm just telling you what the body tells us,' Osborne tapped a button, and a printer in the office's corner started to buzz. 'Got something else for you, though, on that.'

'There's more?'

Osborne nodded, with the slightest hint of a smile on his face.

'Mister Harris here had the same coal traces on the front of his uniform, or whatever it was he was wearing. Second, the stab wound where the Gladius was had something wrong with it. I checked, and I believe he wasn't killed with the sword.'

'What do you mean?'

'Exactly what I said. The sword didn't kill him. He was shot in the back, and from behind. There's gunpowder residue around the wound, and somebody later on took the sword and stabbed it into his back, to make it look like he'd been murdered with a blade.'

Osborne sat back in his chair with a knowing smile and an annoying, "I-know-something-you-don't-know" grin as he placed his hands on the table.

'He also had gunpowder residue on his right hand,' he said. 'Our Roman fired a pistol in the last few hours of his life. If I was a betting man with two people found dead, both of effectively gunshot wounds, both around the same time and both with gunpowder residue, I would say they killed each other. But as you said, how could he if he was already on stage at the same time?'

Doctor Marcos rose from the chair, walked over to the printer, and took the printout.

'Thanks for this, Peter,' she said. 'I don't know if this helps yet, but it definitely gives us something more.'

With that, she turned and started towards the door.

'Hey!' Osborne spoke out, causing her to turn and look back at him. 'If a white-haired Helen Mirren lookalike *does* turn up, I will look the other way because I respect you enough to do something like that. But I really hope that you're joking.'

'It all depends on whether she fulfils her promise or not,' Doctor Marcos said. 'Stay safe, Peter, I'll speak to you soon.'

MATT BUTCHER SAT IN THE CORNER OF THE BAR OF THE Lyttelton Arms in Camden, sipping at his shandy, watching the others standing around him.

Many of them there were re-enactors and history experts, just as they had been in the bar for the last week and a half. But whereas in previous times and events around the country he classed them as friends and allies, people of the same mindset, now every single one of them was a potential enemy.

How long before they work it out, he thought to himself. *How long before they know you lied?*

He shuddered, pushing the thought away. He couldn't think about this. He had to find some other way of getting through what was going on.

Harris was dead.

Dee was dead.

And now Stephens had joined them.

Was this because of Bridget? Had Stephens put this into action without knowing?

He looked around the bar once more, trying to focus on the faces. Although he wasn't drinking strong drinks, he was tired, and the room was spinning a little. It had been a gruelling day, not helped because once the news of the duel murders – and by that he meant duelling murders, rather than two murders – had come out in the afternoon press, people had appeared in the park, more than expected, all hoping to see another murder in front of their eyes. He'd even had to explain to several people that the murders hadn't happened in the Gladiator Arena, and it wasn't going to be some kind of snuff show for them.

But they hadn't cared. All they wanted was to see a body, and they cheered and shouted even louder when the Gladiators fought.

In a way, it was lucky that Nicholas had been unable to joust that day. With the amount of people who had converged onto the park, they wouldn't have had the space to create the jousting arena.

There, in the corner beside the bar, was Susan Cowell; he recognised her immediately from her short pink hair. They hadn't spoken for a while, not since the split.

Not since the murder.

Rising, he quickly made his way over to her.

Looking up and seeing him, Cowell groaned.

'Susan,' he said. 'Can I have a word?'

'Look Matt,' she replied, 'I've had a really tough day. Can I do this tomorrow?'

'It's not about work or anything,' Butcher continued.

Susan shook her head.

'I know,' she sighed. 'I'm guessing you're having a shit-fit about the bodies.'

'Three of them are dead,' Butcher nodded. 'Who knows who's next?'

Susan went to snap a reply and then slumped, her shoulders tired as well.

'Who's left?' she asked resignedly. 'If you believe in conspiracy theories, one of them killed her, one helped with the alibi and the third signed the forms. All the loose ends are tying off nicely for you.'

'It was us, once,' Butcher snapped. 'It was always us.'

'No,' Susan shook her head sadly. 'It was always you and Bridget, trying to screw each other. I was a pawn to be played.'

She leant in.

'And so was Georgia.'

She watched Butcher's face as he stepped back.

'You wanker,' she hissed. 'You bloody knew!'

'No,' Butcher shook his head. 'I suspected, sure, but she said nothing, and I left it. Harris told me about her accounts a couple of weeks back, and I know Stephens had been sniffing around. That's how I worked it out.'

He sighed.

'It was just a terrible accident,' he said, but as he spoke, his eyes narrowed as he leant closer. 'Wasn't it?'

'Curious now?' Susan stopped herself smiling as she stared at him. 'Three years too late, mate.'

'That's not a no,' Butcher pressed. 'You know, hindsight's a bloody good thing. Here I am worrying about the hall and the death, but it wasn't the only death, was it?'

He looked around, lowering his voice again.

'You know Nicholas asked Benedict to send him the case notes, right?' he asked. 'He spoke to me before he died. Said he was going to the police, that he'd worked out who really killed Bridget. Or did you already know that? You used to ride a motorbike, didn't you? Where were you this morning?'

'Don't you dare throw this on me, you arrogant shit!' Susan snapped, and the people surrounding them stopped talking, realising something was going on. 'I've known you for years, Matt Butcher, and I've watched you lose it. They died in duels, and it's all your fault. Don't try to make a conspiracy out of it!'

She straightened as she raised her voice.

'Since your bitch of a wife died – while you were sleeping with me, I'll add – you've avoided using women in duels and battles and one-on-ones. Yeah, sure, we can run around and be in the background. When an explosion happens, we can fall to the floor and play dead. But you won't let us fight. And Christ, if one of us comes near you with a sword, you lose your shit. That's why Georgia had such a problem with you. Because of your sodding wife.'

At this, there was an "ooooh" from the crowd, Butcher reacted backwards as if slapped in the face, and a broad Viking of a man walked over. He was easily six and a half feet in height, with long black hair, cut short in a buzz cut around the sides, and a beard to match. He looked like he'd walked off a Viking war-boat, and had popped in for a quick pint before killing everybody in sight.

'Is there a problem?' Rolf asked, his voice strangely clipped and middle-class in style, going completely against the look.

Susan looked up at him, patting him on the arm.

'Matt was just leaving,' she said.

'Good,' Rolf replied. 'Go on, Matt, piss off.'

'Oh, don't you start,' Butcher growled. 'Just because you're helping run the Iceni event doesn't mean you're better than me. You're doing one thing. I'm doing three weeks' worth of content.'

'My event's going to have the Mayor of London watching,' Rolf grinned. 'The Lord Mayor too, the Aldermen, everybody from the City of London. Who's turned up to yours? Some YouTubers and a person from *Love Island*.'

He leant closer.

'Although I hear that's changing now. Your show's a bit of a success since you've killed half of your gladiators.'

He held a finger up.

'Sorry ... one gladiator and one jouster.'

Butcher didn't mean to. It was an instinctive movement. But his fist landed hard on Rolf's chin, knocking him to the floor.

Even though Rolf was a good foot taller than him, the shock had unbalanced him and he landed on his arse. As the crowd around stepped back in shock, Rolf slowly got up, rubbing his cheek.

'You'll regret that,' he said.

'What, you want to take it outside?' Butcher was now hyped up on adrenaline and ready to go. But Rolf stared at him as if he was a maniac.

'No, you cretin, I'm going to have my solicitor speak to you!' he exclaimed. 'That was unprovoked. We have witnesses. I'm going to have you done for GBH, you psycho!'

Before Butcher could reply, stunned by the threat, Rolf and Susan knocked back their drinks and left.

The crowd, realising their entertainment was over, now turned their attention back to Butcher, who looked around, recognising many of the people staring at him.

People who, usually, were working under him.

'What are you looking at?' he shouted. 'Come on, drink your drinks. It's a party. Remember? It's a festival. Enjoy it.'

This shouted, he then went to the bar, ordered himself a Scotch whisky this time, and went back to the corner, grumbling to himself as he started drinking.

Shandies were fine when you wanted to keep control, but now he had decided control was for pussies.

———

12

HOME TRUTHS

AFTER EVERYBODY HAD LEFT FOR THE DAY, DECLAN AND ANJLI returned to their Hurley house, Declan in his Audi, and Anjli by motorcycle. She was still using it to travel back and forth to work when she knew she wasn't needed to drive anywhere. And on the Friday, when they had arrived, they expected a quiet day and a Saturday that didn't involve murder.

Declan knew it wouldn't last for much longer. Anjli was very much what he called a fair weather rider. That was, she wasn't happy to do it when it was raining, and autumn was already here.

He also had Jess in the car with him. She was staying for the weekend, and before the case had begun, they were going to spend the weekend doing father and daughter things.

Declan had chuckled when he thought of this. In a way, they *were* doing father and daughter things. It was just that Declan and Jess Walsh had a different idea of what father and daughter things actually entailed. If she wasn't helping him with a police crime, she was helping him uncover the story behind her grandfather's murder, or a dozen different things that were probably not the norm for such a thing.

Jess had said that she'd be spending Sunday in Henley with her girlfriend, Prisha, who was also home for the weekend. So Declan knew he had little time to spend with her, although that might have changed now she had a juicy case in her sights.

Without Anjli in the car, however, it did give Declan and Jess time to discuss what she'd been looking through on *Holmes2*. It didn't take long; the conversation was quick. Jess had found nothing.

If the Red Reaper was still alive, he'd either changed his modus operandi, or he wasn't killing any more.

'Do you think he'll come for me?' Jess asked.

Declan shook his head.

'Nah,' he replied. 'I think we're safe. Even if he is alive, there's people higher on a list that he needs to take out. And he has this weird sense of morality.'

'Good,' Jess replied, and Declan could see that she was nervous.

'Look,' he replied, 'if Karl Schnitter is still alive, we *will* find him. And if he decides he wants to start again doing the things that he used to do, we *will* stop him. You and me.'

'And the police,' Jess replied.

'And the police,' Declan reluctantly agreed.

'Because we didn't use the police last time, Dad, and look what happened.'

Declan winced a little at this.

'If we'd have used the police, Jess,' he explained, 'Schnitter would have been in a CIA Safehouse way before he arrived at the police station. The CIA were on their way to pick him up when Tom Marlowe took him.'

'I know, Dad,' Jess said. 'But if you find him this time, we can't—'

'If we find him,' Declan interrupted, 'we'll cross that bridge when we get to it.'

They hadn't continued the conversation; Jess had instead talked about college and Prisha and various teenage things. Declan had nodded and made affirmative *hmph* noises to show he was listening. But, if he was being honest, it was automatic. Because even though he was driving down the M4 with his daughter beside him, Declan's mind was on other subjects. In particular, a German with a secret, and a fixation for murdering in the name of righteousness.

ANJLI HAD BEATEN THEM TO THE HOUSE, WHICH WASN'T surprising because she rode her bike like a woman possessed. Also, to Declan's delight, she'd already ordered pizza, so for the next couple of hours, it felt like normality had returned to the family.

Anjli and Declan, relaxed and laughing.

Jess, enjoying their company, forgetting her worries and talking warmly with Anjli about things, which Declan found quite heartwarming. He'd always worried that Jess would be concerned about his relationship with Anjli. But then, considering the fact that she'd known her before Declan and Anjli had even got together – in fact, had even been telling Declan that the relationship was going to happen before he even saw it – kind of helped in that situation.

After dinner, Jess and Anjli decided they were going to watch a movie, *Practical Magic,* some Sandra Bullock and Nicole Kidman film. Declan, claiming that he wasn't in the mood, had said he'd go down for a pint at the Olde Belle, say hello to Dave the landlord and see if anything had been said about Schnitter lately in the bar.

But he didn't go to the pub.

Instead, he walked through Hurley Village, over to a derelict garage.

He stood staring up at it for a long moment. This had been the workplace of Karl Schnitter for decades. One-time friend of the Walsh family, mainstay of the community, and friend of everybody who spoke of him.

The *Red Reaper.*

When it came out that he was in fact a serial killer East German officer who had been on the run since the fall of the Berlin Wall, the community had been shaken. And in a way, they had blamed Declan for bringing this out; almost as if the people of Hurley had been hoping to keep their head in the sand and ignore it.

Understandably, nobody had wanted to take the garage after he'd gone. And it had laid still in that time.

Declan had a key. He'd kept it since the Red Reaper case, so now he walked over and opened the side door, entering the building.

He'd been in this garage many times over the years. Both as a client, bringing his car to be checked, as a friend, and as an investigating officer. Karl had been there for him when his father had died, and when Declan was accused of terrorism, Karl had even given him a car to use to escape in, without which he'd never have been able to clear his name. It was these things that had caused Declan problems when he learned Karl was actually Wilhelm Müller, the Red Reaper.

He had found out that his mother had been murdered by Karl, but done as a mercy killing. She was in pain with terminal cancer and had asked Karl to do something for her. But by not telling Patrick Walsh, Declan's father, he'd started an investigation that eventually ended with his own daughter, Ilse, killing Patrick, making it look like an accident.

Declan bit back an utterance at that thought. He wanted to scream and shout that his father had been killed, and he wasn't able to do anything.

Ilse had then tried to kill Jess. But Jess, good old Jess, had fought back and had kept Ilse at bay until Anjli and Billy had arrived.

Declan chuckled at this. In fact, Jess had beaten the living crap out of Ilse in the process, and if left alone for longer would probably have done better than Declan could have.

He was proud of her.

But again, that fight had caused problems between Declan and his ex-wife, Liz. It had taken weeks for Declan to be allowed to see his daughter again. In fact, it had taken Teresa Martinez, waiting for her trial, to convince Liz to allow Jess to see her father.

Declan had always found this amusing; that it took a killer to calm his ex-wife down. But he knew he deserved every second of it.

He turned the lights of the garage on. He wasn't hiding, or there in secrecy. If anybody asked why he was there, he could easily say he was checking some information from the case. As far as everybody was concerned, Karl Schnitter had escaped and was still out there. Nobody knew that the CIA had taken him; nobody knew of the witness relocation. If anything, if Schnitter was still alive, it meant that Declan's lie, that Schnitter had escaped and was out in the wild somewhere, was no longer a falsehood.

The garage looked as if it had the last time he was there,

but Declan noticed on the wall to the right there was a spray paint tag. Someone had got into the garage, tagged the wall and left.

He walked over to the shutters and realised they were pulled down, but not locked. Quickly, he locked it, using a chain to keep it down. He didn't want the items in the garage stolen, although there was a curiosity as to why whoever tagged the wall didn't take any items. Maybe they were scared that by taking something, the Red Reaper would come after them. It was a fair assumption, if Declan was being honest, and he was impressed they were brave enough to at least tag the wall.

The tag was more of an image than a name. A roughly spray-painted red man with a scythe in his hand. It was the Ampelmann symbol that the Red Reaper had used. It had been all over the news and Declan hoped it was someone being creative rather than some kind of acolyte showing that they too could do the same things. The last thing Declan needed was a copycat killer, while the original killer was possibly in the same area.

This done, Declan moved into the back offices.

He walked along the corridor, checking the shelving beside him. At one point, Schnitter had stolen Patrick Walsh's iMac, dumping it on one of these shelves, having removed the hard drive from inside, worried that Patrick had information on him being the Red Reaper.

He needn't have worried.

It was only in the back office that Declan really paid attention. The garage could be entered from the rear, but it was a door that had been covered with paperwork and random discarded engine parts. It was a door that had obviously been unused for years, and Declan even remembered

Schnitter giving the excuse that the key had been lost many years earlier, and he'd never bothered getting it fixed. After all, with a massive shutter at the front and a door at the side, why would you need to worry?

But there was something off with the door this time.

The items in front of it weren't against the frame as they were before. Now they were slightly at an angle, as if someone had gently opened the door just enough to slide in, but in the process had pushed the pieces back. They were in a line, a twenty-degree angle from the door.

Someone had been in. Someone who had a key.

Declan crouched, examining the lock. He couldn't see any scratches around it, but then they would have come in from the outside, not the inside. Declan pulled the handle to open the door, finding it locked.

Whoever had come in had locked the door when leaving. This was concerning. As far as Declan knew, nobody had a key. Had this been Schnitter, returning to his location, using a key he had held as a backup somewhere? There was every opportunity for him to do so. After all, saying the door was locked because the only key to it had been lost was great for making sure you could always come back if everything else had changed.

Knowing now that someone else had been in the room, Declan turned, scanning with a detective's eye. There was nothing obviously missing or out of place, as he walked over to the desk. He had stood at this desk several times over the last few months, trying to work out if there was anything he'd missed.

There was nothing.

Opening the drawers, he found the bottom one was locked, but then it always had been. Luckily, Declan had a key attached to the keyring he held in his hand, so he unlocked the bottom drawer, pulling it open. There was nothing in it, bar a few papers, ownership deeds to the land, and a photo of Schnitter at some event, being given an award. It looked about twenty years old, judging from the hair and clothing, and Declan wondered why he found the image so unfamiliar, considering he'd been through this drawer at least half a dozen times over the last year. But, picking it up and looking at it, there was nothing to see.

There was, however, something underneath it, something that fell into the drawer as Declan picked the photo up. It had obviously stuck to the back of the photo, where the tackiness of a onetime piece of Blu Tack had held it on.

It was a business card. A familiar one, Declan had seen many times and hoped never to see again. A red Ampelmann with a scythe, the sign of the Red Reaper.

Declan involuntarily stepped back; he couldn't help himself, as he stared down at the card in horror. He couldn't recall that being here before, but at the same time, he couldn't recall the photo of the event being in the drawer either.

Had someone placed the photo in here for Declan to find? Had the card on the back been placed with it as a message?

Declan looked up, glancing around.

Had Karl Schnitter been here?

The floor of the garage was based around small ceramic tiles, with a rug in the middle; there was no point having carpet when engine oil could be spilt at any moment.

He glanced back at the desk behind him, and Declan could see that there were scuff marks on the tiles where the wood had moved across them. The desk was a heavy one, in the style of a mahogany writing desk. You couldn't see underneath the drawers, but it looked like someone had slid the desk away.

Declan did the same, revealing more ceramic tiles underneath. They were small, each one only six inches square. But underneath the desk, one of these squares had a small chip in the corner. It was small, but it was big enough to wedge a screwdriver, or something of that size, into it.

Declan looked around and saw a screwdriver on the shelf; it was a garage, there were bound to be items that could be used everywhere, so he took the screwdriver, bringing it back to the tile, placing it into position, and levering the tile up.

It should have been glued to the concrete underneath. It should have struggled to come up. In fact, it shouldn't have come up at all, held down over the decades by the heavy desk above it. But it flipped up easily, and Declan could see a small hole chipped out of the concrete underneath.

Taking a torch from his pocket, he shone it into the hole.

There was nothing there.

But at the base there was a newspaper clipping, one that had been pressed into the space. If it had just been placed in there as a clipping, it wouldn't have been forced down; something had been in this hole, had weighed the clipping down under it, and had probably been recently removed.

Declan immediately pulled on his gloves. The latex was a late addition now, but this had suddenly become a crime scene.

Quickly, he pulled his phone out and dialled a number. It was answered on the third go.

'De'Geer, it's Declan,' he said. 'Are you home?'

'Yes, sir?' De'Geer's voice was cautious, unsure why Declan was calling him.

'I need you to come to the garage in Hurley,' Declan said.

'Schnitter's Garage. And bring your forensics kit.'

'Sir?' De'Geer asked.

'I think we've had a visitor,' Declan replied. 'I think he's left a message, and if I'm right, we'll find something that proves he was here.'

As he disconnected the call he knew De'Geer would already be on his way. The man was proficient if anything. Also, thankfully, now he worked for Doctor Marcos, his forensics kit was second to none.

Declan sat back on the floor, staring at the hole under the desk. It'd been there all this time, and Declan had never known. They'd never moved the desk, and even if someone had taken over the garage, the chances are they would never have seen they could pull up that small ceramic tile. Declan looked around, and for the first time in the garage, didn't feel alone.

Someone was watching him.

He didn't know how he knew this, but he could feel the eyes on his back. As he looked around, he saw in the corner a tiny, unobtrusive webcam.

It hadn't been there before.

Declan was absolutely sure of it, and now he rose, walking over and staring up at it.

'Karl,' he said. 'I know you were here. If you're back for anything bad, know I will find you.'

This stated, he reached up and pulled the wire out of the back of the camera. If Karl Schnitter had been watching and waiting, he was now blind once more.

Declan turned and looked at the office.

'That makes two of us,' he said, as he waited for De'Geer.

13

THE MORNING AFTER

EVEN THOUGH IT WAS A SUNDAY MORNING, DECLAN AND ANJLI had travelled to work early separately.

They had the feeling that there'd be a lot of driving today, and chances were they'd need to be going to multiple places, so the decision had been made to go separately, not because of any arguments or problems with the relationship, but more because they knew that two vehicles were better than one.

Because it was a Sunday, Anjli had decided to also go by motorcycle, although Declan was sure this was because she secretly hoped for a motorcycle chase with Nicholas Stephens's killer.

De'Geer, after taking samples had left the previous night, after being sworn to secrecy about the discovery, and now Declan drove back to the office with Jess beside him. She had spoken to Prisha the previous night, and had agreed that they'd meet in London in the afternoon and watch the Boudicca uprising event together, as this way she could come in, at least in the morning, and help with the case a little more.

Declan had chuckled at this. They were still in college, and Prisha had already become a copper's widow. He wondered whether this would actually affect their relationship in the years to come and hoped more than anything that it wouldn't. After all, being a police officer had affected almost every single person's relationship in the Temple Inn Unit. The Last Chance Saloon was filled with divorces and broken relationships.

Although, he thought to himself, *currently things seemed to do okay.* Monroe was eventually going to marry Doctor Marcos, Billy seemed to be in some kind of will-they-won't-they relationship with the forger Sam Mansfield, Declan was with Anjli, and as far as he knew, De Geer was still with PC Cooper, although the two of them never really spoke about their private time.

And, of course, there was always Detective Chief Superintendent Bullman, who they were all convinced was having some kind of relationship with City Police Commander David Bradbury in Guildhall.

In a way, relationships between coppers seemed to work better than with anybody outside of the industry.

Maybe Jess should be convincing Prisha to become a copper as well.

Arriving at Temple Inn, Declan found that Billy and Monroe were already there.

'Any more deaths?' Declan asked conversationally as he walked in through the door.

Monroe looked up at him.

'You almost sound as if you were hoping for one,' he said. 'Briefing room, five minutes. Rosanna's found some interesting new things.'

He paused, watching Declan.

'I also hear that you found some interesting new things as well.'

'Conversation for another time,' Declan replied, cautiously, wondering if De'Geer had given away something.

'We'll discuss it later,' Monroe shrugged. 'You did say, after all, you'd update us when it stopped being a fairy tale.'

'Surely I should decide that? I mean, I'm still the DCI.'

'And I'll let you think that as long as you want,' Monroe smiled. 'You believe you're the important one? Good for you, laddie.'

Declan chuckled as he walked over to Billy.

'Anything?'

'Yes, but I've been told by Monroe I have to keep it for the briefing,' he said. 'Something about surprises and shock reveals.'

'Is it a surprise and a shock reveal?'

'Not really,' Billy looked up. 'But we have found where the van was.'

'Interesting,' Declan said.

Anjli came down from the canteen, two coffees in her hand. She passed one to Declan.

'None for me?' Jess asked.

Anjli grinned, reaching into her pocket and pulling out a can of Coke.

'I know you're not the coffee or tea type,' she said.

Jess grinned, taking it. Anjli noticed the hurt expression on Billy's face.

'You've probably already had your caffeine intake for the day,' she snapped. 'So don't get pissy at me. At the same time, I can see you've got a fresh coffee on your desk in front of you.'

'The offer would have been nice,' Billy suggested.

Declan glanced at the door and saw Cooper and De'Geer enter, Doctor Marcos loitering behind them. Monroe, glancing up and seeing this, walked out of his office, nodding towards the briefing room.

'Come on, boys and girls,' he said. 'Let's get this show on the road.'

'RIGHT THEN,' MONROE SAID, LEANING AGAINST THE TABLE. 'AS DCI Walsh has pointed out, this is his case. But I don't care and I'm Scottish, so I win.'

There was a chuckle at this.

'Before we start the briefing, there are a few things I'd like to state,' Monroe replied. 'First off, yes, the wedding is now delayed from next Saturday. Once we know what's going on with my current marital status, I'm hoping that we'll be able to get some kind of quick fix, on the basis that my wife has been legally dead, or at least missing from all records, for almost twenty years. And that's the last we'll have on this. I don't want to talk about it, neither does she. And if Emilia Wintergreen enters the room, please make sure that Rosanna has no sharp objects in her hand.'

Doctor Marcos, sitting at the back, raised her hands up in defence.

'I've told you I'm fine with this,' she said.

'I'm sure you are,' Monroe replied to his fiancée. 'Didn't

stop Peter Osborne contacting me last night and saying you were asking him to turn his eye if he found Wintergreen's dead body on his slab.'

'It was a joke,' Doctor Marcos replied with the slightest of smiles. 'A *very funny* joke.'

'Right then, let's start with the conversation,' Monroe continued, ignoring her and looking back at the room of officers. 'Last night, Doctor Marcos found out some very interesting things.'

He sat on the table, allowing Doctor Marcos to rise and walk to the front, turning.

She was about to speak, but paused as a figure appeared in the doorway.

'Don't mind me,' Detective Chief Superintendent Bullman said. 'I heard this was a place where excitement was happening. I decided to come in on my Sunday morning and see what was going on.'

'You're avoiding a church service, aren't you, ma'am?' Anjli asked.

At this, Bullman smiled.

That I'm having to miss a church service to help my loyal unit in a time of trouble is nothing that should be considered,' she said. 'Keep going, I'm all ears.'

Doctor Marcos looked back at the briefing room.

'We now have three dead bodies,' she said, as Billy tapped on the screen, and three images turned up on the plasma screen behind her. Those of Adam Harris, Benedict Dee and Nicholas Stephens. 'Adam Harris, believed killed by the insertion of a Gladius into his back. Benedict Dee, shot through the eye with a duelling pistol. And Nicholas Stephens, lanced through the chest with a broken branch in a makeshift jousting match south of Regent's Park. Three completely unconnected events that are believed to be connected to some bet being made several nights ago.'

'Are we sure the bet is the reason for this?' Declan asked.

'Well, I'm classing it as a starting point,' Doctor Marcos said. 'I don't know yet. But I know one thing is for certain. Of the three murders we have, two of them are lies.'

There was a hushed silence at this.

Doctor Marcos smiled.

'I've got your attention now, don't I?' she said. 'We knew Adam Harris had been moved from his place of murder. The lack of blood on the scene and the double positioning of the blade into the back gave us this. I'd passed both bodies over to Doctor Osborne at Lambeth to check into as well. I worried we'd missed things, and we didn't have the space here.'

She looked back at Declan.

'He found some interesting things.'

'Pray tell, what are these interesting things of which you speak?' Monroe intoned seriously.

Doctor Marcos pierced him with a glare.

'Am I still marrying you?' she asked. 'Surely I've made a mistake.'

Before he could quip back, she looked back at the briefing room.

'Benedict Dee had been moved as well,' she started. 'After speaking with Doctor Osborne, we now know that Benedict Dee was killed twelve to fourteen hours earlier, which would place him in a four pm to six pm slot for his death. We also found traces of coal dust and ash on his clothing, particularly his back, suggesting when he died, he fell back onto something sooty that, although had been brushed off, still left traces.'

'Coal?' Anjli was writing this in her notebook.

'We're still looking to see where that was,' Doctor Marcos nodded. 'But there aren't many places that would fit that requirement in London. However, what we also now know is that Adam Harris *also* had the same traces of coal and soot on him. More importantly – and this is the fun part, kiddies – not only did Harris *also* have gunpowder residue on his hand, Peter Osborne believes the blade shoved into the back had been done so post-mortem to hide a bullet wound.'

She waited for the mumbling to stop before smiling.

'Did I mention he also believes that Harris was murdered between four pm and six pm on that day?'

'Jesus,' Declan said. 'Are you telling me that Harris and Dee had a duel?'

'I don't know,' Doctor Marcos replied. 'What I do know is that going on this, we have a new theory. Somewhere between four and six pm, Adam Harris and Benedict Dee were at least both killed by what looks to be duelling pistols in the same location. We can't be a hundred percent sure about Adam, because there was no bullet inside him; whoever shot him had taken the bullet out before ramming the blade in. But, from what we can see, if there was a duel, then Benedict Dee was shot straight through the eye socket, whereas Adam Harris was shot in the back.'

'Either he turned around or it was before he was ready,' Billy suggested.

'Fifteen paces and someone turns on ten,' Anjli muttered. 'Dick move.'

'Well, that explains the note on Dee,' Monroe said,

scratching at his beard. '"Pistols at Dawn. Practice for the real thing. Be there for five." It wasn't five in the morning, it was five in the afternoon.'

'Maybe they shot each other,' Declan suggested. 'They take their duel. They start walking. Ben turns around and shoots Harris in the back. Harris turns and in his dying moments fires his own pistol, killing Benedict Dee instantly with a bullet through the eye socket.'

'True. But then why would you then fake the death of Adam Harris? Or at least doctor it?' Anjli replied. 'Surely just having them both dead at the duel means you don't have to even hide it. Why place them in the locations?'

'Why do any of that?' Declan nodded. 'Perhaps because them killing each other doesn't fit the "duels for cash" narrative people are spreading around?'

'Hold on ...' Cooper said suddenly, checking through her notes. 'The times don't match up, sir.'

'And here we have the second problem,' Doctor Marcos smiled. 'As PC Cooper has just realised from her original conversation with Matthew Butcher, Adam Harris couldn't have died between four and six, because Adam Harris was pretending to be a gladiator around four thirty in Finsbury Circus.'

'So, how do we explain that, then?' Monroe asked.

'It wasn't him?' Billy suggested. 'The second time there was a fight, he wore a helmet. If you remember, Butcher had hinted that it was done to stop people from realising the same person from the earlier fight was back again. They pretended it was a different gladiator. What if somebody took his place?'

'Did anybody film the fight? Do we know?' Declan asked.

'Somebody on social media, perhaps, or someone from the festival?'

'I've already looked into that,' Billy said. 'I'm waiting for some responses. I believe there were people filming at the time. We can then check if there's anything that can confirm or deny it was Adam. He was bare-armed apparently, so if this gladiator's got a tattoo that Adam doesn't have, then that's pretty much a given.'

'Matt Butcher must have known this,' Declan nodded. 'There's no way he would have let a complete stranger go on there.'

'Unless he believed it was Adam.'

'It still gives us a situation though, that Adam Harris had gone to help Benedict Dee with a duel,' Monroe replied. 'As I said, the note Dee had in his pocket read "Practice for the real thing".'

'Georgia Wingate,' Cooper suggested. 'Maybe she *is* the killer. She said she had alibis for dawn and late in the evening, but now we know they were killed between four and six in the afternoon. Where was she then?'

'She said she was planning the finale of the dark ages events,' Monroe said. 'A big re-enactment of Boudicca's uprising later today. Maybe we should check if she was there around that time or even where it was.'

'I'll check into that,' Declan said, noting it down.

'There's something else,' Billy stated. 'I don't know if it's important or not.'

'Go on.'

'So, I looked into Matt Butcher,' Billy said. 'He's been doing re-enactment events for years. Since probably he was a kid. His entire family was involved in it; his father was a lord in some 15th century MSS company. Matt's wife also worked in the Dark Ages and Roman re-enactments.'

'This is Bridget Farnsworth, aka Bridget Butcher, right?' Monroe asked.

'Yes, and she passed away three years ago,' Billy said. 'As we've been told, she was in some massive battle in a field within the grounds of Pennington Hall. Something happened and unfortunately, a spear went into her chest. The armour wasn't placed on properly, or something.'

'The spear was thrown by Nicholas Stephens,' Anjli added. 'According to the coroner's report, it was a terrible accident. She was taken to hospital, and she died later from internal injuries.'

'It was a freak accident,' Billy said. 'From what I read, anyway. There was an inquest that looked into it. A coroner examined all the details, said it was an accident. But here's the thing.'

Billy leant forward.

'According to the coroner's notes, during that battle, Adam Harris was there, and at one point his horse collided with Nicholas Stephens, just as he was about to throw. The spear went wide and struck Bridget.'

'So Stephens and Harris were both involved in a show that led to the death of Matt Butcher's wife,' Declan mused. 'That could explain why he had a problem with it. But why keep using them in shows?'

'Because it was agreed it was a terrible freak accident,' Billy replied. 'The local papers talked about it. Butcher himself said his wife would have wanted him to carry on. But ever since then, he's never allowed women to perform the difficult combat pieces. In fact, one reason why he's not involved in the Iceni Boudicca uprising battle this week is because he didn't want to do it.'

'Let me guess, because Boudicca's a woman?' Doctor Marcos asked.

'Pretty much, yes,' Billy shrugged. 'I don't think they wanted to have a bearded man play Boudicca. They had to use a woman to play the part, and Butcher wouldn't agree – I think his wife used to play her, so it's a triggering subject, perhaps.'

'Hold on,' Declan said. 'Stephens and Harris were both there. What about Dee?'

'Dee doesn't work in that era,' Anjli said, looking at the notes. 'Butcher told me. He's primarily concentrated on 18th century history. He does a lot of American War of Independence stuff. Civil War. Dandies. Duelling. You name it, it's that kind of thing.'

'Then why would he be involved if this was something to do with Matt's wife?'

Billy was typing.

'I'm still going through the court notes,' he said. 'I'm trying to work out how that ...'

He trailed off as he stared at his laptop.

'You're not allowed to find things out without telling us,' Monroe said. 'You know the rules.'

Quietly, Billy tapped on his computer and his screen appeared on the plasma screen behind Monroe and Marcos. It was a record of the trial in a local paper. But there was one sentence that had been highlighted by Billy about the trial.

The coroner, Benedict Dee, agreed that some kind of freak accident had caused the wounds that led to Bridget Farnsworth's death.

'I can't believe that you'd have a name so uncommon that two people would have it,' he said. 'Harris and Stephens were part of the same battle that killed Bridget Butcher. And Benedict Dee was the man who signed off on it being an accident.'

'This isn't a Bitcoin bet,' Declan said. 'This is a revenge killing three years in the making. The question is ... *whose* revenge?'

14

INTERVIEW WITH AN EMPIRE

Matt Butcher stared at Declan and Anjli as they sat across from him at the interview room table.

He was nervous, fidgety, and unsure what was actually going on, which was exactly how Declan wanted it.

'Look guys,' he said, forcing a smile, 'I really don't know why I'm here. I've told you everything I know.'

'I'm sorry,' Declan replied calmly. 'Are you in a hurry to go somewhere?'

'Well yes, actually,' Butcher said, and the slightest hint of irritation was creeping into his voice now. 'I'm performing in the Gladiator Arena before lunch, and I need to get ready.'

'I thought you only organised this?' Declan asked.

Butcher gave a weak smile.

'I usually do,' he said. 'But with Adam now, well, you know ... we're a man short, and it's easier for me to go on.'

'That's okay, I'm sure someone could stand in for you, maybe do a double shift,' Anjli said. 'They could wear a helmet, like Adam did.'

There was something in the way she spoke this that made

Matt Butcher twitch as Declan leant forward and pressed the recording button.

'Interview with Matthew Butcher,' he said. 'Sunday, ten twenty am. Detective Inspector Anjli Kapoor and Detective Chief Inspector Declan Walsh in attendance.'

He looked at Butcher.

'Mister Butcher has no representation, and this will be classed as more of a questioning than an accusation interview ... for the moment.'

Matt straightened as he realised there was something far worse going on here.

'Look, I don't know what's going on—'

Declan held a hand up.

'Science, forensics,' he said. 'I've always been a fan of it. There's something incredible about learning using science. Things that couldn't be discussed or even considered decades earlier. Do you know, we can take a dead body and work out what time it died, almost to the minute it happened these days?'

Matt Butcher nodded at this, although he had the expression of a man who didn't quite know what was going on.

'That's great,' he said. 'It doesn't explain—'

'So, tell us more about Adam Harris,' Declan interrupted. 'On the day he died, Friday, he had two gladiator sessions, is that correct?'

For a moment, Butcher relaxed, as if believing this wasn't the problem he thought it was going to be.

'Yes,' he said. 'He had a morning session – well, by the time he went on it was closer to twelve-thirty, one o'clock, and then he went on again about four-thirty, maybe.'

'Right,' Declan replied with a smile. 'Twelve-thirty and four-thirty. And how long did these gladiator sessions last?'

Butcher scrunched his face up as he considered the question, or at least attempted to look as if he was considering it.

'Fifteen minutes, maybe,' he said. 'I mean, there's a lot of pageantry, you know; they come out, they wave to the crowds, and they run around more than a usual fight would go. We have a good guy versus bad guy thing going, it's kind of the same style as, you know, most re-enactment shows.'

'Right,' Declan said. 'And did Adam Harris take his helmet off at the end?'

'Oh God, no,' Butcher shook his head. 'There were people there who had seen him fight earlier. If he took his helmet off, then people would know it was the same guy who died in the first contest.'

'Adam Harris died?'

'Well, his *character* did,' Butcher quickly altered the comment. 'Adam agreed to be killed by the gladiator in the first round, and as a kind of apology, I let him win in the second.'

Declan nodded at this.

'Do you have photos of the battles?'

'Um, I can check,' Butcher offered. 'I mean, we have a social media person who was doing this – the festival people have their own social media, but we wanted to get a bit of promotion out there. After all, this is only once a year and we like to try to fill up our weekends. It would be on our Instagram page.'

'That's fine,' Anjli said. 'We're looking into that right now.'

'You are?' Butcher seemed taken aback by the statement. 'Can I ask why?'

'To be honest, Mr Butcher, it's more a case of working out how the dead were able to fight,' Declan said, 'You see, as I said earlier on about science and forensics, we learned an interesting thing yesterday. Adam Harris died between four and six o'clock on Friday afternoon. Closer to the former than the latter, which gives us the question, "how did our gladiator fight in the arena at the same time he was murdered somewhere secret and far away?"'

'After all,' Anjli added, 'you're telling us he started at four-thirty, so he would have finished and be back in his changing area by, say, five – while at the same time, according to our pathologist, it's about then he was actually *dead*.'

Before Butcher could say anything, Declan slammed a fist onto the table.

'Who fought in his place?' he shouted. 'Who wore the helmet? Don't tell us it was Adam Harris. We know he was dead at that point!'

'Did *you* know Adam Harris was dead?' Anjli now asked, calmer than Declan. 'Did *you* know he wasn't turning up because he was going to a duel, or at least to meet with Benedict Dee about one?'

Butcher paled as he realised he was way out of his depth here.

'Look, I'm not the only person who deals with this,' he said. 'It's not my fault.'

'Then whose fault is it?' Declan asked. 'If you weren't organising the battles, who was?'

'I was distracted,' Butcher said. 'I'd left it to somebody else. Possibly Aaron. He does a lot of things for me. Aaron Forden. He's my second in command.'

'I spoke to him yesterday,' Anjli nodded. 'He was the one who found the body of Adam Harris, claimed he'd been sent a ticket by Georgia for a walk, with Lucy and Rolf Cowell.'

At the names, Butcher flinched slightly; Declan noted this and filed it away mentally for use later.

'Right. And where was he at the time?'

'I don't know.'

'So, hypothetically, Aaron might have realised that his opponent for the four-thirty slot wasn't there, and found someone else to take the spot?'

'Yes, possibly, I think so.'

'And what were you doing that was so important, Mister Butcher?'

'I can't remember,' Butcher said. 'I was there, though. I was around. I hadn't left.'

'Handy.'

'Look,' Butcher shook his head now, leaning forward. 'I get why you're interviewing me. Two of my men died. But I didn't work with Benedict Dee. And I wasn't the one who made the bet. That was Georgia. She's insane. You should talk to her.'

'Oh, we have, and we will again,' Declan said. 'But we wanted to ask you a slightly different line of inquiry right now. Tell us about your *wife*.'

There was a long, uncomfortable moment of silence as Matt Butcher stared incredulously at Declan, his eyes wide, his mouth opening and shutting as he realised that this was more than he had ever expected.

'My wife,' he repeated.

'Yes,' Declan said. 'Tell us about Bridget. Primarily, what was going on before she died?'

It was a guess, but Declan had noted the flinch, and saw Butcher's eyes flick around the room.

'Let's pretend we don't know about Susan,' he said, playing a hunch. 'Why don't you come clean?'

Butcher sighed, leaning back on his chair, looking up at the ceiling.

'Who told you?' he asked. 'Bloody Georgia, I bet.'

'It doesn't really matter now, does it?' Declan played another card. 'We just want the truth of what led up to that accident.'

Matt Butcher straightened.

'It wasn't supposed to happen,' he said. 'I was happy. We were happy.'

'Go on.'

'Bridget and me? We'd met at an event. Two years later we were married. But we were from different worlds. She was a partner at a massive London firm. High six-figure salary a year, seven with bonuses. I was a painter. Good one, but I always lived hand to mouth. I had a dream of owning a small landholding, a wooded area with some space to build a folly, a barn, stuff like that, then rent it out on weekends to role-playing groups and re-enactors.'

He looked at the table.

'She bought me one the day we got married,' he said. 'Didn't even tell me she did it. But with hindsight, I think it was because she wasn't taking my surname, and she felt guilty.'

'How long were you married?'

'Ten years, but the last two were a nightmare,' Butcher admitted. 'She was stressed at work, she played Boudicca on weekends, and we were drifting apart. And then I met Susan.'

'Susan Cowell.'

Butcher nodded.

'She was way more my speed,' he said. 'Bridget was ambitious. Everything was financial now. The smallholding wasn't making enough, she was looking to sell it to a developer. We fought. And Susan was a shoulder to cry on. And then a shoulder to kiss.'

'We get the idea,' Anjli held a hand up to stop him continuing. 'So, you had an affair for two years?'

'Yeah,' Butcher slumped at the admission. 'I knew if I left Bridget, she'd destroy me. I'd lose the woods, and that was all I had. I was stuck. And if she learnt about Susan, she'd divorce me, and I'd lose everything, anyway.'

'Sounds like a good reason to murder her, claiming an accident,' Anjli's eyes narrowed. 'I'm guessing she had life insurance?'

At the accusation, Butcher half rose from the chair.

'I didn't kill her!' he exclaimed. 'I didn't need to. A week before the event, she admitted to me she'd been having an affair too. I didn't know who it was, but she'd already agreed that if we were to divorce, she wouldn't contest it.'

'You were happy to let her think she was in the wrong?' Anjli was angering now.

'I didn't say I was an angel here,' Butcher shrugged. 'I hadn't told anyone, though. She asked for a couple of weeks to prepare things, make sure she and I could split amicably. She promised me the woods if I did so.'

'You hadn't told Susan?'

Butcher shook his head.

'It'd been a week,' he said. 'There was nothing else.'

'So, you don't think she was murdered?'

At this, Butcher's face darkened.

'She was killed,' he said, and finally Declan saw the anger within he'd been looking for. 'People knew something was going on. Adam came to me the day before, saying he had an issue. A professional quandary. I was a friend, but he was also Bridget's accountant. He said he'd been told by Bridget to help him liquidate some assets. I knew it was so she could make our divorce amicable, but he didn't know this, and he thought she was about to screw me over.'

'And later on, he knocked Nicholas Stephens, causing his spear to hit Bridget?'

'Nobody's that good, detectives,' Butcher shook his head. 'And Adam was middling at best.'

Declan noted this down as he looked back up at Butcher.

'The coroner, he decided instead of being stupidity by a particular re-enactor, it was an accident, that it couldn't be proven to be anything to do with Harris or Stephens.'

Butcher looked around the room now, his eyes filling with tears.

'And the coroner, if we can just confirm this for the record, was Benedict Dee?' Anjli asked.

At this, Matt Butcher nodded again.

'For the record, Mister Butcher has nodded,' Anjli continued. 'He agrees that the coroner who judged on his wife's manslaughter and two of the people accused of the act are the three bodies we now have in our morgue.'

Declan gave it a moment to sink in, and then leant forward.

'Matthew,' he said, his voice soft and friendly. 'I lost my father to a killer, and it made me blind with vengeance. Even now, years after he's gone, I'm still fixated on the man who did it. It's understandable that you might want to kill them, and finding a way to do it ...'

'What do you mean?'

'A drunken bet given in the middle of a pub. One rescinded, but still continued,' Declan said. 'Something you're able to use to get your vengeance.'

Butcher shook his head vigorously, realising the implications.

'No, God no,' he said. 'It wasn't me, I didn't do this. I wasn't there, I couldn't have.'

'Do you know anywhere that has coal floors?' Anjli asked. 'Somewhere within the city limits? Somewhere easy to get to?'

'No, why?'

'Because that's where both Adam Harris and Benedict Dee died,' Declan said.

'The sword fight was there?'

'No,' Declan interrupted. 'Adam Harris wasn't killed by a sword; he was shot in the back with what we believe was a duelling pistol held by Benedict Dee. We currently suspect there's a very strong chance that Adam Harris was duelling Dee, and they both died.'

He leant closer.

'But you weren't aware of that, were you? I can see it in your eyes.'

'Wait,' Butcher replied, now eager to assist. 'Dee had a house in Hackney. Real old. Had a coal cellar. Went on for ages, soundproofed. He could practice duelling there for the shows.'

'That's very helpful,' Declan smiled. 'Anything else?'

'The day of Bridget's death, it was cursed from the start,' Butcher admitted. 'Weather was treacherous, and the owner was a prick.'

'How do you mean?'

'Just that he was an absolute bell end,' Butcher snapped. 'Kept changing the deal, altering what we could do. Because of him, we didn't get ample rehearsal time, which caused the ... well ...'

He sat back.

'Then, after it happened, Crawford-Dunne—'

'Lord Henry Crawford-Dunne?'

'Yeah, it was his house, anyway he kicks off saying that because we had a death on the field – she wasn't even dead and he had the gall to state it – and because we had to end the show early, he was going to lose money with refunds, so he was halving the payment to us. He'd only paid the deposit, and it looked like we weren't getting anything else. There was a massive argument, and shortly after that's when I ended up splitting with Susan. She was convinced we needed to take his family to court, get them to pay us.'

'The family, not Lord Crawford-Dunne?'

'No, the stupid old bastard had a heart attack and died before we could do that,' Butcher shook his head. 'And worse than that, when the inquest into Bridget was done, I learnt she'd moved all her assets into another account, like Harris had said, but it wasn't to help me, it was to stop me getting any of it. Over a million's worth. And she'd cancelled my name on the life insurance. All I ended up with was the woods, and I had to bloody fight for that.'

'Where did the money go?'

Butcher shrugged.

'I have my suspicious, but no facts,' he said. 'Because of that, I'm not throwing assumptions out there.'

Sitting back, Declan glanced at Anjli.

'Any more questions?'

'Not yet,' she replied. 'But the day's still young.'

Declan nodded.

'Mr. Butcher,' he said. 'I would suggest you contact your second-in-command and ask him to find you a replacement, because I really don't think you're going to be fighting today.'

But Matt Butcher wasn't listening, he was staring off into the distance, his expression unreadable.

Exiting the interview room, Declan looked over at Anjli, closing her notebook, and placing it in her jacket pocket.

'What do you think?' he asked.

'Honestly, I don't know,' she replied. 'If it was him, why now? If it wasn't him, is someone using his grief as an excuse?'

'Possibly, but I'm starting to believe Matt Butcher isn't the person who did this, even if he's secretly glad they're dead,' Declan replied. 'That said, I think Mister Butcher knows way more than he's telling us.'

'At that, I agree,' Anjli nodded. 'So, what next?'

'Check into his phone records, see if they can show us where he was,' Declan suggested as they continued along the corridor. 'If he wasn't anywhere near Harris or Dee when they shot each other, then we know he's not worth looking at. Let him stew for a while, then get a uniform to take him into a cell. Maybe it'll shake something loose, even if it's some kind of re-enactment gossip.'

'Affairs and divorces aren't enough?'

Declan grinned at this, refusing to answer. As they walked into the main office, however, Declan saw Billy waving at them to come over.

'I didn't realise you'd missed us so much,' he said, walking across the office.

Billy smiled smugly in response.

'I've got something,' he said. 'The motorcycle, the one that killed Nicholas Stephens.'

He started back on his computer keyboard, pulling up CCTV footage.

'Traffic cameras in the area,' he said. 'I've reversed it, following the bike as it came to Regent's Park. No records of whose bike it was though, as the number plates are missing.'

'Which means this was premeditated,' Declan said.

'Yes,' Billy replied, nodding. 'They were on the bike. They had cause. The question is, did they know Stephens was going to run? Were they waiting for him to do so?'

'Exactly,' Declan said. 'With Stephens being unarmed at the time, this was definitely no contest duel proving themselves. This was murder, plain and simple.'

'At least we have an image of the rider now,' Declan pointed at a frozen image on the screen. 'We can at least rule out anyone tall.'

Billy nodded.

'I have info on the Transit van, too,' he said. 'It was seen in Hackney, near where the Mini Cooper had its plates stolen. A small suburban street named Sutton Place.'

'That's in Hackney?'

'Yup,' Billy grinned. 'And I have something big there, too.'

'I bet I can guess,' Declan smiled. 'Sutton Place is where Benedict Dee lived, right?'

'How—' Billy's face was crestfallen. Declan smiled.

'Matt Butcher just told us, "Dee had a house in Hackney. Real old. Had a coal cellar".'

'I've not looked too close, but yeah,' Billy nodded. 'Wikipedia says about Sutton Place that "As many as three servants would live and work in the basement of each house, hauling coal from the cellars to the grates in the upper house", so if we go there and find a basement with coal dust, I reckon we have it.'

'It's also only half an hour from East London,' Declan nodded. 'That can't be a coincidence. Get De'Geer to go have a look. It's Sunday morning, should be a straightforward route.'

He was about to continue, when the doors to the Unit smashed aside, and Chivalry Fitzwarren stood there, triumphant.

'Rejoice!' he cried. 'I have solved your crime!'

'Oh good,' Billy sighed.

15

MARKINGS

CHIVALRY USHERED EVERYONE INTO THE BRIEFING ROOM, AS IF he himself ran the unit. Even Bullman, amused at this, and having been downstairs with Doctor Marcos, came up for the event, sitting behind Declan as Chivalry tapped on his phone, pointing at the plasma screen behind him.

'How do I get photos on this?' he said to Billy, who now leant back with a smug smile on his face.

'I'm sorry, do you need my help?'

Chivalry replied by folding his arms in a commanding fashion and glaring at Billy until he eventually sighed, holding out a hand to take the phone.

'That was a real Paddington Bear stare,' Cooper said to De'Geer, impressed. Of course, this impressed feeling was also because she hadn't met Chivalry that much, and the look De'Geer gave her, one of hurt and betrayal, wasn't even noted by her.

'Last five photos – don't go any earlier or it might change your opinion of me forever,' Chivalry said.

Billy nodded, and instantly scrolled back past the five photos, raising his eyebrows at what he saw.

'That's unfair,' Monroe muttered. 'Share with the class.'

Billy connected the phone by mirroring the screen and an image of Chivalry appeared on the plasma screen to a collective gasp from the Unit.

'You're a ... a *Morris Dancer?*' Declan was not expecting that, as he stared at the picture of Chivalry, in the white shirt, braces and hat of a Morris Dancer, caught mid clunk of a piece of wood in his hand.

'Of course I am!' Chivalry replied, as if this was the most obvious answer. 'The puritans banned it for being the "devil's music" and "satanic dance", so obviously I was going to try it.'

He looked back at Billy.

'Next slide, before I forget I'm still helping you win your family's love back.'

He looked back at the others.

'I knew I'd seen the marking before,' he explained as, on the screen, the image he'd drawn of the marking on the Gladius appeared. 'This was a punch that had been found on the two weapons found with the bodies.'

'The sword that was in Adam Harris's back, and the pistol that was in the hand of Benedict Dee?'

'Exactly. You might not know this, but Pennington Hall is owned by a family known as the Crawford-Dunnes—'

'We know this,' Declan raised a hand, smiling. 'Lord Crawford-Dunne passed away around the same time as Bridget Farnsworth.'

Chivalry glared at Declan and then searched around the room.

'This will all go far easier, if you forget you know this and pretend I'm brilliant,' he replied. 'Wait. You said *around* the same time?'

'Well, yes, we don't know exactly—'

'Aha!' Chivalry crowed. 'Then I am indeed still the man to solve the case!'

'I don't recall asking you to solve the case, Poirot ...' Monroe frowned. 'How about we start with this image?'

'So, I chatted to an old chum of mine. Timmy. We call him "Tim nice but dim" after that Harry Enfield sketch. But he's actually quite bright, so we probably shouldn't do that. Anyway, he reminded me of an old museum sale I went to a while back. Stately homes and museums often sell off old, battered shit they don't want, and people pay top dollar for it, because they're stupid.'

'Hold on,' Doctor Marcos raised a hand. 'Didn't you say you used to buy pieces from Tim nice but ... Timmy?'

'Yes, but not the shit pieces,' Chivalry replied loftily. 'Timmy worked for Henry Crawford-Dunne. He was a kind of broker for his antique sales and I stopped, as I said to you, when his boss's "mates rates" disappeared.'

He looked back at the others.

'Anyway, Tim nice but ... well, Timmy, he saw the marking and confirmed it was the Crawford-Dunne family's crest, or at least what was on the family's seal.'

He nodding to Billy, who changed the image on the plasma screen.

'You can see here, the circle with the line down the

middle are actually a C and D placed together,' he explained. 'The small hyphen in the middle is the hyphen between the two names. C-D, Crawford-Dunne.'

'So how do antique items from a stately home arrive in dead bodies?'

'Maybe it's because it's where the re-enactors had the event?' Jess said, looking around. 'Of course it was. Sorry.'

'No, small child, you are indeed correct,' Chivalry grinned. 'And this all ends up with that fateful day.'

He looked around, and Declan groaned; Chivalry Fitzwarren hadn't finished.

'You see, there were arguments afterwards,' he explained ominously. Over-ominously, in fact.

'Yes, Matt Butcher said that the Hall wasn't paying them, because of refund requests from the public.'

'Exactly,' Chivalry smiled as he nodded at Declan, who suddenly wondered why he felt he was being patted on the head. 'The house claimed that what happened on the field that lunchtime was nothing to do with them. Understandably, it was re-enactors having an accident, but they claimed that one accident ended the event, and cost the house valuable PR and good relations.'

'Good relations?'

'As far as they were concerned, they'd paid in good faith for an event, which had been cancelled halfway through the day because of effectively an almost death on the battlefield – remember, at this point the woman, Bridget Farnsworth was still being operated on.'

Monroe shook his head.

'Jesus,' he whispered. 'So this house, this Pennington Hall, they were annoyed that someone had almost died and spoiled their wee little Ceilidh?'

'Effectively, yes,' Anjli replied. 'It's what we were just told upstairs. They argued they didn't have to pay, and that they wouldn't finish the payment.'

'They'd paid a deposit when everything had started, but at the end of the day, when the re-enactors went and asked for money, they said no,' Chivalry added. 'Turned into a bit of a complicated event. Henry, the Lord of the house, also had a heart attack and died, which put a real dampener on things, but when the dust settled, they ended up going to court over this. However, during the court case, the house claimed that several items of worth had been stolen from the house on the same day.'

'Do we know what the items were?'

'Timmy – I suppose I should call him Timothy – wasn't sure, but when he looked into the details, it looks like the re-enactors, realising they were being stiffed, had taken items in kind.'

'But this is hypothetical, right?' Declan asked. 'With Henry dead, nobody can prove if they did or didn't?'

Chivalry didn't reply, nodding to Billy to move to the next image, and a picture of a stately home downstairs room appeared on the screen.

It was as a stately home room would look, with wood panelling and flocked wallpaper, but the walls showed swords, axes, pikes and pistols all over it.

'They have an extensive armoury,' Chivalry explained, looking back at Monroe. 'One that goes back many hundreds of years. The family of the late Lord Crawford-Dunne claimed that someone from the re-enacting group had walked in and taken several items worth high six figures to the right collector. The two items downstairs were likely stolen from Pennington Hall three years ago, and now they've been found with two bodies.'

He waved to Billy, who changed the photo once more. Now it was the same room, with at least a third of the weapons now missing.

'They claim the thefts had to occur on the same day, as that was when the re-enactors had vans large enough to steal the items. In fact, they even claimed they had an image of the van from the outside CCTV, but the re-enactors claim this was from when they arrived to collect the non-payment.'

'What kind of van?' Declan asked.

'I don't know. A grey one.'

'Transit?'

'I'll look into it,' Billy said, already typing on his laptop.

'It'd make sense,' Monroe mused. 'The grey Transit that took the bodies would now be part of some kind of revenge. Like we had on the Justice case.'

'Do we know who spoke to Henry Crawford-Dunne?' Anjli asked.

'The people running the event spoke to *Lord* Henry Crawford-Dunne,' Chivalry replied.

'No, that can't be right,' Anjli checked her notes. 'Matt Butcher ran the event. He would have been in the hospital with Bridget, regardless of how he felt about her. Someone else would have had to do it.'

'Timothy said they claimed it was two men and a woman who spoke, and the woman had pink hair,' Chivalry added.

'So we can probably confirm it was Susan Cowell, probably her brother too, and the third could be Aaron, or someone else,' Anjli noted this down in her book.

'I'll ask him when I see him,' Declan muttered.

With that, Chivalry Fitzwilliam gave a little bow.

'I now relinquish the floor back to Detective Superinten-dent Monroe,' he said, stepping back and standing by the door as Monroe rose.

'You sure?' he asked, half-mockingly. 'I'd hate to interrupt your flow.'

Chivalry made a little wave, unaware he was being mocked. Or, more likely, he knew, but simply didn't care.

Monroe walked back to the front of the briefing room.

'So, we need to know who killed the three men, whether it was connected to the death of Bridget Farnsworth, or even the possible theft of thousands of pounds of—'

'I'm sorry to interrupt,' Chivalry held a hand up, and Monroe bit his lip to stop snapping a reply. 'But it wasn't thousands. The Crawford-Dunnes, in the court case claimed there were many hundreds of thousands of pounds' worth stolen. Maybe even millions. A lot of the items were unique, you see. One of a kind creations that had been with the family since Tudor kings gave them the land.'

'What happened to the court case?' De'Geer asked. 'Did they come to terms?'

'No,' Chivalry shook his head. 'The problem was that Henry Crawford-Dunne didn't have children, at least legiti-mate ones, and the extended family couldn't come to terms with who actually owned what. Add to that the fact there was no proof, and it was their word against the re-enactors, in the end it was dropped, and both sides paid their own costs.'

'So there are no Crawford-Dunnes left?' Declan was surprised at this.

'Oh there are,' Chivalry shook his head. 'Not part of the immediate family, that's all. After hundreds of years, you'll have offshoots by the bucket load, all convinced they're owed a piece of the pie. Bit like the Fitzwarrens, really.'

'Right then,' Monroe glared at Chivalry as he continued. 'We need to know who killed the three men, whether it was connected to the death of Bridget Farnsworth, or even the possible theft of *hundreds* of thousands of pounds of antiques, and perhaps even the death of Lord Crawford-Dunne himself, how and where it was done, and what's next—'

He paused as Chivalry's phone went off; raising an eyebrow as the elderly eccentric answered it.

'Hello?' he answered. 'Timothy! So good to hear from you. You what? Oh, that would be capital. How did you find them? Send them to my email.'

He looked up, catching Monroe's gaze.

'Must dash, I have a miserable old Scot glaring at me,' he said into the phone. 'No, not the club. Yes, I suppose they are all miserable up there, aren't they? Cheerio.'

He disconnected the phone and looked back at Monroe.

'As I said, the chap is an old friend,' he explained. 'Spoke to Pennington Hall, they have some PR shots of the fight, asked if I wanted them. I'm guessing you'd like them?'

'Aye, you'd be right.'

'So, answering the phone was important?'

Monroe groaned, nodding.

'Aye, you'd be right again.'

Chivalry sat back with a smile on his face.

'I'll forward them to Billy as soon as I get them.'

'Aye, you do that,' Monroe looked around. 'For the love of Christ, do we have anything else?'

'Do we keep Matt Butcher in a cell?' Anjli asked.

'For the moment,' Monroe nodded. 'He might be useful. But if we can't get anything, we'll have to let him go free. Declan, carry on with visiting Forden at the gladiator arena, see what he says to you. Anjli? Go chat to the pub they had the original bet in, see if we can shake anything out. De'Geer? Go have a look at Benedict Dee's swanky house, see if he had some kind of coal-cellar kill room. Cooper? Go check Nicholas Stephens' house in Surbiton. I'll have a wee look around Adam Harris's place.'

He stopped as the phone in the main office went. Cooper ran out, answered it, and then came back.

'There's a DCI downstairs named Warren,' she said. 'Claims she's here to see Monroe about Nicholas Stephens and Pennington Hall.'

Monroe grimaced.

'It was only a matter of time,' he said morosely. 'Anjli, check out Harris's place after you do the Lyttelton Arms. I'll have a chat with DCI Warren.'

He looked at Chivalry, and a mischievous smile crossed his face.

'With our consultant, Mister Fitzwarren here,' he finished. 'Yes, I think they'll get along swimmingly.'

16

LAST ORDERS

THE LYTTELTON ARMS PUB IN CAMDEN WAS WELL KNOWN IN the area for its connections to the Racetrack Wars of the 1920s, then known as The Southampton Arms. It was here where the Clerkenwell Sabini Brothers, allied with Alfie Solomon and Alf White, fought often with Camden's George Sage, with several shoot-outs happening in the pub, making it a go-to attraction for *Peaky Blinders* fans.

However, for the last two weeks, it had been the de facto entertainment base for the re-enactors and role-players that had been performing in the Festival of London's activities. Anjli had come here herself over the years, and looking up at the building, she felt a wave of nostalgia wash over her before she entered through the main doors.

She also made a mental note to re-watch *Peaky Blinders* again.

It was the start of Sunday lunchtime now, and there was sport on one television, a small crowd of people sitting watching it, but to the right there was more space as it led to the bar. Anjli, deciding to avoid the sports fans, wandered over, nodding to the barman.

'DI Kapoor,' she said, showing her warrant card. 'Is the duty manager around?'

The barman looked about.

'I think he's in today, but he might be on break.'

'That's okay. Is he the manager who would have been on during the evenings?'

'It's either him or Shannon,' the barman replied, pursing his lips as he thought about it. 'What's the problem?'

'I'm trying to find somebody who was here on Tuesday,' Anjli said. 'In the evening.'

The barman nodded at this, already knowing the answer.

'Yeah, that's Neil,' he said. 'I'll go get him.'

He wandered through a door to the side of the bar and Anjli took a moment to look around the bar. In the corner there were a couple of men having a drink, wearing the garb of what looked to be dark-aged peasants. Anjli assumed they were part of the event, having a break before going back.

Well, at least she hoped so.

She considered going to speak to them, but before she could, a tall, large man, stocky and broad, walked through the door, nodding at her.

'I'm Neil,' he said. 'Neil Chapman. I'm the duty manager, and I was on shift Tuesday, so what can I help you with?'

Anjli smiled and turned around.

'I'm looking into the deaths of three re-enactors,' she said.

At this, Neil nodded sadly.

'Yeah, I know the ones,' he replied. 'People have been talking about that all weekend.'

'I understand they came in here in the evenings?'

'A couple of them I saw,' Neil nodded. 'I was also told they were part of the fight.'

'The fight?'

'Re-enactors and live role-players from different times, different areas,' Neil shrugged. 'They were all prissy little queens if you ask me. *"Oh, our time's better than yours. Vikings are better than Romans. Romans are better than dandies. Oh, look at you and your plate armour. You should have leather straps like we do."* It's all one giant pissing contest, usually run by big boys who've run out of toys to buy. Do you know how much a full set of armour costs?'

'A grand?' Anjli offered.

'And the rest,' Neil laughed. 'Had a guy in here, little runt of a man boasting he'd spent over twenty grand on a high-end set. My car isn't worth that much. In fact, my last three cars together haven't been that much.'

He shrugged.

'Never really got the point of it, I'm afraid.'

'I get that,' Anjli replied. 'Tell me about the fight.'

'Oh, there's always a conflict here somewhere,' Neil smiled. 'I wasn't around last night, but I've already been told there was a punch-up at one point. Some small prick punched a giant Viking guy and everyone started expecting a fight to go off.'

'Did it?'

'Nah. It settled down quickly. The one thing about these re-enacting types is they're all about standing on fields and waving their swords, but if you come up to them and offer to punch them in the teeth, they quickly run away and call their lawyers.'

Anjli smiled as she pulled out her phone, opening it up to

a photos app. One by one, she showed photos of Nicholas Stephens, Adam Harris, and Benedict Dee.

'Recognise these?'

'Yeah, they're the three I heard died,' Neil said. 'Harris, Dee, Stephens. It's all over the news. I remember seeing them here and there.'

'Did you see them on Tuesday?'

'I think so, yes,' Neil tapped the photo. 'They were part of a group that was standing over by the bar there.'

'Did you see this person?' Anjli said, scrolling again. Now the image of Georgia Wingate appeared.

'Ha, yeah. Yeah, I remember her,' Neil chuckled. 'She was the one who kicked it all off on Tuesday. Started shouting at one of them, saying it was his fault that she couldn't do the things she wanted to do. She's been lording it up all week. Apparently she's playing Boudicca today in some big event down the road. Pissed the other females off, too.'

'She did?' Anjli asked.

'There's a small woman, pink hair, I think, was bitching about her a couple of times, when it was quieter. You get all the gossip here, standing behind the bar. They forget that you even exist.'

'What kind of gossip?'

'Just that people didn't think she should have got the job. There are better people out there. Apparently, for years, someone else played the role, and they died a couple of years ago and people think Georgia pushed her way into the role because she was sleeping with her. To be honest, I got distracted around then and wandered off.'

'Georgia was sleeping with the woman who played Boudicca?'

'It's just gossip, I wasn't paying attention. Who cares who sleeps with who?'

'Did you ever see this guy?' the picture scrolled again and now Matt Butcher stared out of this phone screen.

'Ha, yeah, we know that guy,' Neil said. 'He was the prick who punched the Viking last night. Sat in a corner, drank loads of whisky after it happened, started screaming out it wasn't his fault. He's the one they were all pissed at.'

'And why would that be?'

Neil looked around, leaning closer as if some dangerous secret was about to be told.

'He's a misogynistic little prick,' he said. 'If you're watching the *Karate Kid*, he's probably rooting for Cobra Kai, you get what I'm saying?'

Anjli did.

'He's the one who wouldn't let women perform in the show,' Neil continued. 'Got really pissed off about it. One guy told me he had a shit fit when he learnt the Queen Boudicca re-enactor was in the event.'

'They don't get on?'

'Christ, no. Every time they've been in the bar together, they've made sure they're at separate ends.'

He considered the question.

'Apart from that Tuesday,' he added. 'Yeah, he was there talking to her during the bet argument.'

'Do you remember much about that?'

'Christ, yeah, we had to pull them all apart. Got really heated. That Queen Boudicca woman had had a few and started mouthing off at him. He was sitting with a few others, two of which were Dee and Stephens.'

'No Harris?'

'He was there, but by the wall,' Neil thought back. 'She

started claiming she could do better than anybody in the room. You know, the usual, what I would usually call dick waggling, "I could beat you in a duel" kind of thing, but obviously without the dick to waggle.'

'So she challenged him?' Anjli let the comment pass.

'Yeah,' Neil nodded. 'Told him she'd pay them money, I think, if they could beat her. Properly laid the gauntlet down.'

'Did anybody take it up?'

'Nah. As I said, you stick them on a stage, and they waggle their swords like bloody kings. You stick them in the real world and they shit themselves and call for their mummies. None of them took it. Everybody knew it was some kind of sick joke.'

'So what happened after that?'

'The argument got boring. People started to wander off. Boudicca took her attention off onto someone else.'

'Do you remember who?'

Neil shrugged.

'Can't remember. Maybe she'd got bored of having to go up against the Viking puncher,' he replied as he thought about this. 'Jenny might remember. Hold on a sec.'

He wandered into the back room, calling out after Jenny, whoever she was.

Anjli stood waiting, considering what she'd been told. From the sounds of things, it wasn't just Matt Butcher who had people gunning after him. And it sounded like Georgia Wingate was closer to Bridget than they realised. Was she the woman Bridget was leaving Matt Butcher for three years earlier?

'Do you remember anything else about that argument on Tuesday?' Neil returned, talking to a ginger-haired woman as they walked out. "Jenny" turned out to be another member of the bar staff.

'Nah, they were just mouthing off lots,' she replied. 'They're always doing that. That and stupid bloody songs.'

'Songs?'

'Each group has their own little campfire songs and they sing them. You ever see *Casablanca?*'

'Sure,' Anjli frowned, not understanding what the connection was.

'You know the bit where the Germans are singing and Victor Laslo stands up and gets all the French people to sing the French National Anthem, and they're all singing against each other, and they all get pissed and angry? It's like that every bloody night, with Viking sea shanties and Tudor sonnets and bollocks like that.'

Anjli chuckled.

'Neil said that after Georgia – the Boudicca woman – had argued with Matt Butcher – the, um, Viking puncher – and challenged several people to a duel, she started on someone else,' she asked.

'Yeah, creepy bald guy. I don't know his name. He's always in here. He's one of the gladiators.' Jenny considered this. 'I want to say his name was Alan ...'

'Aaron?'

'Perhaps. Yeah, that's the one. Aaron. Because Butcher, the guy who was running everything – Viking Puncher – he turned around to him and told him to give it up, that she wasn't worth the argument.'

'So, she argued with Aaron Forden then?'

'I don't know his full name. But he's a creepy-looking bugger with a bald head. Looks like one of those skinless cats, but in human form.'

She considered this for a moment.

'To be honest, I kind of got the impression they knew each other. He was also goading one of the others to take the bet.'

'This one?' Anjli showed a photo of Benedict.

'No, the Roman they found. He was all in his ear, like some evil grand vizier or something. Anyway, they all just postured, and then she got dragged away by some others.'

'He was whispering in Adam Harris's ear?'

'Yeah. I got the impression he was a popcorn guy. You know, wind them up, watch them go, sit back with a bag and enjoy the show.'

Anjli nodded. Looking around the bar, she paused, looking up at one of the corners.

'Do you have the CCTV footage?'

'Not really,' Neil apologised. 'It's a rotating forty-eight hours. If we don't need it, we don't keep it.'

He stared off for a moment.

'We have last night's though, if that helps,' he said. 'I mean, Boudicca woman wasn't here, but most of the others were. And you'll see the fight, as I said, where the short guy punched the Viking. Most anti-climactic action scene I've ever seen.'

'If we could get that, that'd be great,' Anjli smiled. 'Either on a CD or—'

Jenny laughed.

'We've not used CDs here for years,' she snorted. 'We can send you the cloud link.'

'That would be better,' Anjli smiled, but there was no humour in it. Passing over her business card with an email address for the link to be sent to, Anjli gave them a nod and walked out of the pub.

The story that everyone had kept to, that Georgia had challenged people to a duel, was true. But from the sounds of things, there was more going on here than met the eye.

And more importantly, Georgia versus the Duellists didn't seem to be the only problem that was going on anymore.

Anjli sent a quick text to Declan; he was about to speak to Forden, and maybe this could help him.

Looking back up at the pub's frontage, she sighed. There was such a history of violence with this bar, it almost made sense re-enactors would do the same in there.

She was just glad they didn't have any *Peaky Blinders* re-enactors at the festival. That could have got messy.

DCI LENETTE WARREN SAT IN MONROE'S OFFICE, LOOKING around. She was tall and stocky, her once-grey hair now dyed blackcurrant red, but still tied back in a scrunchie. She had an expression on her face of disdain, and Monroe couldn't for the life of him work out if this was because she was involved in the case, or whether it was because she had to deal with him again.

He *really* hoped it was the latter.

'As much as it's lovely to see you, Lenette,' Monroe started the conversation, 'could you explain to us why you're here?'

'Don't get me wrong, Monroe,' DCI Warren replied, 'I don't exactly want to be here, either. You've never been one of my favourite people. And don't think I haven't forgiven you for what you did a couple of years ago in Savernake Forest.'

Monroe hid the smile. He'd deliberately caused a distraction at the forest when he'd arrived with the then-brand new and shiny Declan Walsh, deliberately pissing her and her officers off in the process when they arrived loudly and brazenly at the crime scene, knowing that it would divert them from Doctor Marcos, who snuck in, disguised as a forensics officer. At the time, Doctor Marcos was banned from attending crime scenes, and Monroe needed her there, if only to see what the hell was going on.

'So, what brings you here on a wonderful Sunday morning, then?' Monroe asked.

'Nicholas Stephens,' DCI Warren replied. 'You know about Pennington Hall?'

'Aye, we've heard about it,' Monroe nodded.

'Well, Pennington Hall is in Newbury, which makes it my remit,' Warren added. 'That's why I'm here.'

'It also happened three years ago. Why are you only now looking into this?' Monroe asked, pausing as the door opened and Chivalry Fitzwarren walked into the office, warmly walking over to DCI Warren and holding out his hand.

'DCI Warren,' he said jovially. 'I'm Chivalry Fitzwarren, special consultant to Detective Superintendent Monroe. And who knows, we might even be family, with "Fitz" being "son of" and us both sharing a surname!'

'Bloody hell, no offence, but I hope not,' Warren shook her head as if the idea was abhorrent.

Chivalry simply gave her a grin and sat down beside Monroe.

'So, where were we?' he asked conversationally.

'DCI Warren was just about to tell us why she waited three years to investigate a death.'

At this, Warren looked a little embarrassed.

'Honestly?' she said. 'We hadn't been looking into this. It was a mistake, an accident on a field, and it was before my time as a DCI there. It was written off, the coroner's report cleared everything.'

'And then what happened?'

'Nicholas Stephens started looking into it again,' Warren replied, shrugging as she did so. 'It was a little bit of armchair detective work if you ask me. But it was good stuff. He'd contacted me asking for the details, the information we'd gained and obviously as a member of the public we couldn't do that, but as he was also part of the case itself, we assumed he was looking to appeal and offered to pass it on to his legal team if he was doing anything. The next thing we know, a lawyer had contacted us and we passed it across. What we didn't know was the lawyer was a friend of Nicholas's who had done this as a favour.'

'So, what you're saying is Nicholas gathered his crime information from you without your knowledge?' Monroe raised an eyebrow.

'Don't start,' Warren snapped. 'I'm not in the mood for you to play one-upmanship. Nicholas Stephens was absolutely convinced he'd been set up.'

'He's had three years. Why now?' Monroe asked.

'New evidence,' Warren replied. 'Apparently, when the accident happened, Nicholas was new to the scene and had only been around six months or so. He was shiny and eager to please and knew little about the gossip and politics of the industry.'

'What you're saying is he didn't know who was shagging who,' Chivalry replied with a smile.

'Pretty much,' Warren shifted in her chair. 'For example, he didn't know that Matt Butcher at the time was shagging Susan Cowell.'

'So, I'm guessing he found something out then?'

'I don't know,' Warren replied, still shifting uncomfortably in her seat. 'We weren't taking him that seriously. This was something that had happened ages ago, and to be honest, he sounded a little extreme.'

'Go on.'

'He was saying that it was part of some massive conspiracy, that his spear had been stolen before the event, and replaced with an exact duplicate.'

'Okay, and why would this happen?'

'Nicholas Stephens was absolutely convinced that somebody in the re-enactment group had taken his spear, replaced it with an exact duplicate so he could throw it without realising, and then kill Bridget Farnsworth with his own spear, aiming the murder at him because of the identification on its base,' Warren replied. 'He had his own initials etched into it. A good deal of re-enactors do, because that way they can find their items after a battle, but if someone had stolen his spear, then this made it premeditated.'

'Did he know who it was?'

'He believed it was a man named Rolf.'

'Rolf Cowell?'

'Do you know him?' Warren replied, surprised at this. 'Makes sense, you've probably gone quite into this already. But, although he was focused on Rolf, he was also convinced it could have been one of several other people.'

'Go on,' Chivalry now said, leaning closer. Monroe wasn't sure if he was interested in the story or the gossip.

'Well, he believed it was Rolf, because Rolf and him had had an altercation earlier, and during this Rolf had the opportunity during that time to swap spears.'

'But surely the spears would be different?' Chivalry frowned. 'If Stephens was on the side against Bridget, then he'd be playing a Roman, going up against Boudicca, and the Roman's spears were different to the Dark Ages spears. The Iceni had different styles, and that's the one that your man Rolf would have had, which meant it had to be someone on the Roman's side.'

Monroe couldn't help it; he was actually impressed by this.

'So, he was thinking someone else?'

'A chap called Aaron Forden was an option, as he was the re-enactor playing the head of the Romans, but I'll come to him in a second,' Warren replied. 'Nicholas was absolutely convinced it was Adam Harris, who during the battle bumped into him, causing him to let his spear go flying. Again, it was claimed to be an accident, as his horse was spooked by something. But now Stephens started believing that Adam Harris had been told to knock him.'

'And why would Adam Harris do this?' Monroe asked.

'Because Adam Harris was part of a theft. A theft that included both Rolf and Susan Cowell, and a coroner named Benedict Dee. Well, he thinks the coroner was involved.' Warren shrugged. 'I'll be honest, we weren't paying that close attention, but he was convinced that the coroner had been bought off. And being honest, it was sounding a bit conspiracy theory. Tin foil hat-wearing time. There he was, telling us that the accident, an actual accident, confirmed by a whole inquest and everything, and for an act he wasn't being blamed for in any way possible, was murder.'

She shifted on her chair.

'There was nothing on him. He wasn't even being blamed by the husband of the woman who died. He had decided that it was some kind of immense conspiracy involving multiple people, an exact duplicate of his spear, a theft of items, and the death of a lord – many of which were happenstance and coincidence at the same time.'

'Jesus,' Monroe muttered to himself. 'Did you look into any of this?'

'Of course I did,' Warren snapped. 'I'm not a bloody rookie. And he called us yesterday.'

'He did?'

Nodding, Warren removed her phone, scrolled to her voicemail and played the message.

'Hello? DCI Warren? It's Nick Stephens. I was the chap you talked to in the Pennington Hall ... well ... debacle. Could you call me back? I have new information about the accident. I think they're on to me.'

'Interesting. Did he ever say who he thought was going to kill him?' Monroe asked. 'I'm particularly drawn by the usage of "they're" used there.'

Warren nodded.

'He'd said before it was obvious who it was,' she replied. 'But they wanted him dead and there was nothing he could do about it.'

'Let me guess,' Monroe smiled. 'Was it by chance either Rolf or Susan Cowell?'

'We thought that too,' Warren replied. 'But actually, he was more scared of Aaron Forden right then.'

'And why would that be?'

'Because Aaron Forden was somehow connected to Pennington Hall and Nicholas believed it was revenge,' Warren replied.

'And that's why you said you'd get to him later.' Monroe nodded. 'What don't I know about him?'

'Did you know about his criminal past?' Warren leant

forwards now, smiling. 'I'd expect not, it was wiped from his record when he came of age. You have to really hunt for it.'

'What kind of criminal record?' Monroe asked. Anjli had mentioned Aaron had claimed to have spent nights in cells, but there were no actual records to this.

Warren shrugged.

'Juvenile shit,' she replied. 'But he was done for burglary once. Posh home in Newbury. Only reason I know is because one of my uniforms was there at the time. Said he was the first safe-cracking teenager he'd met, although he claimed he hadn't cracked it.'

'Newbury?' Monroe scratched at his chin. 'Interesting he was caught near the Hall.'

'Oh, didn't I mention this?' Warren shook her head. 'Sorry. The house he broke into as a teen *was* Pennington Hall.'

17

LEG BEFORE WICKED

By the time Declan arrived at the cricket ground at Shoreditch, it was already gathering a small crowd, even though the events of the Boudicca uprising were likely to be a good four hours away.

Though it was getting dark in the early evening, the plan was to have torches around the outside of the battle, following the cricket pitch boundary area to give a kind of spooky atmosphere to the event, so that the battle would be seen in a half-light. This meant, first that the re-enactors within the contest didn't have to fight so hard, but second, having it during twilight gave more of an impression that it was people fighting, and less of the fact they were watching this happen in the middle of what was effectively a cricket ground.

There wasn't much you could do to hide the giant pavilion to the side, however, and Declan assumed they hoped that the fire torches and darkness would at least give it something a little more authentic.

Declan had parked his Audi outside, nodding to a security guard who, when they asked him to move it, had stopped quickly as Declan showed his warrant card. Walking into the event itself, he noticed there were several tents to the side, and a changing room that looked as if it was part of the building where the cricketers themselves prepared. Declan wondered if the owners of the cricket ground were happy that a place for people who once would slap on padding and cricket whites was now being used by people placing woad and leather armour on, or Roman cuirasses and metal helmets.

As it was, nobody was getting changed as Declan arrived. There were still several hours to go, and even the most excited of re-enactors was unlikely to dress up in such a costume for a long time with nothing else to do.

A man, tall and stocky, with his head shaved apart from the topknot, walked over to Declan as he entered.

'Have you got an ID?' he asked, only he stopped as Declan held up his warrant card.

'And you are?' Declan asked.

'Geoff,' the man said, 'G-E-O-F-F, not with a J. I'm sick of people saying it's with a J.'

Declan nodded.

'Thanks. I'm looking for Rolf and Susan Cowell.'

At this, Geoff frowned.

'What have they done?' he asked.

'What do you *think* they've done?' Declan replied with a smile.

Geoff didn't answer. Instead, he turned and pointed back down a corridor, to the other side of the door that Declan was about to walk through.

'Third door on the right,' he said. 'I'm not anything to do with this. I don't want to know.'

He left and Declan carried on through the door, heading down the corridor, where on the third door on the right, he knocked three times and opened it.

There were six people sitting around a table, having some kind of takeout lunch. Declan could see fast food containers on the table itself, and as he stepped through, three of the people rose quickly.

'We were told we could eat in here,' they said.

'I wasn't going to stop you,' Declan replied, holding his card up once more. 'DCI Declan Walsh, City of London Police. I'm looking for Rolf and Susan.'

He didn't say anymore. Susan and Rolf Cowell, obvious by their pink hair and large appearance respectively, stood up at the back and nodded.

'I'm Rolf, this is my sister Susan,' Rolf said. 'I'm guessing you're here about the body we saw.'

'Yes,' Declan replied, walking over. 'Sorry to bother you, I know you're preparing for your big event tonight, but I just needed to get some questions answered.'

'Of course,' Rolf said, smiling, waving for Declan to take a chair. 'Anything we can do to help.'

'And we're grateful for that,' Declan took the provided chair, smiling back thankfully as he sat down, pulling out his notepad and placing it on the table, his tactical pen next to it. 'I understand you were given tickets to a walk on Friday?'

'Yes,' Susan glanced nervously at Rolf before speaking, and Declan couldn't quite work out if this was support or permission to speak. 'We thought it was from Georgia Wingate, but we confronted her yesterday about it and she said it wasn't her.'

Declan opened the notebook, making a point of noting this down, even though he'd already heard this from Georgia herself. He wanted the questions to draw out, give the two people in front of him time to think about them. The nervousness, mixed with the fear of a police officer asking questions, even if they were innocent, was always enough to loosen a tongue, especially if they were eager to answer.

'And you expected Georgia to send you this because …?'

'We didn't expect anything, to be perfectly honest,' Susan replied. 'We don't really talk to her that much. We assumed she'd been given some tickets by the council, or whoever was organising the walks, and we were probably very far down a long list of people who didn't want to go.'

Declan noted this down.

'Why did you go?' he asked.

Rolf barked a laugh at this.

'Because we like history and we work with Romans,' he said, as if Declan was some kind of idiot.

Declan patiently wrote this down and smiled at Rolf.

'I don't mean that,' he said. 'I mean, why did *you* go? Why did you accept tickets from somebody that you don't seem to like?'

At this, Rolf froze.

'Who said we didn't like Georgia?' he asked suspiciously. 'I just said we didn't talk much.'

'Well, I was under the assumption that she'd taken Susan's spot,' Declan smiled at Susan as he looked across at her. 'Weren't you a shoo-in to play Boudicca when Bridget passed?'

Susan's demeanour changed. Her eyes narrowed and her lips pursed as she leant forward.

'Bridget didn't pass,' she said. 'Bridget was killed in a

terrible accident.'

'True,' Declan replied calmly. 'A terrible accident which Nicholas Stephens seemed to contest.'

'What do you mean?' Rolf asked.

'I mean, he was investigating the accident,' Declan said. 'Or didn't you know that?'

Rolf and Susan looked at each other, but there was no surprise visible to this revelation. Declan waited.

'My boss has been talking to one of the Newbury police officers,' he continued. 'She was working with Nicholas. He'd been contacting her, discussing the case, almost like some kind of informant. Seems he had started to believe that he *hadn't* done this.'

'He threw a spear, and it killed my friend,' Susan growled ominously, her face reddening with fury. 'Don't you dare belittle what happened.'

'Oh, I'm not belittling anything,' Declan replied, leaning forward to match her. 'But you have to understand this. The coroner's report stated that Nicholas had been nudged, or knocked when he went to throw the spear, and the simple act of the knocking made him throw the spear at an angle, hitting Bridget. But Nicholas was convinced someone had swapped his spear, and that someone else had used his spear to kill Bridget – and only when the dust settled had it been revealed as his, because of his initials.'

He gave a second before continuing.

'How well do you know the coroner, Benedict Dee?'

'Look, what's this about?' Susan frowned, leaning back, looking back at Rolf as she continued talking to Declan. 'Why are you talking about Benedict? He's not even a Dark Ages re-enactor.'

'No, but you know him, don't you?' Declan said. 'You

know him and Adam Harris, the man who knocked Nicholas Stephens in that battle, causing such a terrible, life-changing accident for him.'

'We met occasionally,' Rolf said, leaning into the conversation now as if trying to divert away from his sister. 'But he was always doing the duelling things. He's a pedantic little prissy.'

Declan held a hand up, one finger in the air. It was a simple gesture, but it was enough to stop the larger man.

'Let me stop you there,' Declan smiled. 'Because any second now, you're going to treat me like an idiot. And be aware, Mister Cowell, at this point I've been very careful to *not* be an idiot.'

He looked back at Susan.

'Did you know Benedict Dee before this?' he asked. 'And be aware, the answer I have may differ from what you think I have.'

It was a bluff, but a worthwhile one, as Susan sighed, leaning back in her chair.

'We did know him a few years back,' she muttered.

Rolf placed a hand on her arm, and she shook it off, glancing back at him.

'No, they need to know,' she said. 'We knew Benedict Dee. We knew him when he was just starting. He'd joined the Dark Ages group we were members of, but he hated the battles. He wanted to be the king, not the little person who ran out there and died.'

'Was that common?'

'We used to have ways of doing the battles where, when an explosion happened, if we were doing an event with gunpowder or things like that, we would shout a letter out, and if your surname started with that, you fell down. This was a way to give a kind of random death; if your letter began with S, and we called it out, then you'd be the first people stabbed. It didn't matter what letter it was, but it was a lot easier when doing an event to have something that meant that you couldn't argue about why you were dead so soon.'

'Benedict didn't like this?'

'Benedict thought he should have been surviving on his own actions,' Rolf shook his head. 'Do you know what that prick did once? We were in the town of Battle, you know, where the Battle of Hastings was, doing an event there. He decided he didn't want to die when he was supposed to, and he kept going. We had to literally tackle him to the ground to stop him saving Harold from the arrow to the eye, because in his mind he'd become this hero who was going to change history.'

'After that he was kicked out,' Susan added. 'He wasn't a team player, and he looked for more solo activity. Duelling was quite good for that.'

Declan nodded at this.

'So, you didn't agree with what he said?' he asked. 'When he said in his coroner's report it had been an accident?'

'No, I didn't mean that at all,' Susan replied, and Declan felt she was starting to backtrack a little. 'We were on his side on that, as it was an accident, a terrible one. Nicholas had been accused, and then cleared, and Benny made a big thing of it, playing the mighty hero, finding out the clues.'

'He thought he was Poirot, in the way that he acted, and he made everybody's life a living hell,' Rolf added.

'Benedict Dee wasn't at the event, was he?'

'No, it wasn't his thing.'

'We have nothing to explain why Benedict Dee was the coroner,' Declan looked into his notes. 'It just seems strange that somebody with a connection to the people involved happened to be working on the case.'

'I can't answer that one,' Susan said. 'I don't know how he got involved.'

'Not at all?' Declan pushed. 'Nobody explained it in any way?'

'I believe someone connected to the family asked for him,' Rolf said. 'Said they trusted his judgement. But if I was a betting man, DCI Walsh, I'd think you suspected we were something to do with this.'

At this, Declan smiled.

'We're looking in many directions,' he said. 'And, as you can understand, one of them seems to be involving you.'

At the statement, Rolf straightened up angrily.

'Are you saying you think that I—'

'Don't get pissed at me,' Declan snapped, rising. 'I'm asking questions. You seem to get very agitated about something that I haven't even got to yet. But if you want, I could move over to it. Nicholas Stephens, before he died, became a bit of an amateur detective. And during that time, he'd decided *you* had been the person who stole his spear on the day of the accident in question.'

If Rolf was surprised at this, he kept it quiet as Declan continued.

'I've heard there was a very strong chance that you and Nicholas had some kind of altercation before the event, when you could, if you'd been so inclined, have taken his spear and swapped it.'

Rolf shook his head vehemently.

'No,' he said. 'I mean, yes, there was a point where I could have done that. But I didn't because I wouldn't have done that. Look, we had loads of things going on that day. The last thing we wanted was a terrible accident. That would cause major problems. For not only the community, but for poor Matthew.'

'Matthew Butcher?'

'Yes.'

'Why *poor* Matthew?'

'His wife died in a senseless accident. Why do you think?'

'I can see that,' Declan replied. 'And I do feel sorry for Matt Butcher. Apart from the fact I know that not only was he trying to find a way of getting divorced at the time, he was also having an affair with *you*, Susan.'

There was a long, awkward pause at the table.

'You can't choose who you love,' Susan eventually said.

'No, I suppose you can't,' Declan replied, placing his notepad down. 'But it makes me wonder how connected you still are to all of this.'

'I was one of the closest spearmen to Bridget in the battle,' Rolf replied. 'But if the spear was taken, there were six or seven people it could have been. It was a hectic time.'

'Do you have any photos of the battle?' Declan asked.

'There were some taken at the time, I'm sure,' Susan replied. 'And there were the ones sent for the Coroner's Report, but they didn't really show much, just the battle, and from the wrong angle. But, as you can understand, anything that was taken after the accident would have likely been deleted, as we wouldn't have stuck them on social media.'

'Something else,' Rolf added. 'Nicholas played a Roman, and I was Iceni. The spears would have been different, so even if I did swap, I would have stood out in the battle. You should look at the Romans, to see who could have done it. Start with Aaron, he was there as the leader of the forces.'

Declan nodded, rising.

'Before I go,' he said. 'How did you take your kit to these events? I mean, you have costumes—'

'It's armour,' Rolf corrected.

'Sorry, yes, you have your armour, your tents, your weapons, your food, drink, all that kind of stuff. I mean, that's got to be a lot to take with you. What is it, an SUV? A van?'

'We had a van,' Susan replied. 'Rolf, me, Adam, a couple of others who have faded away now, I think. We all chipped together and bought one.'

'Do you still own it?'

'God, no,' Rolf replied. 'That went a year or two back. The alternator collapsed on the M25.'

'Yeah,' Declan noted this in the book. 'They do that. Can you remember what make it was?'

'Oh, I don't really know cars,' Susan started, but Declan placed his hands on the table, leaning forward.

'Was it by chance a gunmetal grey Ford Transit?' he asked, staring directly at her.

'Adam looked after it. I think he painted it blue, but it could have been grey at some point. I never really used it, I just dumped my kit there and Rolf sorted it.'

Declan glanced at Rolf, who shrugged.

'One last thing. You informed me that somebody pretending to be Georgia Wingate sent you tickets to a walk where, at the end, you found the body of Adam Harris.'

'Yes,' Rolf nodded. 'We've said all we know.'

'We were told by Aaron Forden you arrived late,' Declan continued. 'In fact, you arrived very near the Cripplegate part of the walk, effectively across the road from where the body had been found. Was there a particular reason why you arrived so late?'

'Why should this be a problem? I didn't realise it was illegal to turn up to a walk later than everybody else.'

'Usually, I would say it's not,' Declan smiled. 'But, when you arrive five minutes before the body is found, and from the same location where a van remarkably like your old one was seen, you can understand why it raises alarm bells, yes?'

Rolf went to snap a reply, but Susan held up her hand.

'I can explain that to you very easily,' she said, opening her phone. Scrolling through her notes, she found the email.

It was from the Georgia Wingate Hotmail address.

Susan, I have two spare tickets for a walk, Friday night. Parking is available off Silver Street, meet us by the London Wall. Click the link to confirm.

Declan read the email, looking back at Susan.

'So whoever sent you the email wanted you to appear there?'

'Yes,' Susan said. 'So, as you can see, Detective Chief Inspector, we were set up as much as anybody else.'

'Interesting,' Declan replied. 'Aaron Forden received no such message. I wonder why you were targeted as such?'

He turned and walked to the main door.

'Good luck today,' he said. 'I hope it goes well.'

'Thank you,' Susan said. 'And I hope you find the man, or woman, who killed Adam and Ben.'

Declan nodded.

'And Nicholas Stephens?'

'Yeah, him as well.'

It was a reluctant agreement, and Declan noted this.

Walking out of the room, Declan saw Geoff with a G, standing by the door.

'Are you ready for today?' he said, as he walked through it.

Geoff shrugged.

'It's a show like every other,' he said. 'The fact we're in a weird cricket ground doesn't really change it. We've done battles in other places, weirder places. As long as we've got our items and our tents and everything, we're fine.'

Declan looked around, once more seeing the tents to the side that he'd seen earlier.

'Is that where the stock is?' he said.

'Stock?' Geoff laughed. 'You mean all the weapons we use? Yeah, that's pretty much where it is.'

'Aren't you scared of losing your personal items in all that?'

'Oh no,' Geoff replied with a smile. 'We don't leave that in there, we bring that with us. This ain't like those knights in armour who bring their stupid sodding plate mail. We've got our own leather straps and armour and weapons and we'll bring those with us.'

As Declan went to move, he shook his head.

'Apart from a couple, though, Rolf usually brings Susan's stuff.'

'Really, why's that?' Declan asked; she'd mentioned similar in the meeting.

At this, Geoff laughed.

'It's really hard to carry a spear on a motorcycle,' he said, walking off into the back room.

Declan stopped. He looked back at the room and almost turned, but instead he walked out into the car park, walking along the line of cars and vans that were there.

There were three motorcycles on site. He wasn't sure

which one could have been owned by Susan Cowell, but he took photos of all three bikes and sent them to Billy.

If Susan Cowell had the same motorcycle as the one that killed Nicholas Stephens, that would be a very interesting conversation to be had later.

But first, he needed to speak to Aaron Forden.

18

COAL SELLERS

THE JOURNEY TO HACKNEY HAD BEEN QUITE FAST FOR DE'GEER, although it was both a Sunday morning and a journey by motorcycle, which could nip through the more complicated areas of the London traffic system.

Arriving at Sutton Place, De'Geer examined the area. He knew this was where the van was believed to have stayed the night but, looking around the Georgian street, he couldn't quite work out how something like that wouldn't have stood out.

The street was filled with expensive cars and motorcycles; this was a street where the average house was close to "two million pounds" in price. If you lived on Sutton Place, the chances were you didn't need a grey Transit van.

He didn't have a key, as Benedict Dee didn't have one on him when he was found, but De'Geer knew the neighbours would likely have one. In fact, before De'Geer had even walked to the door of Benedict Dee's terraced house, with soot-washed brick, white painted windows and black doors, the door next door had opened and the neighbour had already offered to help in any way they could.

De'Geer had smiled at this and thanked them for their help. Usually "their help" meant they wanted to know what gossip was going on, but De'Geer, being seven feet tall and looking like the scariest Viking you've ever seen, knew he didn't have to worry too much about people pressing for gossip. Weirdly, however, the house next door wasn't an even numbered one like Dee's house; Sutton Place seemed to be one of the few places around that numbered the houses sequentially along the terrace.

The house itself was a three-storey house, with a basement. It was large, and TARDIS-style spacious for the postage stamp ground floor it occupied, looking out onto an incredible patio garden, with a tall fence at the back. From the plans that De'Geer had seen of the place, he knew this led out to a path at the back, known as a "nightsoil" path. Historically, this was where waste from the houses was removed, which would be collected by cart; meaning the "path" was actually quite wide and secluded.

Walking through the house, he paid little attention to the furnishings. He wasn't here to examine a bedroom or kitchen, for example, after all, he was here for something different and more subterranean.

Eventually he found a set of stairs that led to the basement, or cellar. Many of the houses on Sutton Place had utilised these, turning them into downstairs kitchens or extra rooms, or even home cinemas, leading out into the raised back gardens. But Benedict Dee had been a traditionalist, it seemed, and had left the cellar pretty much as it had always been, the garden still above it.

The cellar itself was low-ceilinged and built of more soot-washed brick. It was dark, with only a strip of light, running down the centre of the space giving any illumination to the downstairs area. It was probably only fifteen metres in length, which De'Geer believed was probably almost to the back of the patio garden above.

The cellar was quite basic, considering the high-end look of the floors above. There was no wallpaper or even fancy furniture down here. This was more of a workroom than anything else, which fitted what they'd been told about Benedict Dee, and how he would practice his duelling shots here. In fact, down the end of the cellar space was indeed a target dressed in the clothes of a Regency gentleman, torn bullet holes in the jacket.

De'Geer paused before moving any further now, pulling on blue latex gloves and placing disposable forensic baggies over his feet. He didn't want his footprints affecting anything he found, and with these on he bent down, crouching over the floor, using a swab to test it.

The floor was dirty and looked to be a mixture of soot and black coal dust. Coal hadn't been used in this house for many years, but the cellar had obviously never been cleaned. Perhaps Benedict Dee had preferred a more original look, or maybe he'd just not bothered. Taking a small sample, De'Geer placed this in a baggie, and slid it into his fluorescent police vest. This done, he rose, pulled out a torch, and shone it on the floor.

Even though the fluorescent light strip illuminated the room, it was still a half-light, and De'Geer couldn't make out anything on the ground; but with his torch now on it, he could see several footprints and movements in the dirt. He wasn't as expert at this as some people in forensics, but looking at the footprints, he could see that the more fresh ones there differed. There was a more refined boot, with a heel, possibly Regency style, as it stepped around one end of the room, and on the other, a more flattened sandal style, which could have been Adam Harris, who had come here to work with him.

To the side, there was a third set of footprints, however, distinct from the other two. These could, of course, have come from any other time, and in fact all three sets could have been Benedict Dee's, although the more basic style did seem larger.

Either way, he knew this was something he wanted to check into at some other time, maybe even get Doctor Marcos in to look, and so took some photos.

There was a box on the counter of a workbench desk against the wall, a wooden one made of what looked to be walnut. As De'Geer opened it with his left hand, he saw green velvet inside, with space for two duelling pistols, one of which was now missing. Picking it up and examining it, he saw both the pistol maker's name, *Wogdon and Barton,* and a familiar marking, that of the Crawford-Dunne family.

This was exactly where the duelling pistol found in the hand of Benedict Dee had come from.

De'Geer again pulled out a large evidence baggie and placed the entire box into it. He wasn't going to take much with him, but this was something he would want to take later, if only to confirm the pistol they currently had matched the one inside the case.

There was nothing else on the desk either so he continued on.

He paused, however, as he saw that a piece of paper was sticking out of one drawer underneath the desk. Pulling out the side drawer, he noticed a pile of paperwork pushed into it. Carefully removing it, he flipped through the pages and realised this was the coroner's report for the death of Bridget Farnsworth that Dee had obviously written. Flicking through it, he realised that this too was something important, and so rolled it up and placed it in his pocket. He didn't know if it would be something worth looking at, but if he *didn't* take it, he knew it would be. That was the way Sod's Law worked in forensics.

He took a moment to examine the scene, and then stopped as he glanced to the opposite side of the cellar – there was a small shelf placed into the brick, with what looked to be a small webcam on it. Walking over, he picked it up, seeing that it was indeed a freestanding house webcam connected to a small, external SSD. Placing these in a baggie too, he added this to his collection.

At the end of the cellar, De'Geer saw two slots in the ceiling, most likely from when the coal would have been poured in. There had been talk, when discussing Sutton Place back at the office, that in Georgian times the coal would be placed down here, and the servants would have to bring it across into the house. Underneath the holes, however, were scuff marks, and more importantly, drag marks. Something heavy, and what looked to be body-shaped, had been pulled to the bottom of one hole.

Looking up, De'Geer could see that a body could easily fit through it, and at the base of the left-hand coal hole, he could see what looked to be rope scrape markings in the dust.

Could someone have taken a body, tied it, and winched it up through the hole?

De'Geer crouched, examining the markings, and paused. This wasn't a case of one person being dragged up through the hole, from the scratches and scuffs this looked very much like *two* bodies, distinctly separate, being pulled up.

De'Geer stood, staring from the ground to the hole above, and then back to the ground. Did someone remove Benedict Dee and Adam Harris this way? It was a possibility.

De'Geer quickly walked back to the entrance, taking the wooden case in the baggie as he did so. Moving upstairs, he hurried out of the back door, passing into the back garden, following it to the end. There was a tree at the back of the garden, cut low so as to not affect anybody's vision, but it was sturdy and had a large branch that jutted out almost over the coal holes. De'Geer went and examined the branch, and could see scrapings on the bark where rope and tackle had been attached to it, and what looked to be scuff marks on the grass leading to the back gate.

It was quite obvious, if you looked carefully, that someone had attached some kind of pulley device to the tree, using it to winch up whatever was down in the cellar.

Could one man have done this? Was it a two-man job?

That would have to be decided later.

De'Geer took photos with his phone and then, following the scuff marks, ones that could easily have been body-shaped, maybe thrown into a sheet to stop the mud and grass rubbing on them, but too late to prevent the soot, walked out into the back alley.

It was wide enough for a Transit van; they could have winched out the bodies, put them in the van, and no one would have been any the wiser, especially if it had been done in the early hours of the morning. But Adam Harris was left in the early hours of the *evening*, which meant that somebody somewhere could have seen the van. De'Geer made a mental note to have some officers canvass the area, to see if any witnesses had seen anything.

With this done, he walked back into the house. There were photos on the walls, and as he walked past, he glanced at a few of them idly, thinking about the cellar as he did so, but then stopped as one photo caught his eye.

In it were four people: Susan Cowell, her brother Rolf, tall and imposing, Adam Harris, and Benedict Dee. It was obviously not a re-enacting event, more likely a fancy dress party, as the costumes they wore were cheap and homemade. But they were happy, and they were young. This had to be ten, maybe even fifteen years old.

De'Geer took another photo of the frame then stood back and stared at it.

How had they met back then? Was this *before* the affair that Matt Butcher claimed he had had with Susan Cowell?

One thing was for certain. Benedict Dee may have been killed in a duel, but there was something more going on here than what people had been thinking.

A duel where two men died was a terrible affair.

A duel where two men died, and then a third man took the bodies, screamed *murder*.

19

BURGLARS

COOPER ARRIVED TO FIND THE POLICE ALREADY AT THE DOOR TO Adam Harris's Surbiton house.

'I didn't think we'd called for backup,' she said, frowning as she climbed out of her squad car. One officer, a tall, stick-thin man with short, spiky grey hair and a rough beard, glared at her.

'Who the bloody hell are you?' he snapped.

'I'm PC Esme Cooper, Temple Inn, City of London Police.'

'What the bloody hell are you doing in Surbiton?'

'I came to check Adam Harris's house, as it's part of *our* murder enquiries,' Cooper replied, pointing at the door. 'But it looks like you guys beat me to it.'

'Yeah, sorry about that,' the officer nodded, finally relaxing and holding out his hand. 'Sergeant Goldman, we had a call this morning. One of the neighbours noticed yesterday that the door had been opened. They thought little of it, it's quite a peaceful place around here. But then they saw on the news that Harris had been killed so they were worried that someone may have come in and stolen stuff.'

'Did he have anything to steal?'

The sergeant waved around.

'We're in Surbiton, love,' he said. 'Everybody's got something to steal. Either way, we came in and, well ...'

He nodded at the door.

'Feel free to go and have a look, make your own decision.'

Cooper, suspicious already, walked to the door and opened it.

Entering the house, it didn't take her long to realise that the entire place had been ransacked.

Walking through the house, she saw that every room had been turned over, with the franticness of somebody desperately looking for something. What it had been, Cooper had no idea.

Eventually, she wandered into a home office, where to the side was a large metal safe, which had also been opened. This, however, was spectacularly done. Whoever had opened the safe wasn't some teenager in a crime of opportunity. This was somebody who knew how to open a safe, and who knew what to do to find items of worth. What items they found inside, she didn't know, but this also had the franticness the rest of the house had, so she had a good idea it wasn't a separate occasion here.

One thing she noticed, however, was on the wall.

There was a space with a hook. Something had been hanging there until recently, as the paint behind the item was slightly darker than the paint around, where the sun hadn't been hitting it.

It was sword-shaped, short, and possibly Roman in size and shape. And PC Esme Cooper knew without a doubt that whatever had hung there until recently, probably had the initials CD stamped on it somewhere.

This was the sword that probably ended up in Adam Harris's back.

Moving away, she walked over to the desk. It hadn't been touched by the police, and interestingly, the paperwork hadn't been touched by whoever had come to steal, either. It was almost as if they had come looking for particular things, and the information on the desk wasn't relevant to them.

Perhaps the sword was?

Flipping through the paperwork, she paused as she started to read. A lot of it was numbers and spreadsheets. After all, Adam Harris had been a chartered accountant when alive. But there was one page of numbers and information that caused her to stop and re-read the sheet. Reading it, she deliberated, ignoring the officers now entering and checking around.

She knew why Adam Harris had died.

She pulled out her phone, dialling.

'Guv,' she said. 'It's Cooper. I think I've worked out what's going on.'

Nicholas Stephens owned an apartment in Canary Wharf. Anjli had his keys and identification to get through, as they'd been on his body when he died, but on entering, she felt a strange sense of déjà vu.

These were the Circus Apartments, the same location where Johnny Lucas had been accused of murder over a year earlier. She wondered idly as she headed for the elevators, whether Nicholas Stephens and Johnny Lucas had ever met each other while walking through the lobby.

On entering the apartment, however, Anjli found herself

in what seemed to be less a modern-day professional's apartment, and more some kind of set from the *Addams Family*, with taxidermic birds and fake wood panelling on the walls, chandeliers hanging from the ceiling, and large oil paintings of knights and what looked to be Tudor princes everywhere she could see. It reminded her of a Disney ride she'd been on when in Paris, called the *Haunted Mansion*, and the juxtaposition of this inside to the outside building actually made her chuckle.

She didn't know what she was going to find, or if there was anything that *would* lead to an answer. But the thing that she didn't expect to find was a crime wall.

Anjli knew what a crime wall looked like. Declan had one when they first started working together, trying to work out who had killed his father. This was almost exactly the same; a board wall made from cork, with pictures and scraps of writing linked by pins and red thread. It was as stereotypical a cork wall crime wall as you could have, and Anjli wondered if Nicholas Stephens had been watching a little too many Swedish crime dramas when putting it together.

But why would he need a crime board?

Walking up to the wall, she examined it, and after a moment of reading, she pulled out her phone and had snapped photos. This seemed to be Nicholas Stephens' personal crusade to prove he had been innocent of the murder, accidental or not, of Bridget Farnsworth. There were pictures of the scene, printed from video screen captures. There was information on the scene, and links to various people there on the day. And lines of written text, notes he'd obviously considered, placed and pinned beside pictures.

It was the pictures that interested Anjli the most, though.

There was a photo of Matt Butcher in full armour, one of

a pink-haired lady that Anjli believed was Susan Cowell, the woman that Matt Butcher had had the affair with.

A tall Viking man with a spear in his hands and a blue woad on his face. This, Anjli believed, was Rolf Cowell, Susan's brother.

Adam Harris was next, in his Roman armour, and next to him was Benedict Dee, in full Regency regalia. And to the right, away from all the others, was an image of Aaron Forden and Georgia Wingate, talking together in a field, obviously taken candidly from a distance.

But it was the text beside the photos that drew Anjli's attention now.

Next to Aaron was a note that simply said *'Crawford-Dunne?'*

Next to Georgia was a second note that said, *'Gained Her Money?'*

Under Rolf, and connected to both him and his sister, was a red thread holding a note that said *'Had My Spear? Did They Return It?'*

Under Adam was a note, *'Was It Accidental?'* which could have meant the death or the so-called accidental nudging of Nicholas that caused the spear to go flying.

And under Matt Butcher, underlined three times and in capital letters; *'Did He Kill Her?'*

Anjli was going to walk away, see if anything else was in the house, but stopped as she saw one last part of the crime wall, shadowed by the bookcase beside it.

It was a photo, taken at a costume party, and in it were Adam Harris, Susan and Rolf Cowell, and Benedict Dee. Under it was another note, with the line *'They Profited From Him, Did They Kill Him?'* written in a red pen.

Anjli noted this down, taking another photo. 'Did They

Kill *Him?*' didn't mean Bridget Farnsworth, but could it have meant Lord Henry Crawford-Dunne? And why was his name next to Aaron's picture? Had Aaron been involved in the death as well?

One thing was for certain, Nicholas Stephens had been very active in hunting down the truth of what happened that day, and now Anjli could understand why someone had killed him – if only to keep him quiet.

20

GLADIATOR, TOO

DECLAN ARRIVED AT FINSBURY CIRCUS GARDENS SHORTLY after the second wave of Gladiator performances. The crowd was easily three times what it had been the previous day from the photos he'd seen, now pushing back against the railings around the edge, and even trying fruitlessly to gain purchase on the trees to get a better view, and he was surprised at this as he walked across to the main tents at the bandstand end of the arena. Maybe the fact it was a Sunday helped.

Or maybe they hoped to see another body.

There were a couple of re-enactors in Roman armour standing outside the "backstage" area, who looked at him with suspicion as he walked towards them. One of them, bald and muscled, wiry rather than weights trained, stepped forward.

'No press,' he said. 'If you want to see anything, go stand around there.'

He pointed at the barriers on the other side of the arena.

Declan instead pulled out his warrant card and showed it.

'DCI Walsh,' he said. 'You Aaron Forden?'

'What if I am?' Aaron, obviously correctly named from the description Anjli had given from when she saw him, asked.

'Well, for a start, speaking in such a suspicious way doesn't help you,' Declan snapped. 'Thought I'd let you know your boss, Matt Butcher, is currently helping us with our enquiries, so won't be here today.'

'That's great,' Aaron muttered, looking around. 'For a start, he's not our "boss". He's just the organiser, for what he actually does here. And second, you've screwed the next show up, because we need somebody out there.'

He sighed, walking off before Declan could speak. Realising he had to follow, Declan continued after the smaller man.

'Can't you do it?' he asked.

'I am bloody doing it,' Aaron replied. 'I've been filling in for sodding Adam Harris all day.'

'I thought he was only doing one or two duels a day.'

'Yeah, but we're not just being gladiators,' Aaron said. 'We're doing talks about the history, we're doing marches and things like that. Anybody connected to the Roman side is being worked off their bloody feet at the moment. Doesn't help when one of our main guys dies and you guys nick the other one.'

He paused as Declan grabbed his arm.

'You haven't asked if he did it,' Declan said softly, staring directly at him. 'Usually when people hear someone's been brought in for enquiries, especially ones connected with murders, there's a kind of morbid curiosity. But you don't seem bothered.'

Aaron shrugged.

'I know he didn't,' he said. 'He's been here all the bloody time. Guy never leaves the park.'

'Apart from when he goes to the pub,' Declan replied.

'We all go to the pub,' Aaron smiled. 'It's the only bloody thing we do that we actually enjoy at the moment.'

'You're not enjoying this?'

Aaron waved around.

'Look at them,' he said. 'All they want to see is people dying. Christ, they'd wet themselves if they saw you. Yeah, I know who you are, DCI Walsh. I've seen you on TV and on the news. I get this is a big case for you.'

Declan wasn't sure where Aaron was going with this, so he folded his arms and waited.

'But I'm at work, and usually it's fun, but at the moment everybody wants to see another death, everybody's expecting another injury. It's bad enough having to perform in front of people who don't give a shit, and are waiting for the dog display – it's another thing to have everybody here expecting you to fail in front of their eyes. And now you've taken away the person I was going to fight, which means we now have a gladiator arena with nobody in it.'

'Sorry about that,' Declan said.

'Yeah, well you can help out,' Aaron smiled.

'Oh, and how's that?' Declan raised an eyebrow.

At this, Aaron walked over to a rack on wheels, picking up a gladiator helmet and placing it on his head. Then, reaching in, he pulled out a sword.

'I'll talk to you after the fight,' he said. 'I'm running late.'

With that, he then walked onto the grass arena.

Declan frowned as he watched him go, turning to one of the other gladiators standing there.

'Who's he fighting?' he asked. 'He literally just said he didn't have anybody.'

'We've been waiting for Butcher, but if he ain't coming, then that fight ain't happening,' one of them said. 'And we can't fight, the two of us, as we've only just come off.'

When Declan turned back, he noticed Aaron Forden walking up to the speakers at the back, stopping beside a man in a toga, obviously one of the "commentators" for the show. He took a wireless microphone from him with a small nod of thanks, tapped it and started speaking, his voice echoing around the arena.

'Ladies and gentlemen,' he said. 'We know why you're here. It's not to see the gladiators. It's mawkish. It's creepy. You want to see pain. You want to see actual death. Well, that isn't happening. We're proud of what we do. But what we do is dangerous, and it takes a lot of skill. To show this, instead of a gladiator arena, we're about to turn this into a classroom. And one of you will have the opportunity to learn what it takes to be a gladiator.'

Declan felt a gnaw in the pit of his stomach as Aaron Forden glanced back over at him.

'Ladies and gentlemen, I want to bring onto the stage right now Detective Chief Inspector Declan Walsh of the City of London Police.'

At this, the crowd started muttering and talking; the voices raising in interest. Declan was, after all, a name they recognised from the news.

Declan shook his head.

'Come on everybody, DCI Walsh is a bit shy, it seems,' Aaron laughed. 'Let's give the Detective Chief Inspector a big, loud cheer.'

As the cheering started, Declan saw cameras and phones

being aimed at him. Grimacing, he straightened and walked out into the arena.

When he hears about this, Monroe is going to have a bloody field day.

Aaron walked over, still waving to the crowd, now excited to see a show. His face was all smiles, but it didn't reach his eyes as he walked up to Declan.

'You want me to answer questions?' Aaron said to him softly, the microphone in his hand now aside, and turned off for the moment. 'You beat me? I tell you everything.'

'Come on,' Declan said. 'I'm in a shirt and tie, you're dressed in armour.'

'Let's get DCI Walsh some armour!' Aaron shouted. And Declan watched as the two gladiators he'd just spoken to came running over to him.

'Take your jacket off,' one said. 'We'll throw this over the top.'

Declan sighed, pulling off his jacket, passing it to the first of the two gladiators, while taking what looked to be some kind of stiff leather breastplate and cuirass, pulling it over his chest, securing it at the side with a buckle.

'It'll keep you safe from blows to the front, but it's shit when hit from behind,' one of them said. 'So don't let him get behind you.'

'Pick your weapon,' ignoring this, Aaron pointed at the rack that had been pulled out onto the pitch by the second gladiator.

Declan sighed, walking back over to it. There were a few swords there; the last time he'd used a sword was while at a Robin Hood convention, fighting a murderer with a fake Excalibur, but he wouldn't say he was an expert at it. Next to that was some kind of spiked mace. It reminded him of his police-issue extending baton, and he almost considered taking it before grabbing the sword.

If he was going to make a fool of himself, he was going to make a point of looking like Russell Crowe as he did so.

Holding the sword up, he walked out into the arena as the crowd got even louder.

'I'll take it slow,' Aaron said with a smile. 'See if you can keep up, yeah?'

Declan gave a smile.

'I have a lot of questions,' he said. 'I'll talk slow when we get back.'

'Only if you win,' Aaron mocked.

'He needs a helmet, too!' one gladiator said, passing across his own metal helm, one that covered his eyes, nose and cheeks, placing it on Declan's head.

'He aims low but loves his headshots,' he whispered as he secured it onto Declan's head. 'It'll batter you about, so take him out quick if you can, or just lie down and yield, it'll all be over.'

'If you think I yield to anyone, you don't know me,' Declan smiled as he turned away, walking into the middle of the arena – well, the grass field surrounded by barriers – with Aaron Forden.

This wasn't Declan's first fight; it wasn't even his first fight with weapons. He'd spent years in the military police, and he'd trained in a multitude of martial arts. Funnily enough, since he'd started work at the Last Chance Saloon, he hadn't needed to use it that much, so, with a sick realisation, he knew he wasn't anywhere near the fighter he used to be.

Still, this was all pretend and make-believe. This wouldn't be—

Aaron launched at him, swinging his sword with a force that Declan hadn't expected.

He only just moved to the side, the sword's flat edge smacking against the side of his head, sending him stumbling.

'As you can see, Aronus, our gladiator, has decided to go for a headshot,' one commentator spoke out on the speakers, now having regained the wireless microphone. 'In Roman times, this was actually frowned upon by the gladiators, as the whole point of the fight was to give a show to the paid customers, mainly rich dignitaries who had come to see the event. So, to kill a rival gladiator fast was removing their enjoyment, and deemed dishonourable.'

Declan wasn't sure how historically correct this was, but the crowd didn't seem to care, as they now booed Aaron, walking around waving his sword at them. He'd decided, obviously, from the audience's reaction to Declan's involvement, to play the part of the heel in this; if it had been a wrestling show, he would have been picking at a chair and trying to smack it into Declan's back by now.

Declan shook his head to stop the ringing, glanced back at the gladiators who were watching him, remembering what they'd said, and shifted his grip on the sword he held.

It was a Gladius, the same sword that had been left in Adam Harris's back. It felt heavy in his hand, even though it was not a "real" sword as such.

Or was it?

He didn't really have time to think about how re-enactors' swords differed from the real thing as Aaron was already moving at him. He was, however, moving slower this time, giving Declan a chance to back away, batting away the constant attacks, as Aaron over played the role, pantomiming to the audience. No matter how he felt about Declan destroying his gladiator event by keeping Butcher at Temple Inn, he still had an element of professionalism in him. Something he'd decided to lean into, to give the audience a show – even if it was at Declan's embarrassment and expense during this play fight.

But Declan was *tired* of playing.

As Aaron swung hard, once more aiming for the head, Declan brought his sword up, connecting – using the force of the upward swing to knock Aaron, who hadn't been expecting such a forceful response, backwards.

Declan followed in quickly, moving with three swift slashes. In his mind, the sword was an extendable baton, and he used it as such. It was heavier, but at the same time, he could feel the movements that he had used and learned so well over the years.

A clang of swords echoed across the park, and Declan continued to move forward.

Aaron was obviously more experienced at this, but he had underestimated Declan, played him for a fool, and now had suddenly realised that there was every chance that Declan could take this momentum and defeat him.

Aaron quickly shifted grip, blocking one of Declan's blows with a double-handed hold, and before Declan realised, Aaron had swung his leg out, sweeping Declan from behind, sending him back first onto the grass.

'And here we see Aronus is using his other limbs to take down his foe,' the speakers announced as the commentator continued. 'At the end of the day, many gladiatorial contests weren't to the death. After all, with the amount of money spent training the gladiators, the last thing they wanted was dead bodies. A body meant a new gladiator had to be trained. Even major injuries could cause problems to the bottom-line profit. Therefore, gladiators were allowed to use whatever they wanted to take down their foe, and anything that wasn't a weapon was appreciated by their patrons, the people that had paid for them.'

Declan rolled to the side as Aaron slashed down with his sword, but it was a theatrical, slow movement, deliberately made so that Declan could move out of the way.

Declan rolled to his knees and then clambered to his feet as Aaron gave him the moment to do so, once more playing to the crowd.

Up to that point, Declan had been struggling to keep up, but Aaron, in this one violent act, had shown Declan how he could win. The Roman gladiators of the turn of the millennium might not have known Krav Maga, but Declan knew it very well. And Aaron Forden, for all his skills, wasn't a trained martial artist, from his movements.

With that, Declan shifted his grip on his sword again. Now it wasn't just a Gladius. It was part of him.

Aaron went to move, but Declan rolled forward, a circus-style tumble, something that was against everything you would have expected a man with a sword to do. Aaron swung around, spinning, as Declan carried on moving, keeping the man off balance as he tumbled around him, slapping out with his sword, catching Aaron in the knee before moving away again, and slapping Aaron on the arse.

The audience was cheering at this. Their underdog, DCI Walsh, was starting to win and Aaron, Declan could see even though he wore a helmet, was getting angry.

'You're going to tell me everything, Mister Forden,' he said as he moved again, dipping under a swing, Aaron now getting more sloppy with his movements. 'You're going to squeal like a piggy for me.'

He didn't know why the line from the film *Deliverance* had come to mind, but it did the job, and Aaron gave a guttural scream as he attacked again, his movements sloppier now. Declan had assumed that although Aaron probably learned all the skills he used now many years ago, he had coasted with the gladiator work, spending time with re-enactors, working to predestined outcomes; even if Aaron had been fighting any free-form battles, the chances were he'd have been fighting people less experienced than he was.

Declan *was* less experienced than Aaron was, but unlike the other re-enactors who probably didn't care if they lived or died in their character roles, or had even been told when to fall, with predetermined outcomes, Declan wanted more than anything to wipe that smug grin off Aaron Forden's face.

Aaron moved in quickly, thrusting his sword forward—

But Declan, moving to the side once more stepped into it, getting close as he grabbed his wrist, pulling the sword even further forward and kicking out, taking Aaron's feet out from under him, sending him tumbling to the ground, face first.

Declan still held on to the wrist, however, and yanked it back, rolling Aaron from his front onto his back, looking up at Declan as he held the sword to Aaron's face.

'I believe this is the part where you yield,' he said.

'It looks like DCI Walsh has bested Aronus!' the commentator said, with more than a smidgen of glee in his voice, and Declan wondered whether this was because Aaron was disliked as much as Declan was believing.

Either way, Declan was the winner, and he raised his sword up.

'This is *Sparta!*' he cried out to rapturous applause and cheers.

'Christ,' Aaron muttered. 'Ask your bloody questions, but please don't quote that bloody film.'

Declan laughed, the adrenaline coursing through his body right now.

'You cheated,' Aaron hissed, the crowd still cheering.

'How could I cheat when there are no rules about being a gladiator?' Declan smiled warmly. 'All I did was survive.'

'Let's give it up to the winner of the event, DCI Walsh,' the commentator shouted as Aaron angrily clambered to his feet, pulling off his helmet, glaring at Declan.

'Take your helmet off,' he said, 'and let's finish this properly.'

Unsure what he meant, Declan pulled his helmet off as the crowd cheered again.

Aaron held Declan's hand up and turned him around in a slow circle, eventually stopping so he faced the seats at the end of the arena. Declan hadn't realised, but there were people sitting in them, probably people from *Love Island* or Instagram influencers, something like that. One of the people, however, was dressed like a Roman senator, and he smiled as he stood up and gave the ...

Thumbs down.

21

THUMBS DOWN

THE AUDIENCE GAVE A COLLECTIVE GASP AT THIS, BUT THE commentator, still on the microphone, laughed.

'Don't worry, ladies and gentlemen, this isn't the movies,' he said. 'In real Roman times, the thumb down was actually the sign to *save* the life. If the Emperor wanted to spare the life of the Gladiator who lost, he would either make a closed fist, or a thumbs-down gesture, showing the winning Gladiator should lay down their sword. Thumbs up only turned up in films, but I can understand why you were confused!'

The audience laughed at this, and Declan, snapping his hand back from Aaron's grasp, gave a wave to them.

Aaron had resigned himself, slumping his shoulders slightly as he looked at Declan.

'Let's clean up,' he said. 'Then I'll answer your questions.'

Declan walked back to the tent, the two other gladiators patting him on the back as they helped remove the leather armour. As Declan grabbed his suit jacket, he realised with a trace of annoyance that his trousers now had grass stains running down the back leg.

'Nice work,' the first gladiator, the one who had given him the heads-up about the headshots, said. 'He won't fight us any more, he knows we'd kick the shit out of him.'

Declan nodded.

'Thank you,' he said. 'Did either of you know Adam Harris well?'

'I did,' the taller of the two said. 'It was a damn shame what happened to him.'

'Who do you think did it?' Declan asked.

At this, however, the taller gladiator shook his head.

'I'm not saying anything,' he replied. 'There's too many people out there with their own opinions, and all it does is muddy the waters.'

'Hypothetically?'

'If I'm being honest, I think it was because of the woman, the one that died.'

'You think Harris was involved in that?'

'No, but I still think it was because of her,' the gladiator shrugged. 'Speak to Aaron about it,' he said. 'He was closer at the time, playing the rival general. He would have seen up close and personal who did it.'

Declan nodded, and after thanking the two men, he started walking over to the other tent where Aaron was. He found him sitting dejectedly on a stool; he'd pulled his armour off and was currently tending to a cut he had on his arm.

'I didn't catch you, did I?' Declan asked.

Aaron shook his head.

'You wish,' he replied. 'This was from earlier. It's why you beat me.'

'Of course,' Declan smiled. 'That's the only answer.'

Aaron couldn't tell if Declan was mocking or not, and

eventually sighed as he leant back on the stool, glared at the ceiling of the tent, and then returned his attention to Declan.

'What do you want to know?' he said. 'I promised I'd answer anything.'

Declan went to speak, but then paused as his phone beeped. Holding a finger up to pause Aaron, he read it. It was a note from Billy, collecting some information that they'd recently picked up from DCI Warren.

'Tell me about your misspent youth,' he said, looking back. 'I understand you were arrested for burglary?'

'Burglary, safe cracking. I was a bit of a tearaway,' Aaron replied, and Declan was surprised at the lack of secrecy. He'd expected Aaron to deny it, or at least play it down. 'But I was a kid, you know, a teenager.'

Declan carried on reading.

'You were arrested for breaking into Pennington Hall,' he said.

'Yes,' Aaron nodded, not hiding this at all.

'Was there a reason you picked that place?'

'I lived nearby, it was a big house,' Aaron shrugged.

'And years later, you were there as the head of a Roman army, facing off against Boudicca on a day when items, priceless items, were taken from that location.'

At the comment, Aaron's eyes narrowed.

'When I was a kid, I went looking for money,' he replied. 'I knew nothing about antiques or weapons or things like that. I didn't go in the weaponry room, or the armoury, or whatever they call it these days. I went to the office where the takings were.'

'How did you break the safe?'

'It was an old safe,' Aaron shrugged. 'I'd watched movies. My dad was a GP, and he had a stethoscope. I'd borrowed it, taken it with me. To be honest, I didn't need it because when I got there, the safe was ajar and it was easy to open.'

He chuckled.

'I was fifteen years old, DCI Walsh. I didn't have a clue what I was doing, and I was angry.'

'Why were you angry?'

'Because I was fifteen years old,' Aaron said, as if this was an obvious answer. 'My family was broke, and *they* had everything.'

Declan could tell there was something more but couldn't quite work out what it was. There was definitely an anger at the Crawford-Dunnes.

'I understand,' he said, looking back at his message, 'that even though you were arrested and pretty much bang to rights for the act, Lord Henry Crawford-Dunne didn't press charges. In fact, if anything, it was this high connection that got you off.'

'I hadn't stolen anything when I was captured,' Aaron said. 'When the police were alerted by a silent alarm, they turned up and found a half-cut fifteen-year-old kid, who had smoked a couple of joints, finished a bottle of Thunderbird and drunk a can and a half of Tennents Super, absolutely convinced that he was on a righteous cause.'

'And what would this righteous cause be?' Declan then asked.

Aaron looked up, went to look away, and then he sighed.

'It's a historical grudge,' he said. 'My family and theirs.'

'Really?' Declan said. 'And would this historical grudge have affected you years later when stealing items?'

'I stole nothing from my family!' Aaron shouted, and then paused as if realising he'd said too much.

Declan stared at him.

'Forden,' he replied. 'Ford-Dunne. How distant from the Crawford-Dunne family is yours?'

Aaron grimaced a little and nodded.

'My great-grandfather's brother was the lord of the manor,' he replied. 'Pennington Hall and the Crawford-Dunnes ran Newbury, but then my great-grandfather fell in love with a divorcee – and an American at that. This was deemed unacceptable.'

He spat on the grass.

'I'm not even going to mention the fact that her *colour* wasn't the same as the family. There was a fight, he was disowned, and as a response he removed the "Craw" from his name. Crawford-Dunne became *Ford-Dunne*, and then became *Forden*.'

'Ballsy move.'

'Stupid move. He had nothing. No money, no status. There's no "lord of the manor" in a council estate in Berkshire.'

'How much of this did you know?'

'When I grew up I didn't know any of this. We even went to Pennington Hall on a school trip, and I looked at people on these paintings and I didn't recognise any of them. But my teacher did,' Aaron shook his head. 'I don't know how, but apparently my great-great-great-uncle Edmund, or something like that – I never paid attention – bore a striking resemblance to me. She even commented on this. When I went home, I jokingly said I must have been adopted and then I learned everything.'

'How old were you?'

'I was fourteen. I spent a year falling off the rails, annoyed that they had everything and we had nothing, and then I broke in.'

'Why did they drop charges?' Declan asked.

'Because I was family,' Aaron chuckled again, but this time there was a bitterness to it. 'They wouldn't give us a pot to piss in, a penny to our name. But they also knew the moment it came out that the penniless cousin of the Crawford-Dunne dynasty had resorted to stealing shit from his own family, the press would have a field day. They bailed me out, sat us down and said they'd sort things, make things right. The problems of my great-grandparents shouldn't be dealt with by me and my generation. My family was welcomed back.'

He leant closer, glaring at Declan.

'My family was welcomed back,' he repeated. 'Which basically meant we were given a little land, and a pitiful amount of money, but even though we were effectively told to sit down and shut up, we were looked after by Lord Henry Crawford-Dunne. So no, DCI Walsh, I didn't steal from him, and I didn't cause him to have a heart attack the day of the theft.'

He sat back, and his face was dark as thunder as he spoke.

'But if I knew who it was, I wouldn't bother going to the police, because you did nothing. I'd damn well dispense the justice myself.'

'Murder?'

Aaron smiled and held up his hand, raising his thumb.

'No mercy,' he said. 'Eye for an Eye. The Romans called it "Vindicta," and it's where both "vindicate" and "vendetta" come from. And the Romans were very good at vendettas.'

Declan nodded.

'Change your clothes,' he said. 'You're coming back to the station.'

'Your DI told me I didn't need to come to the station,' Aaron replied.

Declan grinned.

'This happens when you lose a fight with a minor celebrity,' he said. 'Do I have to arrest you or will you come willingly?'

Aaron rose, already unclipping his armour.

'I have nothing to fear,' he said. 'I killed no-one.'

Declan watched Aaron as he said this, and a sliver of ice ran down his spine. He couldn't yet work out whether Aaron was telling the truth, or just believed it.

One thing that was for certain, though, was that Declan was very glad the fight had been in front of an audience. He didn't know how well he'd have fared if Aaron hadn't needed to hold back.

AARON FORDEN, ALTHOUGH DECLAN WASN'T SURE IF HE WAS technically now a Crawford-Dunne, glared at Declan and Monroe across the table.

'I'm not a killer,' he said. 'I wasn't there. I didn't do the things you seem to think I did.'

'I don't know if you've noticed, laddie, but we've not actually accused you of anything,' Monroe smiled as he leant forward, placing his elbows on the table. 'Because the problem we have here isn't that you've not done anything. It's the fact that you kept your mouth shut when there were areas that we should have known about. And I understand the whole family thing because we've got a wee laddie out there who's the child of a rich family, trying desperately to get back into the will. We see exactly how this can be for you, and we have some sympathy.'

'But Lord Henry Crawford-Dunne died three years ago and his items were stolen,' Declan added ominously. 'Now, you might not have been part of the group of people who did it, but now we have a motive for you to get revenge. "Vindicta", as you say.'

Aaron nodded.

'I get that,' he said.

'Tell me,' Declan said, changing the subject slightly, pulling out his notebook and starting to write. 'Was it you who set up the event at Pennington Hall?'

'I suggested to Butcher that it would be a good idea,' Aaron nodded. 'Nobody knew I had family connections, and I wanted to keep it that way. But Matt was looking for a place to do the Boudicca uprising and I knew that Uncle Henry was looking for something to help make some money for the home. The Crawford-Dunne clan weren't exactly as flush as they used to be.'

'Aye, but they're land rich,' Monroe grinned. 'A lot of houses could be built on that land.'

'There's the ability to have money, and there's wanting to make money regardless of the cost,' Aaron replied. 'Henry Crawford-Dunne wasn't the latter. He was a good man; he showed me a way to live that wasn't one of thievery and lies.'

'And yet here you are, still lying,' Declan muttered.

'Everything we hear about him is that he reneged on the deal,' Monroe said, changing the subject before Aaron could reply.

'He reneged on the deal because those guys were absolute pricks,' Aaron snapped. 'I was there front and centre, I saw it all. The night before the battle, we were all camping on his land. There was a fight, a big argument.'

'What was the argument about?' Monroe raised an eyebrow.

'Bloody Matt and Bridget kicking off. Susan having a go at somebody else, as well. I can't remember what it was, I wasn't paying attention.'

'Matt Butcher had a fight with his wife?'

Aaron slumped back in the chair.

'Look, the worst kept secret in re-enactment was that Matt and Bridget were about to break up. She was a very vocal person.'

He chuckled to himself.

'She once turned around and complained at an event that Japanese snacks were being sold at one of the stalls. She claimed she didn't like the Japanese because they hunted whales but it just came out of nowhere. When people started asking whether she was racist, it was pointed out that this was just the way she was. She liked whales. She spoke her mind. She was never one to turn away from a confrontation. The problem we had was she was never one to turn away from a situation, either.'

He sighed, shaking his head.

'Unfortunately, Matt gave her as many situations as he could possibly give.'

'Do you know what the fight was about?'

Aaron shook his head but then stopped halfway through mid-shake and reluctantly nodded.

'She was the rich one. Matt was broke,' he said. 'Matt didn't care about her. He was shagging Susan Cowell and everybody knew that – even she knew that. There were a lot of rumours bouncing around that she was cucking him with someone else. That night, she commented in passing she was looking into changing her will, mainly to get a rise from Matt. It worked. Matt was suspicious, assumed that she was pissed at him being with Susan.'

'*Was* she pissed at him being with Susan?' Monroe asked. 'After all, you just said it was a badly kept secret. A lawyer like her must have known.'

'Oh, she knew. She didn't care,' Aaron replied. 'From what I could work out, I think they had some kind of written deal that stated that, you know, all the money she made was her own, whether or not he liked that.'

Monroe wrote this down.

'So, what was the change in the will?'

'I think Bridget knew she was about to break up with Matt. And she knew if something had happened to her, this would cause a problem because Matt would still get everything, and at the time they absolutely detested each other.'

'Enough to kill her?'

'Matt didn't want her dead. The will would have meant he got nothing.'

'What about life insurance?'

Aaron shrugged.

'I wasn't close enough to ask,' he said. 'But what I do know is that Adam Harris started this. He was a sneaky little shit. He always enjoyed stirring the pot to see what happened.'

'How would he know?'

'He was her accountant,' Aaron replied. 'He'd been involved in converting her bonuses money into cryptocurrency. Like, a *lot*. And at some point he had been talking about crypto to somebody else, and stating what coins should be used, telling them as if he was some kind of expert on where they should go. And when they said "well, how do you know all this", he kind of let it drop that he'd been working on behalf of somebody converting almost seven figures worth of cash into crypto.'

'And Matt put two and two together?'

'Matt was annoyed, but he kind of understood. I mean, he was more worried that she would have gone for him with the affair. Susan and him being together meant that she could have divorced him with cause and kept everything.'

'So, why didn't she?' Declan asked.

'Because she was shagging Georgia Wingate,' Aaron said. 'It wasn't public, but I knew, as I'd seen them together. They were subtle, "best friends". No one considered that the woman married to Matt might actually shag another woman.'

He sighed.

'But I wasn't the only one to see it, and the following day, she died.'

———

22

PLAY THE PART

NODDING, MONROE NOTED THIS DOWN.

'Did Matt know?' He asked, looking back up from his notebook.

'Honestly, I don't think he did,' Aaron replied. 'Or if he did, he was superb at keeping it quiet. And Matt isn't that good an actor. All I can tell you is that the night before the event, Adam was boasting he was moving money into crypto and was therefore an expert. People worked out it was the money being given to him by his client, Bridget Farnsworth. And people knew this meant things were going to go really badly for Matt Butcher. It was a five car pile-up in slow motion and we were all there to watch.'

'Do you think hypothetically Matthew Butcher could have killed his wife to gain insurance, or even possibly to catch it before the will was changed?'

'You speak as if he's some kind of supervillain,' Aaron said. 'Matt Butcher only gave a shit about a piece of land. He didn't care about money. He wanted the land. He wanted to do the things that he enjoyed.'

'What about Susan?' Declan said. 'I've met her. She seems quite ambitious. And her brother—'

'Oh, don't even start about Rolf,' Aaron started to laugh. 'He dresses like he's from *Vikings*, but he acts like he's the most wounded animal around. You do anything near him and he'll have you sued. It's an absolute joke.'

'Could they have killed him?'

'What, do you think Rolf would have stabbed the spear?' Aaron looked surprised for a split second. 'Yeah, I heard Nicholas Stephens' conspiracy theories. He was spouting them off on Tuesday.'

'At the pub?'

'Yeah. Going off on one. Around the same time as Georgia was doing her stupid bet idea. I swear to God they're like children.'

'But you were nothing to do with this.'

Aaron smiled.

'I'm a lot of things, Detective Superintendent Monroe. But what I'm not is an idiot. When I was a teenager, I almost destroyed my life. But I had it fixed for me. There's no way in hell I was going to allow somebody to take that back.'

He shrugged.

'Besides, if I had ... the Crawford-Dunnes could have taken away everything.'

'WHAT ARE YOU STILL DOING HERE?' ANJLI SAID TO JESS AS SHE arrived back in the office. 'Haven't you got a date you're supposed to be going to?'

'Trisha's coming here,' Jess replied, looking up at Anjli from her laptop. 'I'm just going through some photos.'

'What sort of photos?'

Jess nodded at a USB stick jutting out of the side of the laptop.

'Chivalry gained some photos of the event,' she said. 'The Crawford-Dunnes had meant to use these for PR and press, but never did. His contact emailed them over around an hour ago.'

'Anything exciting?'

Jess shook her head.

'The exciting thing is with Billy, in Monroe's office. That is, he's showing it to Bullman, as Monroe and Declan are upstairs.'

Anjli frowned. That Billy had gone to the office to show this was something important.

Nodding, she left Jess to the photos, and carried on through, pausing at the door as she realised that Bullman and Billy were both staring at Billy's laptop.

'What have I missed?' she asked.

'A pretty bloody important thing,' Bullman said. 'Come look at this.'

Anjli walked around and saw CCTV footage of what looked to be some kind of cellar.

'This is Benedict Dee's dungeon,' Bullman explained. 'Or whatever you want to call it. The basement of his house. When De'Geer went looking, he found a wireless Wi-Fi camera in the corner. It had been recording for days onto a solid state drive. Mister Fitzwarren here has been going through that aforementioned drive, looking for things that we can use.'

Anjli looked at Billy.

'Am I thinking that you're seeing the murders?'

'In a way, yes,' Billy said. 'He's angled the camera down

the cellar, so it wasn't to monitor his items. This wasn't used for security. I think this was actually used for learning.'

'You're going to have to explain that one to me,' Anjli pursed her lips. 'Most security cameras I know aren't here to teach things.'

'This case I think it was,' Billy replied. 'If you notice, the angle shows the main cellar area. This is his shooting range. At the end, you can see a couple of figures. These are what he uses as targets when he duels. I think he has his one-sided duel, shoots the figures and then uses the footage to work out how better to change his aim, or things like that.'

'So, effectively he's filming his duels and working out how to be better?'

'Exactly,' Billy said. 'However, it's a motion sensitive Wi-Fi camera, so every time there's movement, it'll start recording, unless he's deliberately overridden this to record something, like duel training.'

Anjli nodded.

'So, what do you have?'

Billy turned, pressed a few buttons, and a file opened on the screen.

It was a different file to the one he was looking at, but this one still showed the end of the cellar, still lit the same as it was in the first image.

'Watch,' he said.

There was some movement to the edge, slightly off centre, and Anjli watched as a blurry figure to the side moved back out of shot and then a couple of moments later reappeared.

It was Adam Harris wearing his Roman armour, a duelling pistol in his hand.

He looked back and laughed as if having a conversation

with somebody else in the room, motioning that he was going to walk ten steps.

A second figure now appeared; their back was to the camera, but it was obviously Benedict Dee, also speaking.

Then, after turning back around, Adam Harris carried on walking. It was in all intents and purposes a duel, but from his attitude and his laugh, Anjli wondered whether Adam Harris had realised the severity of the situation.

However, before the ten steps had occurred, he suddenly lurched forward as Benedict raised his pistol, firing it, a puff of smoke appearing on the screen.

Anjli knew what had happened; he had been shot in the back.

He staggered forward another step, turning, his expression one of shock.

He grabbed at his spine, pulling back his hand, with blood appearing.

He started shouting and raised his pistol at Benedict – who was now raising his own hands to try to stop this – then fired, Benedict falling backwards, out of shot.

This done, he slumped to the floor.

'Do you know what we've just seen here?' Bullman whispered.

'Adam Harris was believed to have gone to help Benedict Dee prepare for a duel,' Anjli nodded. 'It wasn't supposed to be a real one.'

'No, you're right there,' Bullman shook her head. 'He believed he was assisting him, and you can see there that they were having a conversation, discussing the number of steps, how far he should walk. However, before he reached his number, Benedict Dee shot him in the back.'

'But he didn't kill him immediately,' Billy added, rewinding the footage to when the bullet had obviously hit. 'The chances were, it would have killed a normal person in the back, but Adam Harris had put on armour, and that armour saves him, but not quite enough.'

'He turns, and he fires, and I think we know where that bullet ends up,' Anjli leant closer as she looked. 'Benedict Dee fires early, catching him in the back. But why?'

'That's a question we need to check,' Bullman replied, shifting position as she spoke. 'But here's something else. Benedict Dee shoots Adam in the back, thinking he'll kill him instantly, but what he doesn't consider is the armour that Adam's wearing. It's only leather, but it's enough to stop the bullet a little, enough to allow him time to turn around and angrily shoot back. An inch to the side, he probably would have missed with his own shot, and collapsed dead to the floor in front of Dee, but he didn't, he shot Benedict through the eye, killing him instantly.'

'The two killed each other. In all intents and purposes, it was a duel,' Billy whistled.

'But someone had to be there,' Anjli shook her head. 'There's no way they could kill each other in a cellar and then appear in other locations.'

Billy returned to the original video and started scrolling through it again. After a moment, the video stopped.

'This is where the motion detector stops,' Billy explained. 'We think that Benedict Dee hadn't meant to film this, he'd forgotten that he had his wee motion detector thing on. The camera only records movement, so it's a good hour before *this* happens.'

On the screen, a figure appeared. It was close to the

camera and hidden. The figure reached down and dragged the body of Adam Harris away.

It wasn't hooded, it wasn't masked. The person doing this hadn't realised there'd be a camera watching him.

Anjli didn't need to see the face, from behind she recognised the bald head of Aaron Forden, the gladiator she'd spoken to the previous day.

'Aaron Forden. We need to get him in,' she said.

'Already done,' Billy replied. 'It's who they're talking to upstairs.'

'Have they seen this?'

Billy shook his head, and Anjli grabbed the laptop.

'Then let's go show them,' she snarled as she left the office, heading for the interview rooms.

'LET'S TALK ABOUT THE CRAWFORD-DUNNES,' DECLAN SAID.

'What would you like to know?'

'Who do you think stole from them that day?' Declan asked. 'I'm guessing you had a bit of an inroad into what was going on.'

'Not really,' Aaron shrugged. 'We were welcomed back into the family, but that didn't mean we were family.'

'What would you have called yourselves? Reluctant relatives, perhaps?'

'We never got invited to the table at Christmas, but we received a card. And they knew our name. That seemed to be good enough for my mum and dad.'

He considered the thought.

'All I know is that when Bridget died, it wasn't fast. The

ambulance was called. They took her to the hospital, where she died. Matt was with her every moment of that time. Matt had been organising everything, and when Henry argued the cost ...'

'Because there'd been a murder, which had caused bad PR?'

'That was the bollocks the re-enactment society said,' Aaron shook his head. 'It wasn't like that at all. The reason they got angry at Henry was because he was refusing to pay them the full amount. And the reason he was refusing to pay them the full amount was because he was charging them for the damage they'd done the night before in their drunken piss-ups on his land. He wasn't a monster. He wasn't going to turn around and say he wasn't going to pay them because of someone dying. That was insane.'

'So what did happen?'

'I don't know,' Aaron admitted. 'Honestly, I wish I could help you. All I can tell you is that with Matt gone ... it was Susan, Rolf and Adam that went to speak to him.'

'Susan, Rolf and Adam,' Monroe frowned. 'Not you?'

'I was keeping out of it. Susan and Rolf went to speak to him first. Then, half an hour later, they came back and said that Adam needed to speak to them. There had been some kind of argument, and they wanted a third person involved. An hour later they came back and said he was refusing and that we'd be dealing with it in the courts.'

'Did you?'

'Did I what?'

'Deal with it in the courts?'

'By that point everything had fallen apart,' Aaron admitted. 'I don't even know if they ever got the money back. And I'd gone full Roman. Didn't play with those pricks anymore.'

'What do you think happened at that point?' Declan asked.

Aaron sat forward.

'I have my suspicions,' he said.

'Tell me your suspicions,' Declan said. 'Be honest, because whatever you tell us here is going to affect what we think of you right now as a suspect.'

If Aaron saw the look between Declan and Monroe, the look that hinted at more, he didn't act on it as he nodded, cricked his neck as he looked around, and then looked back at Declan.

The look that he gave him was the same look he'd given him in the gladiator ring, and Declan knew this was a new mindset that he had taken on. It was confrontational, but this time it wasn't confrontational against the police officer opposite him.

Now he was about to start a fight against other people.

'I think that Rolf and Susan argued about the money,' he said. 'I think Susan went in heavy-handed. She believed she was the de facto queen of the re-enactment group.'

'How so?'

'Matt was the leader. His wife was likely to be dead soon, and she was shagging Matt. She knew once the smoke cleared that she would be the head of the group.'

'Do you think that's why she was with him in the first place?'

'I don't know and I don't want to know,' Aaron said. 'But I think she kicked off. There was an argument. Henry wanted to give them less money, they wanted more money. He argued about the fight, they argued about everything else. And I think he had a heart attack, there and then in front of them.'

'You think that they caused his heart attack?'

'I didn't say that,' Aaron replied carefully. 'You'd have to ask them. But it seemed mighty strange that on the same day that they both confronted him, he has a heart attack and dies. They then find Adam.'

'Why do you think they brought Adam in?'

'Because he part-owned the van with them,' Aaron replied. 'Grey Transit; the van he was driving to every event. Big enough to place all the items in. Adam was about to leave, so they called him over. He parks up next to the house, they go in to continue their "discussions". An hour later, Adam leaves, Rolf and Susan come over and tell us, "Pack up, we're leaving, he's not paying."'

Declan sat back. It matched. Susan and Rolf could have done this, Adam Harris taking the items away. The gun that was found in Benedict Dee's house would have been there, likewise the Gladius, the markings matching the Crawford-Dunne branding.

'When did Benedict Dee get involved?' he asked.

Aaron shook his head.

'I never really knew Dee,' Aaron shrugged. 'He didn't get on with them, they were Dark Ages and he was a dandy with a pistol. From what I'd worked out, they'd kicked him out of their club a while back, so he had every reason to turn round and tell them to go screw off. But he stepped forward, fought to get this case, because Georgia Wingate asked personally for him. And once he'd looked at everything, he sat down in an inquest and announced Bridget had died of an accident. And then he stated my uncle had simply passed away from a heart attack, and the items believed to be stolen were nothing more than items he had sold to people over the years, and not told anyone.'

He looked away.

'Handy that Dee gained an antique pair of duelling pistols around the same time, though, wasn't it?'

'You think he was bribed?'

'I think he was part of it from pretty much the start,' Aaron said. 'To be bribed, you must be coerced to be involved and paid to look the other way. I think Benedict Dee was involved from the moment they got out of Pennington Hall. He knew what Pennington Hall had. He'd seen it many times as well. Probably spent ages working out how to get a slice of that pie. When Georgia asked for his help, he probably thought it was Christmas.'

'And at no point did you think to get revenge?'

'Oh, I wanted revenge,' Aaron said. 'I wanted revenge from the start. I was fighting constantly. I even had friends I knew on the force who owed favours to my family and I got the paperwork.'

'You were the one who gave Nicholas Stephens the results of his case,' Declan realised.

Aaron nodded.

'Stephens' "accident" was a handy lie. I knew it had to be sorted out a different way,' he said. 'So, yeah, I found and then gave him paperwork that made him doubt what he saw. The problem was that all eyes pointed at him. The only other people who wanted Bridget dead were Rolf and Susan, and they both were on her side of the battle. Sure, you could have had a spear go through from either side, but Rolf's spear was a Dark Ages spear. Nicholas's was a Roman. Different styles.'

'You were front and centre, leading the forces in that battle. Who else could have used a spear—'

Declan paused, surprised, as Anjli entered the interview room.

'Sorry to interrupt, sir,' she said, nodding to Monroe as

she spoke. 'But we have a recent development in the case and it involves Mister Forden here.'

Declan glanced at Aaron, who now looked a little sick, as if realising something was about to come out into the open.

'Spit it out, lassie,' Monroe said. 'Don't be shy.'

Anjli walked over and placed the laptop onto the table.

'For the record, Detective Inspector Kapoor has entered the room with a laptop,' Declan said. 'She is now opening the laptop.'

'Mister Forden,' Anjli continued, looking at Aaron. 'How well did you know Benedict Dee?'

'Barely knew him at all,' Aaron replied.

'Had you ever been to his house?'

'I think he had a dinner party once I might have been at.'

'Dinner parties are quite intimate, aren't they?'

'Not Benedict's ones,' Aaron laughed. 'There were usually fifteen to twenty people there. Half the time it was because he wanted to suck up to somebody else. I honestly can't remember.'

'You never remember going into his cellar, then?' Anjli asked.

Aaron frowned at this.

'I didn't even know—'

Anjli held a hand up.

'For the record,' she said. 'I am holding my hand up to stop Mister Forden from lying further. I am now showing him the footage we have.'

She pressed play on the screen, and the CCTV footage played.

'Do you know what this is?' she asked.

Aaron Forden looked at the image and paled.

Silently, he nodded.

'For the recording,' Anjli smiled, 'Mister Forden has acknowledged that he knows what this video is, with a nod. He also knows he's been outed as a liar and is pretty much utterly screwed right now.'

23

___

BODYSNATCHERS

Anjli turned the laptop so now Monroe and Declan could both see it.

'Billy found the footage of the webcam Benedict Dee had in his cellar,' she said, looking back at Aaron. 'He'd film his one-man duels, working out how to aim better. It was motion detected and by pure chance, when Adam Harris and Benedict Dee had their rehearsal duel, it filmed the whole thing.'

Aaron Forden said nothing.

Anjli looked back at Declan.

'We see in the video that Benedict Dee shot Adam Harris in the back. He was laughing before it happened, and we believe he was practising a duel with Benedict. But when the shot was fired, a ball struck him between the shoulder blades.'

She returned her attention to Aaron.

'The armour stopped the bulk of it, but it was a fatal shot. It did, however, give him long enough to turn and fire his own pistol. We believe this was the shot that entered Mister Dee's eye, travelling into his brain and killing him instantly.'

'Roman armour,' Declan realised. 'In the gladiator arena, they said it was great from the front, but pointless from behind.'

Aaron looked away, unable to match her gaze as she continued.

'Then, around an hour later, Mister Forden here is seen pulling Adam Harris's body out of the camera's angle. I wondered if he had any explanation for this?'

Monroe glanced back at Aaron from the screen.

'It looks like we've got some more questions to ask you,' he said.

'Oh, there's more,' Anjli added. 'You see, we've had a look around some other houses, Mister Forden. We've had a bit of an exciting morning if you're asking. We know, for example, that Nicholas Stephens had a crime wall. He'd been aimed at people in relation to the death of Bridget Farnsworth.'

'I've already admitted that,' Aaron said, looking at Declan for confirmation. 'I gave him information, Berkshire police gave me it, I've got no problem with that.'

'The paperwork at the crime wall included printed scans of sheets of paper matching papers found in Dee's cellar drawer, where it could only have been gained from someone there. It's even got Dee's handwritten notes,' Anjli leant closer. 'Sergeant De'Geer is checking it for your fingerprints, Mister Forden. What do you think it'll find? That you held each one as you took photos? I also understand you were once a burglar and a safecracker.'

'I've talked about that as well,' Aaron replied, now uncertain, floundering. 'I was a teenage kid, I didn't know what I was doing. I broke into Pennington Hall because I was angry.'

'But you still knew how to do it, didn't you?' Anjli asked.

'Because that wasn't the only time you've ever broken into a house, and you've been making a habit of it recently.'

Aaron didn't reply.

'You broke in to Adam Harris's house, didn't you? You went through his things and opened up his safe. I don't know if you took anything from there, but I know for a fact you removed a Roman Gladius from the wall. The Gladius that was later found embedded in his back.'

Declan replayed the video on the laptop, and everyone watched the first scene in silence.

'They joke on that video,' he eventually said. 'Adam Harris acts like he's okay, but he's deliberately placed on armour, as if distrusting of Benedict Dee. Minutes later, he's dead.'

Aaron looked from Declan to Monroe to Anjli and then back.

'You have nothing on me,' he said. 'Yeah, I was there after the attack. I found the bodies. I moved Adam into a better position so that when the doctors found him, they might be able to heal him. I was under the assumption he was still alive and I could save his life. So—'

'Please be aware, Mister Forden, that lying while being recorded isn't exactly going to help you,' Anjli spoke sweetly. 'Especially as I can tell you that several of the items found around the space where the Gladius once was have your DNA on them, and we also have footage of you dragging both bodies to the coal chutes, where, out of sight of the camera, we can guess you removed them.'

Declan looked to Anjli as she said this, and he knew from her expression that she was lying; the chances were the camera missed this, or even didn't detect the movement if it was to the side.

But Aaron didn't know that.

Slowly, he almost seemed to melt into the chair, his head bowed forward.

'I wanted them dead,' he whispered. 'I'll admit that. I've got no problems admitting that. But I didn't kill them. They shot themselves in a stupid duel.'

'I broke in an hour or so after they started,' he explained. 'I knew they were coming in to have their duel. Georgia had primed them for me. She knew Benedict wouldn't be able to turn down a duel. Arrogant prick could never say no, but she couldn't ask him directly. That would be too obvious. So she made a point of kicking off against everybody else.'

Aaron leant forwards now, arms on the table.

'I didn't kill them,' he said. 'I let them do that themselves.'

'If you're going to admit to it, laddie, you might as well tell us the full story,' Monroe replied.

'Georgia came up with the idea,' Aaron sighed. 'It was incredibly simple. She challenged everyone to a duel. She knew that most people would laugh it off, or say she was a crazy person. But Benedict, good old Benny Dee, he wouldn't be able to. That arrogant, misogynistic prick would take her up on the offer. Not for the money, but because he could say he beat her in a duel.'

'So the argument on Tuesday was done purely to set up Benedict Dee?'

Aaron nodded.

'I was there. She made the argument. Even offered it to me, Nicholas, Adam, a whole load of people to sell the bloody thing. But I didn't accept. All I did was whisper into Benedict's ear how wouldn't it be great if he could take that smile and smack it from her face.'

He laughed now, and it was a bitter, unhappy sound.

'I reminded him that Georgia was one of the people who kicked him out of the Dark Ages group. How she didn't understand the ways a true creative would work in a re-enactment setting. I knew what had happened with him; everybody did. He wasn't shy about telling anyone. So, over Wednesday and Thursday, I kept at him, suggesting this, reminding him of that ... I even brought Adam Harris into it.'

'To help him?'

'Adam wasn't a massive fan of Benedict's anymore. They'd been close back in the day, but not since Benedict had become a dandy. But with Adam, I pointed out that there was no way Benedict would beat Georgia, as she was simply too good.'

Aaron sighed as he remembered.

'I even gave him a tell that Georgia did when she duelled, having seen her play Princess Metternich in a recreation of the Vaduz "Emancipation" duel at an event a couple of years ago. It was all lies, of course. I wanted Adam to go to Benedict with a suggestion. And Benedict, as I knew, would want to train and train and train. Meanwhile, I told Adam he should duel her too, as she'd hurt her arm and was favouring her right side. It was all lies, but I wanted them both to want the money. Really want the money.'

'Then what did you do?'

'Simple,' Aaron replied. 'Once I had Adam agree to help Benedict, I told them I'd cover Adam's second duel. I wanted them to get in there, train up and beat Georgia that night.'

'And Adam agreed?'

'Of course he did. At no point did he think I was going to screw him over. I'd agreed to put a helmet on and take his place. I was his best friend.'

'But you did, didn't you?' Declan asked.

Aaron nodded.

'I went to Benedict,' he replied. 'Said I knew Adam Harris was going to try to kill him. I explained I'd been told by Adam how Benedict knew he'd stolen items from the Crawford-Dunnes and he was about to out him, cop some kind of plea deal as they'd found out about the theft. Said there were problems in the re-enactment group, and Adam was planning to squeal on everyone. Benedict was furious.'

'Because he'd lose everything,' Declan nodded at this. 'His reputation, his job ... I can see that weighing heavily.'

'I suggested perhaps Adam should fall in the duel,' Aaron continued. 'Empty cellar, easy to hide the body, nobody need know, and Benedict would have an alibi, as "Adam" would be fighting as they duelled.'

'Let me guess, you even convinced him to load his pistol with a bullet while leaving Adam's empty?' Anjli suggested.

However, at this, Aaron shook his head.

'No. You'd think convincing someone to cold-bloodedly kill another would be a difficult thing, but Benedict took to it like duck to water,' he explained. 'I think he secretly wanted to shoot Adam in a duel, to see how it felt in real life. But then I went and found Adam, and warned him that Benedict was looking to screw *him* over.'

'Same story?'

'Why break what isn't broken?' Aaron smiled. 'Adam didn't believe it, of course, but the fact I seemed to know all about it made him suspicious that perhaps Benedict had been talking. I suggested that he too pack a bullet just in case, pointed out again that me being "Adam" gave *him* an alibi, then I gave my farewells and returned to the arena, where I performed in Adam's stead.'

'The masked gladiator.'

'Exactly. Once this was done, I returned to Benedict's house. But by now it was gone six, and when I arrived and broke in, I found two dead bodies on the floor. I saw Benedict had realised Adam was wearing chest armour, put two and two together, deciding he wore this to stop Benedict shooting him, realised I was obviously right and then shot Adam in the back. Cowardly prick. Either way, the armour had still helped. He'd lived long enough to turn and kill Benedict.'

'Was he alive when you arrived?'

'No,' Aaron shook his head. 'I went over to the body and found Adam was dead as well.'

'Which you weren't that unhappy with, I'm guessing,' Declan said.

Aaron looked up at him, and his eyes were red and angry.

'Adam Harris was there when my Uncle Henry died,' he said. 'He didn't call an ambulance, didn't call for help. He let my uncle die and then stole his items. And Benedict Dee? All he did was look the other way for a shiny pair of duelling pistols, the same duelling pistols he used to effectively end his own life in a pretend duel.'

'Okay, then what did you do?'

Aaron shrugged.

'I knew I had a couple of hours to kill, so I booked some tickets on a walking tour. I'd seen the guy before, he was a bit of a knob, but I wanted an alibi, so I was going to be a bigger knob, just so he'd remember me.'

He chuckled darkly.

'I also invited Rolf and Susan. I wanted them to see Adam dead.'

'And the plan to get them to arrive later?'

'If it put them in the crosshairs of the police, that was even better,' Aaron replied dismissively. 'I didn't want them dead, I wanted them to be punished for what they did. I wanted you guys to do your job and work it out.'

'So you used a van to move the body?'

'Yes,' Aaron nodded. 'I had a Grey Transit. I remembered the make and model because Adam took it everywhere. Once I had the van, I placed the bodies in and I drove to the car park beside the gatehouse where, with the hood on, so no one could see my face, I moved the body to where I would find it later.'

He shrugged.

'My first plan was to give the items back to the family, but then I realised I couldn't without incriminating myself. The easier way would be for the family to find that the police had them, and have them returned that way; so I decided to leave his stolen pistol in Benny's hand and place his stolen sword in the back of Adam.'

He leant back on the chair, staring up at the ceiling.

'There were other items stolen, but I couldn't find them when I looked around. I guessed, realistically, that Rolf and Susan probably had the bulk of it. And when they were arrested, we'd find the rest.'

'This wasn't about items,' Declan said. 'This was about vengeance. "Vindicta."'

'My family was in the wilderness for so many years and the Crawford-Dunnes, Henry Crawford-Dunne in particular, brought us back in. And then they killed him.'

He glared at the floor now, and the intensity of the stare made Declan wonder if he was about to try to fight it.

'I did what anyone else would do.'

There was a moment of silence.

'No,' Anjli shook her head at the statement. 'I think even you don't believe that. You killed them both, even if your finger wasn't on the trigger, and you placed Adam Harris in a public location, before dumping Benedict's body the following morning in Pickering Place.'

'I did both of those,' Aaron nodded. 'I'd reloaded the pistol, and I fired it in the air. Then I left before anybody could find me. Drove the van to some desolate warehouse area. Parked it up, walked back. It might even still be there, let me give you the address.'

'I understand you were in this for revenge,' Monroe spoke now. 'But you mentioned Georgia had helped you with the bet. What was her part in this?'

'She wanted Susan and Rolf removed as well,' Aaron replied. 'She'd been the partner of Bridget Farnsworth. And when Stephens started finding out the information showing he wasn't to blame, he told Georgia what he'd found. Then it all went wrong.'

'But Georgia doesn't want to kill anyone, though?' Anjli frowned. 'As the bet was all make believe?'

Aaron started laughing.

'Did I not mention? Georgia wants to kill *everybody*.'

'And exactly how is she going to do that?' Declan asked.

Aaron leant closer.

'Let me explain to you how re-enactment works,' he said. 'Especially when important people in an event have to be replaced.'

'Tell us what we need, and it'll help you,' Declan said.

'Oh, don't worry,' Aaron replied. 'I'll be fine, and I intend to tell you everything.'

And Aaron did.

Georgia Wingate stood staring out from the pavilion at the Boudicca's Uprising set-piece. It was rough and hastily made, but the candles had been lit, and the sky was darkening when she turned back to face Rolf and Susan Cowell.

'He's not here yet, and I'm not sure if he will be,' she said. 'The guys at the gladiator arena said the detective took him away after beating him in a fight.'

'I'd have paid money to see that,' Susan muttered. 'Aaron Forden, the mighty Aronus, scourge of gladiators, forced to kneel before a civilian.'

'Well, whatever happened, with Matt and Aaron both being questioned, we currently don't have a Gaius Suetonius Paulinus for her to fight against,' Georgia moved closer, patting Rolf on the arm. 'You're the only person I trust to do it, Rolf. I know your sister wants to be Boudicca. And I'll be honest, I'm tired of what's going on. So I'll make you both a deal.'

This was now said to Susan, sitting beside Rolf, as Georgia spoke.

'You know the parts. You've played them enough times. Why don't we, tonight, have Rolf play the part of Paulinus, and you can play Boudicca?'

'Are you sure?' Susan asked, surprised by the offer.

'I've done it enough,' Georgia nodded. 'And everything that's happened this weekend has just made me lose my interest in – and my taste for – re-enactment. I'll be your bodyguard in the same way that you're usually mine in the arena. And then at the end of the event, I think I'll be stepping down, and you can replace me, just like I ... well, like I replaced Bridget.'

She looked back at Rolf.

'You can play her bodyguard from then on,' she said. 'Or

maybe even stay with the Romans. God knows what's going to happen to the other two, maybe you'd make a better General than them, anyway.'

Rolf smiled.

'Thank you, Georgia,' he said. 'With everything that happened this weekend, this means a lot to us.'

'I know it does,' Georgia smiled. 'And I'm sure it's what Bridget would have wanted. If she hadn't been killed.'

'Come on, Georgia, it was an accident,' Susan winced a little at the statement.

'I know,' Georgia shrugged. 'I just find it hard to see it any other way. Either way, the two of you need to get ready. I've got Keisha sorting out the costume to make sure that it fits you better, and the wig is pretty much "one size fits all" as I don't think we can really have a punk Boudicca just yet. Let's get out there and give them a show they'll never forget.'

Susan smiled widely now, beaming, as she looked back at Rolf.

'Do you know the part?' she asked.

At this, Rolf laughed.

'Gaius Suetonius Paulinus? I've known that part for years,' he said. 'Just like you've known yours. I'll go tell the Romans that I'm their new commander. I know a few people there who will be pissed when they hear it's me. And I want to see their faces when I tell them personally.'

He paused.

'I don't have any armour, though.'

'I wouldn't worry,' Georgia smiled. 'You can use Matt's, he's close enough in width, if not height. We can mix and match the rest. And just use your own spear. It'll be dark, nobody will see. Not like our usual lunchtime shows.'

Rolf grinned, nodding as he walked back into the pavilion. Susan gave an impetuous hug to Georgia before running off to join her brother, looking back and mouthing one more excited "thank you" before continuing.

Georgia stood alone, staring back out across the battlefield.

Aaron, by now, would have been found out, and had probably told the police what was going on. There was every chance they might arrive to arrest her, too.

But Georgia had been very clever with what she'd done.

She'd made a drunken bet, which Aaron had worked from.

She had stepped down as Boudicca, which Susan had taken on.

There was nothing that could link Georgia Wingate to the deaths of Benedict Dee and Adam Harris. And there was *nothing* that would link her to the upcoming death of Susan Cowell, at the hands of her own brother.

She sighed, pulling her cloak around her.

The funniest thing was, she'd always intended to keep either Rolf or Susan alive, mainly as the last person to know what had *truly* happened that day. And now, with what Georgia believed about the death of Nicholas Stephens, there was an even better reason for keeping Rolf alive.

Because, as he grieved the death, accidentally, of course, of his sister, Rolf would be arrested as an accessory to Susan's role in killing Nicholas.

Georgia, of course, hadn't been involved in any of that. Nicholas had made his own bed there, the bloody idiot. She told him to leave it alone.

If he'd gained justice, she wouldn't have been able to gain revenge.

'This is for you, Bridget,' she said, staring up at the sky. 'Today, your killer dies.'

With that, Georgia Wingate turned and followed the others back into the pavilion.

There was still a lot to plan and very little time to do it in.

24

COUNCIL OF WAR

MONROE STOOD AT THE FRONT OF THE BRIEFING ROOM, THE plasma screen behind him showing a variety of images; the recently dead Adam Harris, Benedict Dee and Nicholas Stephens were at the top, and below them were older photos of Bridget Farnsworth, Lord Henry Crawford-Dunne and an image of one room of Pennington Hall, complete with armoury on the wall.

'Okay,' he said. 'We need to look at this and work it out quickly.'

Sitting in front of him was a full house. Doctor Marcos and De'Geer sat at the back, next to Cooper and, strangely, Chivalry Fitzwarren, while in front of them were Billy and Jess in their usual places – Jess beside Billy and Billy on his laptop – and Declan, sat to the side with Anjli. Monroe was at the front of the briefing room and Bullman had returned to her usual spot of standing beside the door.

Monroe pointed at the photos on the screen.

'Adam Harris,' he said. 'Killed by?'

'It looks to be Benedict Dee,' Declan replied. 'The video shows him firing his pistol into Adam's back, and is time-stamped to the same time that Aaron Forden, who we know found the bodies later, was on stage, so to speak, pretending to be Adam Harris, complete with helmet to hide his face.'

'Which leads us to Benedict Dee,' Monroe said, nodding at Billy.

Billy pressed a button and a red X appeared over Adam Harris's face.

'Benedict Dee looks like he was killed at the same time, in the same duel. What can we say about this one?'

'Georgia Wingate created a bet on Tuesday night,' De'Geer said from the back of the room. 'Claimed she would give money to anybody who could beat her in a duel. Nobody took it up, but Aaron Forden had convinced Adam Harris and Benedict Dee that Benedict was the likely person to defeat her. Benedict, as arrogant as he was, believed this as well, and arranged with Adam Harris to practice, but Aaron wound them both up, playing on their paranoia, leading them to kill each other. They each secretly placed balls in their pistols, and then shot each other.'

'Okay,' Monroe looked at the third picture. 'Nicholas Stephens. Killed Saturday morning.'

'Motorcyclist still yet to be decided,' Declan said. 'Chances are it could be Susan Cowell as she matches the size. Or it could have been Aaron Forden, he's of a similar build.'

'Or maybe even someone we haven't even thought of yet. Why was he killed?' Monroe asked, looking around the room.

'Possibly for reasons other than the first two,' Billy looked up from his laptop. 'We know that Harris and Dee were both killed because of a connection to the murder of Bridget

Farnsworth, whereas Nicholas, from his texts, had found something out about it. That made him a target, but possibly from the original killer.'

Declan nodded.

'Which leads us back to possibly Susan or Rolf—'

'Rolf's too big for the motorcycle, based on the footage,' Doctor Marcos shook her head. 'And we know Susan has a motorcycle.'

Billy brought up the images that Declan had taken from the cricket ground.

'There's three motorcycles currently at the cricket ground. Only this one here seems to be a similar make and model,' he said, pulling up an image of a Triumph motorcycle taken at the grounds.

De'Geer and Anjli both leant forward, staring at it with an interest given of that of a motorcyclist.

'That's a Triumph Street Triple. A 675cc inline three-cylinder engine added to the agility of a lightweight, Daytona sports bike chassis,' De'Geer whistled as he looked at it. 'That's the same bike that killed Nicholas Stephens, I'm sure of it.'

'The licence plates are back, I see,' Monroe replied. 'Is there a way we can prove it's connected as the ANPR didn't help?'

De'Geer nodded.

'Can we see the CCTV from the attack again?' he asked.

'We don't see the actual attack, just a moment before,' Billy opened up another file, and a frozen shot of a motorcy-cle, a broken branch being used as a lance, was shown on the plasma screen passing the CCTV camera on its way to kill someone.

'There,' Doctor Marcos nodded as she pointed at the

screen. 'They rest the branch on the crossbar, the handlebar thingie.'

De'Geer nodded, looking back to the others.

'If the branch was on the handlebars, it would have scraped bark on it,' he said. 'Chances are they wouldn't have seen it. But, if we can check the murder weapon against any traces on the bike ...'

'Susan Cowell does seem to be the likely option,' Monroe nodded. 'We should get that done as soon as we can.'

He then looked down to the bottom row as another red "x" appeared over Nicholas above it; now the top row was all red-crossed by Billy.

'And now we look at Bridget Farnsworth,' he continued. 'Killed by Nicholas Stephens, although now possibly *not* killed by Nicholas Stephens. Thoughts?'

'Matt Butcher wanted her dead, but at the same time Matt Butcher seems to be someone who's more reactive than proactive,' Declan replied. 'Susan Cowell, if she killed Nicholas, has the opportunity to do such a thing during the battle. Rolf Cowell could have done it as well.'

'Nicholas was convinced that Rolf had swapped spears, but as we now know, Roman and Dark Age spears look different,' Anjli added.

'So, if that's what's happened, it would have to be someone on the Roman side, Guv,' Cooper spoke, if only to prove she was listening. 'That leaves Matt Butcher and Aaron Forden.'

'Aaron was working with Georgia. He was angry at the people who had stolen his uncle's items, but at this point, he wasn't involved in the group that much. And he'd seen Bridget and Georgia together, claiming he didn't care.'

'If it has to be a Roman spear, I would say we should look at Matt Butcher,' Anjli replied.

'True,' Declan nodded. 'Do we have any photos of the battle?'

'Actually, Mister Fitzwarren helped there,' Jess said. 'I've been going through the images he gained for us from Pennington Hall, and there are a few that have the Iceni side in them. I've placed them on the cloud, Billy.'

Billy tapped on the keyboard, and after a moment, a few images of the battle of Pennington Hall appeared.

Clicking through them, they could see that the re-enactors playing the Iceni were well armed and in full costume. There were shots of Bridget, in full armour, standing on the chariot, with Rolf, her bodyguard beside her as they rolled forward, plastic blades on the wheels, a couple of action shots, and finally two candid shots of the re-enactors laughing as they waited to start.

'There, stop,' Declan said, pointing.

Rolf was standing triumphantly beside Boudicca, his spear up in the air. It was a strange, almost trident design, and definitely not the same as the one that was found inside her.

'Strike Rolf off the list then, it seems,' Declan said, but then held his hand up. 'Wait, there.'

He pointed at the last image, one of the candid shots. Behind Rolf, to the side, was Susan Cowell. She was in the shot's background, waiting for the battle to start, and only half visible, but the spear that she had – held down so it wasn't showing – was almost identical to the ones that the Romans used, and while the others were staring at the marshals, ready to begin the re-enactment, she was glaring at the back of Bridget Farnsworth.

'We've been looking at the wrong person,' Monroe said. 'Susan Cowell yet again seems to be a person of interest.'

'Susan Cowell seems to be at the heart of all of this,' he said. 'If we believe what Aaron says, then she, Rolf, and Adam Harris stole items from Lord Henry Crawford-Dunne, causing him to have a fatal heart attack in the process. They then used some of this to bribe Benedict Dee to keep them in the clear, and it's possible she also killed Bridget Farnsworth, maybe to gain the money from the life insurance for Matt.'

He checked his watch.

'The event is about to start,' he said. 'Susan won't run until the end of that, so we've got time.'

He paused as a worrying thought crossed his mind.

'Chivalry, did anyone else see these photos?'

Chivalry nodded.

'Timothy said they were only found because Nicholas Stephens had been asking for anything Pennington Hall had,' he admitted. 'But he also said Miss Wingate had seen them, too.'

'Georgia Wingate saw this?' Monroe looked back at the image on the screen. 'There's no bloody way she didn't realise what was happening. We need to get to the battle fast.'

'But DCI Walsh said the battle would be starting soon,' Cooper frowned. 'Surely that means we have time before Susan and Rolf try to escape?'

'It's not about that anymore,' Declan looked at Billy. 'Check the socials for the festival. Are there any changes?'

Billy tapped on the keyboard, and then read the screen, his face paling.

'Two,' he said. 'Rolf Cowell is now playing the part of Gaius Suetonius Paulinus, and Susan Cowell is playing Boudicca.'

'We need to get there right now,' Declan was already rising from the chair. 'I thought Aaron was being dramatic, but he was right. Georgia Wingate intends to finish what Susan Cowell started!'

25

UNDERSTUDIED

THE FORCES OF QUEEN BOUDICCA LINED UP ON ONE SIDE OF the cricket ground, on the other the forces of the Roman Empire led by Gaius Suetonius Paulinus. There were only a hundred or so soldiers on each side, but it was still a spectacular event, and the surrounding seats were filled on this Sunday evening. It was darkening, but the battle would be over before the night drew in. Nevertheless, flaming candles were placed around the edge to give emphasis to the battle, while also hiding the boundary line of the cricket ground.

On one side was Boudicca herself, her long red hair flowing, held onto the pink shorter hair by a variety of hair clips and wig tape.

Susan smiled as she looked across the field at Paulinus, already speaking to his troops.

Looking across at her, Rolf smiled back before he straightened his breastplate, checking his sword. Beside him, one of his legionnaires patted him on the shoulder.

'Glad you could do this, Rolf,' he said. 'Although I was looking forward to killing you.'

Rolf laughed at this, still moving the armour about.

'You've never taken me down, so I can't see you doing it any time soon,' he grinned. 'Maybe if I'm on this side, I can teach you a few things.'

'You okay?' the legionnaire asked as Rolf fidgeted.

'Yeah, the bloody armour's too tight,' Rolf muttered. 'Must have been a midget using this.'

'To you, mate, everyone's a midget,' another soldier muttered, as the surrounding re-enactors laughed.

'You, um, did check the choreography, didn't you?' The first legionnaire asked. 'I mean, you know where we go with this, right?'

'It's not my first time in this battle,' Rolf looked back across the field.

'Yeah, but usually you're on the losing side.'

Rolf thought about this.

'I'm exactly where I need to be,' he said, shifting his spear.

'Mate, you can't use that,' the legionnaire, spying it, muttered. 'That's your Iceni one.'

Rolf glanced back at it.

'I know,' he said. 'Trust me, there's no way in hell I'm swapping that right now. You don't know where the one I'd be given has been. And, as the General, I can claim I took this in battle, and is a trophy.'

The legionnaire mouth-shrugged at this, unconvinced.

'Your funeral,' he said. 'People will notice.'

'Don't you get it?' Rolf laughed as he climbed onto the horse his character would ride, as another soldier held it steady for him. 'Aaron and Matt aren't here. I get to be Paulinus. I'll probably never get to do this again, so I want everyone to notice me!'

GEORGIA STOOD TO THE SIDE OF THE CHARIOT, SHIFTING THE spear in her hand.

Beside her, nervously preparing herself, was Susan, while across the way Rolf looked as uncomfortable as she'd hoped.

She turned away, looking out across the field, to the rows of spectators, ready to watch a fight.

If only they knew what they were getting instead.

One of the Iceni, a short man with frizzy blond hair, walked up to her.

'Is it true?' he whispered. 'Are you stepping down?'

Georgia turned and smiled at him.

'Why would you think that?' she replied, nodding at Susan. 'This is only so that Susan and her brother can have their moment.'

'Oh,' the man frowned. 'There's a rumour bouncing about you're considering stopping all this.'

Georgia hefted the spear in her hand; it was a custom-made model, almost a trident in looks. And, at the base, she knew there were initials – not her initials – to provide the identity of the owner.

'I'm considering it,' she admitted. 'But let's just say I'm stepping down until Susan there stops, or gets bored.'

'Susan Cowell stop being Boudicca?' the man laughed. 'She's wanted this for years. She won't be stopping soon.'

'You'll be surprised,' Georgia smiled, but there was no humour to it. 'But for tonight, everything goes as planned.'

'And what's that then?'

'It will end exactly as it should, with the destruction of Boudicca and all she loves,' Georgia replied enigmatically. 'Better get ready. We're about to begin.'

DECLAN HAD WANTED A SQUAD CAR, BUT DE'GEER HAD pointed out that on a Sunday evening, especially with the event happening, the traffic would be an absolute nightmare getting out towards Shoreditch. So now two vehicles weaved their way through the traffic; De'Geer on his police motorcycle, sirens blaring and lights flashing, Declan holding on for dear life behind him, and Anjli, on her own motorcycle right behind them, beeping her horn and flashing her own lights as she followed. The others would arrive later, as soon as their cars could get through the traffic, but this was a strange procession that carried along.

'Can this thing go any faster?' he shouted to De'Geer, who started laughing.

'The last time you were on a bike, you wanted me to go slower,' he shouted back.

'The last time I was on your bike, we weren't trying to stop a murder.'

'Fair point, Guv,' De'Geer said and slammed his foot down, changing gears as he throttled harder and the bike lurched forward. Declan almost threw up, managing to just about hold it together. He regretted with every iota of his soul getting on this bike. He couldn't understand how Anjli could do this for fun, but at least they were finally getting closer to where they needed to go.

Declan risked a glance back and saw Anjli behind him. He nodded at her, and then turned back, waiting for his stomach to settle. Ahead of them, they saw the gates of the Honourable Artillery Company's pavilion, and Declan turned to De'Geer.

'We need to stop this before it goes too far,' Declan

shouted. 'Do whatever you need to do, don't take no for an answer.'

'Agreed,' De'Geer said as he twisted his throttle and the bike sped up even faster. The bike almost went over as it skidded into a left-hand turn, taking him towards the guards and security at the front who, seeing a police bike in full sirens bursting through the middle, dived to the sides as De'Geer took no prisoners, carrying on through.

'Just don't kill anyone!' Declan yelled.

'I haven't yet!' De'Geer cried out, but the glee in which he said it, and the use of the word "yet" didn't fill Declan with confidence right now.

On the pitch, the torches were lit, and the two sides were ready to fight; Boudicca's chariot was moving along her army, which was a sign of the battle about to begin.

'They're about to start,' Declan shouted. 'We have to stop them!'

'I know just how to,' De'Geer said and his foot went down, changing the gear. Declan felt a lurch in his stomach as the bike mounted the kerb and hit the grass of the pitch.

SUSAN HEFTED HER AXE IN HER HAND, PREPARING HERSELF FOR battle.

Beside her, she could see Georgia standing, with what looked to be Rolf's spear in her hand – but one look across the field saw he had his spear ready in his own hand.

So why was Georgia's so familiar?

With a sickening feeling, she realised. It didn't "look to be" Rolf's spear, it *was* his spear. She remembered the words Georgia had spoken no more than an hour earlier.

'Just use your own spear. It'll be dark, nobody will see. Not like our usual lunchtime shows.'

They'd only ever performed one lunchtime show. At Pennington Hall, three years earlier.

Where Bridget Farnsworth had died.

There had been rumours of Georgia and Bridget, and Georgia had quit her job shortly after the death. Had she been the one that gained the crypto? Adam had never known who it was, but it had to be someone Bridget cared for.

Bloody hell. She's killing everyone connected. And now she's going for you.

Susan glanced across the battlefield; how could she tell Rolf? Maybe she should just get off the chariot, leave right now, let him know to do the same?

No. You might be wrong. You might be overreacting.

No. You might never get a chance to play Boudicca again.

Setting her jaw, Susan Cowell prepared for battle.

The only problem was, she wasn't sure *which* battle she was preparing for.

————

ROLF TRIED TO HIDE HIS NERVOUSNESS BY CHECKING AND RE-checking the harness of the saddle. He had a horse purely for show, mirroring Boudicca on her chariot at the front of her own army. They couldn't really use them here; if they did, within seconds, they would have hit the middle of the cricket ground and the battle would be over. This was mainly so the leaders could be seen above the melee, and it was enough for him.

He looked across the field at Georgia, narrowing his eyes as he considered her.

This was too easy, too convenient.

He wasn't a fool, he'd noticed she was holding a spear like his own. She'd outplayed him there; he'd deliberately not taken a Roman spear in case she was trying something, but she'd called his bluff.

But now he knew he could change the narrative. All he needed to do was control the horse with one hand while ramming a spear, accidentally, of course, into the chest of Georgia Wingate, before she did the same to Susan.

But what if it wasn't Georgia?

Rolf glanced back at his sister, watching him. *Could she have done this?* It wasn't like this was the first time; was she about to throw him under the bus, having him kill her problem while she walked away?

He shifted the spear in his hand. He wasn't ever going to kill his sibling, but could he say the same of her?

He looked to the side and saw the organisers, referees, and marshals stepping aside. The event was about to begin. They expected a firework or a loud bang to begin the festivities, as this battle was being termed; but instead, he heard police sirens, with flashes of blue and light coming down the main street.

Then, before anything could happen, a police motorcycle with two riders on it burst onto the Honourable Artillery Company's cricket pitch, speeding between the two armies and pulling to a stop in the middle.

The audience, unprepared for this, paused, watching curiously before bursting into applause and cheers when Declan climbed off the back and removed his helmet.

This was an unexpected, they concluded, and intriguing part of the show.

At this, Rolf yanked on the reins, and the horse surged forward. But, without hearing the expected bang, his army didn't follow.

On the other side, Susan, seeing Rolf moving, started her own chariot, Georgia standing on it beside her, towards Declan as well.

Now, in the middle of the two armies, Declan found himself encircled by Romans on one side and violent Iceni with their tribal war paint on the other.

This could go south real quick, he thought to himself.

One of the commentators was already running towards them, microphone in hand as Susan arrived, stepping down from the chariot and storming over to him.

'You've got some nerve, coming here now to ruin everything we've planned—'

Declan raised a hand.

'Shut up,' he said simply. 'I've had enough of all of you. Was it you or your brother that killed Bridget Farnsworth?'

'Neither,' Susan blustered. 'I think you're overreacting to anger and suspicion.'

'I'm not overreacting, as I know everything,' Declan said. 'I know who killed Adam Harris. I know why the others died.'

'You know nothing,' Susan retorted.

Declan grinned.

'Let me enlighten you then,' he said. He was aware his backup had not yet arrived, and with over two hundred hostile re-enactors around him, he had to defuse the tension. 'Anyway, you should be thanking me, because I just saved your life.'

'Oh?' Susan asked. 'And how does that work?'

'I'm glad you asked,' Declan replied, as he now looked at

Georgia Wingate, currently staring at him as if he'd gained a second head. 'Let me explain.'

At this point the commentator arrived, holding the microphone up.

'DCI Walsh,' he started. 'Are you here to take part in another battle...'

He stopped as De'Geer removed the microphone from his hand with a growl, as Declan turned to more cheers from the audience and waved for them to quieten down, taking the microphone as he did so.

'Ladies and gentlemen,' he said into it, his voice echoing through the speakers. 'I'm very sorry to tell you this, but tonight's entertainment has had to be paused, while we fix a slight problem with the cast.'

This stated, he looked back at Susan and Rolf, as he turned the microphone off.

'Susan Cowell, Rolf Cowell, Georgia Wingate, I think you three need to come and have a chat with me in the pavilion.'

'We're not going anywhere,' Susan said. 'We have a show to do. You might not give a damn, but we do.'

'You should let them continue,' Georgia said, now walking up. 'You've got some nerve trying to stop this.'

Declan stared at her for a long moment.

'I'm surprised you turned down playing Boudicca,' he said.

'I'm not,' Georgia smiled. 'I needed a break after everything that happened. Today, I'm Boudicca's bodyguard.'

Declan laughed, looking back at Susan.

'Is that what she told you?' he asked. 'That she's the bodyguard of you, keeping you alive?'

Susan frowned at the laugh and glanced back at Georgia.

'Yes,' she replied. 'Why?'

'Because all she wants to do is see you die,' Declan glanced back at Georgia. 'Aaron Forden told us everything. How you wanted him and Matt to not be here for this. How you wanted her to be facing her brother on the pitch. How you even planned to have him kill her, accidental or not, with a spear throw?'

He looked back at Rolf.

'I'm guessing that's not your spear,' he said.

Rolf shook his head.

'It looks like mine, but I think I was played,' he said.

'Who by?' Declan asked.

Rolf didn't really have an answer for that, and instead just glared at Georgia.

'I think I can guess your answer,' Declan smiled. 'Let me tell you a story, one that's been private for many years, but actually should be told.'

He didn't really want to talk in front of a crowd, but he was also still aware that currently it was him, Anjli and De'Geer, against about two hundred armed and angry re-enactors. And there was a very strong chance that, hopped up on adrenaline, all it would take is for either Susan or Rolf to give the command, and this could turn into a war.

'Let me take you back three years,' he said. 'A battle at Pennington Hall. Do you remember it?'

'Of course, I remember it,' Susan shook her head sadly. 'It was a terrible day.'

'It was, wasn't it?' Declan replied. 'For all intents and purposes, a tragic accident, when Bridget Farnsworth, the current Boudicca of the uprising, was accidentally speared with a rogue weapon thrown from a horse, the spearman knocked aside during an accident. But that wasn't what happened, was it?'

At this, the crowd made a noise, as they realised that the entertainment that they didn't think they were getting was now being replaced by something possibly more interesting. The cricket pitch wasn't that expansive, after all, and a raised voice could just about be made out.

'You see, to look at those events,' Declan continued, 'we need to look at *earlier* events.'

He turned and looked at Georgia.

'Matt Butcher was having an affair with Susan,' he said. 'Bridget was aware. Apparently, they weren't that discreet. But then, apparently, neither were you.'

'I don't know what you mean,' Georgia pouted.

'I mean, Pennington Hall,' Declan replied calmly. 'When Matt married Bridget, all he really wanted was a simple life. A woodland to turn into an event location, something that people could book and role play in, or re-enact in, whatever you want to call it. A chance to do his own thing, and Bridget provided him with that, gave him the autonomy and the freedom to do such things.'

'They were happy until they weren't,' Georgia snapped.

'Until they weren't,' Declan agreed. 'Because what we've heard is that both Bridget and Matt started looking elsewhere for their love and attention. Matt started sleeping with Susan Cowell.'

He looked back at Susan, glaring back at him.

'You had quite a relationship,' he said. 'But it had to be a secret. If anybody found out about it, there was a very strong chance that Bridget would take away the money that you were enjoying so much.'

Susan said nothing, still glaring at Declan as he continued.

'And that's where the problem started,' Declan said.

'Because Matt was trying so desperately to keep his relationship with you quiet, so that he didn't lose all the money he was being promised, he wasn't paying attention to what his own wife was doing – while she started her own affair with Georgia Wingate.'

26

SHOW-STOPPER

THIS LAST PART OF HIS SPEECH HAD BEEN QUIETER, AND THE crowd hadn't quite heard what was being said, but they could still tell by Declan's tone and the responses given by the two women that something big had been said.

Declan looked back at Georgia.

'You'd been friends for a long time, and sometimes these turn into something more,' he stated. 'No one's begrudging your love. But Bridget had a problem. She couldn't kick off against her husband having an affair when she was doing the same. So, she made sure that if he *did* find out about you, there was nothing he could do. She decided that her bonuses, around seven figures worth, should be removed, taken elsewhere, placed into something that nobody could touch. And three years ago, one of the principal places for this was the decentralised area of cryptocurrency. She turned to her accountant, Adam Harris, and asked him to do this.'

At this, he turned back to Susan.

'Adam Harris was also a very old friend of yours. You'd known him a good fifteen years or so, I reckon, judging from a party photo we'd seen. And when he saw what was going on, he realised that Matt – and more importantly, you – were about to be screwed over. So, he told you what she was doing. He didn't know who was getting the money. He just knew that Bridget was making sure that Matt wouldn't gain it in any nasty divorce case, and therefore, neither would you.'

Susan bit her lip, looking around.

'She called me a money grabber,' she said. 'Never to my face, but I heard it.'

'And you confronted her the night before the event, making sure she knew you were the true love of Matt Butcher's life.'

'Matt was furious.' Susan nodded. 'I shouldn't have mouthed off to her, but she just pissed me off so much, and I'd had a little too much mead.'

'But here's where the problems started,' Declan said. 'You see, you complained to Bridget, giving her a piece of your mind, but by doing that, you gave away your cards. Bridget now knew you were looking to do whatever it took to keep Matt's money, while the attitude you'd given her and the threats you'd made, convinced her you'd not allow her and Georgia to walk away unscathed.'

He looked back to Georgia now.

'She was a lawyer, a good one, and she understood it'd become very messy, and very costly,' Georgia shrugged, no longer denying anything.

Nodding, Declan now looked back at Rolf.

'Was it you or Susan that worked out that Georgia was with Bridget?'

'Actually, it was Aaron,' Rolf replied. 'He'd seen them together shortly after the fight, Georgia was consoling her. He mentioned it as a passing comment; he didn't really know what was going on, but we did. We knew Bridget wasn't going to be the wronged party anymore; she was going to be caught in a very messy divorce case as soon as we had a chance. Sure, Susan was having an affair with Matt, but Georgia and Bridget were just as guilty.'

He shrugged, lowering his spear as he looked around the battlefield.

'I went and spoke to Bridget too, that night,' he said. 'Said I was an interested third party, knew that everything had gone to shit, apologised on Susan's behalf for what she'd said. I knew I had to defuse the situation somehow.'

'How did that go for you?' Declan asked.

'Bridget told me she was going to destroy Matt, Susan and anyone who hung out with her,' Rolf shook his head. 'She effectively accused me of setting her up for this. All I'd done for years was to be her bodyguard. I wasn't even involved in this bloody drama, and now she's telling me she's going to destroy me, and everything I'd done. I was angry. I got drunk, told Susan what had happened. I thought she would tell Matt, and that they would have their own argument, but instead, Susan came up with a new plan.'

'One you agreed with.'

Rolf, at this, shook his head.

'I didn't think she was going to murder her,' he said. 'I thought there'd be an "accident" on the field, maybe enough to make Bridget realise that if she *did* something, there would be consequences. I didn't realise how far my sister would go—'

'Don't you dare throw this on me,' Susan shouted back. The audience still couldn't hear what was going on, but Susan's raised voice brought a murmuring of interest once more.

'You were just as guilty as I was,' Susan stepped forward. 'You were the one who got Adam involved.'

'And *why did* Adam get involved?' Rolf retorted angrily. 'I've known Adam for as long as I've known Matt. We'd done a lot of events together. He was an excellent accountant. Knew how to make money, and more importantly, how to hide it. Adam got involved because of you!'

He looked back to Declan, and there was something in his stature, a straightening that showed he'd made some subtle decision here.

An alliance between brother and sister had now broken.

'We'd had a tour of Pennington Hall the day before the event. The Lord was showing off his items,' he explained. 'Adam had worked out how much many of them were worth, and there'd been a running joke about whether we should steal some before going. We'd realised there was literally no security at all. They even left the building open at night, so we could use the toilets.'

'Shut up,' Susan hissed.

'Anyway, I'd spoken to him about this, and he explained to me what he'd already said to Susan; that he knew Bridget removed a lot of her money into some untraceable crypto account, and he also knew that she was planning to do a few other things with her assets, including selling off the land that she'd given to Matt. Adam was unhappy about this, he had a loyalty to Matt, as well as a loyalty to Bridget. He was caught in the middle, so I suggested that in the battle, when Nicholas Stephens was about to throw his spear, he nudged him and let the spear go wild. We knew it wouldn't do any damage, but I had a plan.'

'The plan was that when Nicholas Stephens threw it, you or Susan would stab Bridget.'

'Yes,' Rolf looked back at Susan, who glared at him angrily. 'They know everything, there's no point lying.'

He sighed, took a deep breath, and continued.

'We picked Nicholas because he was new, still getting used to the horse and the style of riding. The problem was, we thought he was a newbie, didn't know how good he was with a lance, as well as a spear. Nobody had told us he was an expert. We assumed it would be classed as an innocent accident.'

'So, what happened on the day?'

'Lunchtime on the Sunday, Nicholas went to throw his spear, Adam knocked him, just as we had agreed, but I wasn't anywhere near Bridget. I'd worked out earlier on that I wouldn't be able to do this, and Susan had offered to use her spear for it. They were all unified, so I swapped my spear with hers, so that when the spear was thrown, she could stab Bridget with it. The idea was to slash her arm, a nasty wound, but a message saying we could get to her whenever we wanted and, if she blamed us, we could point at the spear and Nicholas's initials, and start telling everyone she was mad and paranoid.'

He looked back at his sister.

'I've never asked whether or not it was an accident that you gave a killing blow.'

'It was an accident,' Susan looked back at Declan. 'I didn't mean to kill her. As you said, it was supposed to be a warning. You know, "don't screw around with my life" and all that. But I was above her, and the stabbing downwards... the whole thing...'

Declan looked back at Georgia, now staring at Susan as she faded off, her eyes red and filling with tears.

'When did you find out?'

'Not for a while,' Georgia said. 'Other things happened first.'

'Would those other things be the theft of hundreds of thousands of pounds' worth of antique weaponry from Pennington Hall?' Declan asked, looking back at Rolf. 'Because we know you, Susan and Adam Harris took it.'

Susan sighed and looked back at Declan.

'The old guy wouldn't pay us,' she said. 'He was being a dick. Usually, Matt does this, and he's a lot more level-headed, but, well, we were angry and hyped up on adrenaline.'

'Well, I'm sure you would be,' Declan replied. 'After all, you had just tried to kill someone.'

'It wasn't that,' Rolf said. 'We were going against the group's wishes when we argued. We knew it would come out, and that the group would have settled for the deposit and run off with their tails between their legs. So, we argued and there was a bit of a scuffle, and it got physical. I ... I pushed the old man, knocking him backwards. He didn't fall or anything, but the shock was enough to kick off a heart attack.'

He looked at the grass, his eyes now hooded.

'And in front of us, Lord Crawford-Dunne died.'

'You could have called for an ambulance,' De'Geer growled. 'You could have called for help.'

Rolf nodded, looking at De'Geer as he spoke.

'We could have,' he said. 'But we didn't. We stood there, and we watched him die. Then, realising that we only had a finite amount of time, Susan and I ran back with Adam to get his van. Returning into the drive, we grabbed as much as we could before anybody could say anything, dumped it in the back of the van under some blankets and then returned to the others, told them that the Lord had effectively told us to piss off, wouldn't pay us and had stomped off. They were angry, but still in a state of shock following what had happened to Bridget and we drove out.'

'And then the inquest started.'

'The inquest started,' Susan nodded. 'We didn't know it was the requirement of any unexplained death, and at the time we hadn't realised how it would play out.'

She glared at Georgia now.

'The problem was, Georgia had decided she wanted somebody she trusted to run it. Benedict Dee. He was somebody with an axe to grind against us; we'd been friends years ago, but he'd been kicked out of the group. Georgia thought he was her new best friend, and had petitioned the authorities to use him, while he did the same. He had some contacts in the office taking the case on, and they didn't want anything to do with it, as it looked to be a bit of a minefield.'

She chuckled.

'What Georgia didn't count on, though, was that Benedict had been kicked out of the Dark Ages group by Bridget Farnsworth and Matt Butcher, not us. He had no loyalty to them and we had a pair of recently gained antique pistols that suggested otherwise.'

'You bribed him with pistols to make it an accidental death?'

'Everything was there,' Susan replied. 'We'd swapped spears, so the spear inside Bridget had been Nicholas's. He was accused of manslaughter, but we always knew it wouldn't get to that, we knew it'd be changed to a sad, terrible accident, mainly because Adam held up his hands and said that it was he who accidentally knocked into Nicholas.'

'And Adam did this because Adam was one of the three of you selling the items,' Anjli muttered. 'The last thing he wanted was for anybody to know what had happened that day. It might lead to more questions about Henry Crawford-Dunne.'

'Is this why Nicholas had to die?' Declan asked. 'After all, you thought you'd got away with it for three years.'

Susan slumped back against a chariot.

'Look,' she said, 'I'll admit it. I didn't expect Bridget to be killed. I was angry. And yes, when I rammed my spear into her, it felt good, I won't lie, and not even because Bridget didn't realise I'd even done it, distracted by something else as I drove down. But after that, I knew I couldn't stay with Matt. He went with her to the hospital rather than staying with me.'

'He was her husband.'

'He was divorcing her. He should have left her. We should have been together, not him and her.'

Declan stared sadly at Susan.

'You genuinely believe that,' he whispered.

'Anyway, it was three years ago,' Susan continued, looking back at Georgia. 'Water under the bridge, so I thought. Until this traitorous bitch kicked off.'

Georgia smiled at this.

'You're just angry I played Boudicca after she died,' she said. 'After Susan made a point of breaking up with Matt, he left, going full-time Roman, leaving her all alone with nobody to vouch for her.'

Susan kept her mouth shut.

'Maybe you should have slept with him some more, gained the role before dumping him—' Georgia mocked.

'So, you stole items from the Crawford-Dunne estate,' Anjli interrupted, before a fight could break out. 'You, Rolf, and Adam. You gave Benedict Dee items to look the other way. You thought everything was fine. But what you didn't expect was Nicholas to check into his own case.'

'Aaron Forden had already started his own investigation,' Declan added. 'Did you know he was a member of the Crawford-Dunnes? A distant member, but one, nevertheless. He learned, somehow, you'd taken the items. He worked it out. Realised who had done what. And then went and spoke to Georgia about it.'

Georgia reddened with anger at this.

'Are you about to say I killed—'

'I'm not saying you killed anyone,' Declan interrupted. 'The death of Adam Harris and Benedict Dee looks to be a terrible accident. But you helped, didn't you? Aaron explained what had happened, and you helped him lay the foundations for the duel. You challenged everybody, offering money, knowing that no one would take you up. But Aaron, meanwhile, whispered into the ears of Adam and Benedict, suggesting that *they* should take you up. That they should work together. Gain the money. Defeat you in whatever duel you were looking to do.'

'So they started practising in Benedict's little murder cellar,' Anjli took over. 'The problem was, Benedict had been convinced by Aaron that Adam was going to try to kill him. Adam, meanwhile, had been convinced that *Benedict* was going to kill him. Both had placed musket balls in their own weaponry to end their rival. Both killed each other. Then, an hour later, Aaron arrived and took the bodies, and sent an email. You weren't involved in the deaths of Adam, Harris, and Benedict, but you were happy to see Aaron do this. You were happy to see Aaron gain his revenge on the stolen items of his family.'

'What if I was?'

Declan shrugged.

'That's a question for a higher judge than me,' he said. 'But there's still one more person we need to talk about. Nicholas Stephens.'

Now he turned his attention back to Susan.

'He'd worked out by now that you and Rolf had been the ones to kill Bridget. He wasn't a stupid man. He had a crime wall in his house. He knew you were the killer, and he was going to out you. But you second-guessed him, sending him a USB stick, claiming there was money on it. For you, it was a payoff. For us, we thought it was Georgia, paying for a duel. But it was neither, was it?'

'It had a tracker in it,' Susan admitted. 'It was so we knew exactly where he was. But it was a trust thing, not a death thing.'

'However, when he said he was going to tell the police everything, you decided it was time to remove him,' De'Geer spoke now, as he looked back at the pavilion. 'Nice motor-cycle you have. Shame you didn't have time to find another one.'

'I don't know what you mean,' Susan said. 'Saturday morning I was busy.'

'I know,' De'Geer replied. 'Interestingly, your phone was here and didn't move.'

'You took the bike and removed the registration plates,' Anjli snapped. 'You knew where he was going. You grabbed a lance made of a tree branch and you rammed it through his chest. This, Susan Cowell, was premeditated.'

'As you said, this mysterious bike had no registration plates on it,' Susan replied. 'Therefore, unless you can show proof that it was me, then—'

'We're doing that right now,' De'Geer interrupted, smiling. 'You see on the video, you rest the branch against your cross mount beside the grip. When you stab him, you've risen it away from the bike. But there is a point where the bark of that branch would have rubbed against the leather, chrome, and rubber of your handlebars. If there's residue, we'll find it.'

At this comment, and as any chance of escape evaded her, Susan's face paled.

'It wasn't my idea,' she said. 'Rolf suggested doing it.'

'Now listen—' Rolf said. But as he went to speak, Susan started running, pushing through the other re-enactors, already heading for her bike.

'I've got her,' Anjli said, running after her. Declan spun back to Rolf, to find Rolf already swinging his spear down at him.

'You won't take me!' he shouted, but then stopped as a second spear, grabbed by De'Geer, blocked it in a two-handed staff action.

'I've got him, Guv,' he said, swinging back, catching Rolf around the back of the legs with his makeshift spear quarter-staff. The two men started fighting as Declan stepped back, noticing that Georgia was moving away from the audience.

'I would suggest you don't move,' Declan said. 'We haven't finished.'

SUSAN HAD TO TRY TO FORCE HER WAY THROUGH HER ARMY, most of whom had stopped, and were forcing her back by sheer weight of numbers. Many of these re-enactors had fought beside Bridget, and what they'd just heard, proven or not, was enough to make even the brightest expression turn dark. As she did so, she stumbled and was tackled to the ground by Anjli, forcing her forward into the dirt, arms held behind her.

'Queen Boudicca,' she said. 'You should be lucky I'm doing this. We just saved your life.'

Susan glared back up at her.

'I could have taken Georgia,' she said.

'Really?' Anjli looked back at the crowd in the stands, who were now cheering, having seen something exciting happening. 'No offence, but she'd kick the living shit out of you.'

DE'GEER SPUN HIS STAFF, SWINGING IT UP IN A TWO-HANDED blow to the base of Rolf's jaw. Rolf staggered back; he was more experienced in the fighting, but his armour was smaller, more restrictive, and he couldn't get the range he needed to fight back.

'You might be some really kick-ass Dark Ages re-enactor,' De'Geer snarled as he continued attacking, 'but I've been Little John for my Robin Hood cosplay group for the last four years. And if anybody can beat me with a staff, I'd be impressed.'

Rolf, at this point, had decided to give up fighting and tried to run, knowing now, as the sirens could be heard in the background, that even if he had defeated this mad Viking, he'd still be captured. Turning, he went to escape, but found himself blocked by a line of re-enactors, spears aimed at him.

'You've brought us into disrepute,' the legionnaire who had been standing beside him said. 'You've made us look like murdering fools.'

'Get out of my way!' Rolf shouted. 'I am your general!'

'You're nothing but a scumbag thief and killer,' the legionnaire repeated.

Rolf, realising he was surrounded, finally slumped his shoulders, dropping his spear to the ground.

'You're nicked, Sonny,' De'Geer said with a smile, glancing back at the Romans, who, as one, clamped their fists to their breastplates as a salute to him.

'You know what, Guv?' De'Geer smiled, looking back at Declan now, as the audience around the cricket pitch burst into rapturous applause and cheers. 'I could get used to this!'

EPILOGUE

Following the events of the Boudicca uprising, the rest of the festival seemed to go without a hitch, apart from one section during the Great Fire of London event, where the accelerant being used, turned out to be a little more enthusiastic than people had expected, resulting in a small amount of property damage and a few singed eyebrows and red faces.

As for the fallout from the event, things were quite anticlimactic.

Declan had once more been on the front page, seen standing in the middle of a Roman battle, a flashing police motorcycle next to him. He found it quite embarrassing, but De'Geer, seen in the photo standing heroically beside him, spear in hand, was quite impressed and had asked for copies of the photo from the newspaper.

Declan had also heard, off the record from Anjli, that Esme Cooper had also asked for copies, although why she wanted them he had no idea, or rather, would prefer not to know.

As for the accusations and arrests, they were light

compared to what had happened. Benedict Dee and Adam Harris were on video killing each other, their own paranoia having caused them to load their pistols and prepare to fight. Adam had even worn armour on the off chance that Benedict would try to kill him. Unfortunately, the chest plate he wore was on his front, not his back, and was likely the reason Benedict didn't wait for him to turn.

The only thing that Aaron Forden could be accused of was removing the bodies and placing them in new locations. Although hindering an investigation, which was a crime that could give some serious prison time, Aaron had played the system, explaining simply that he had been confused and in a fugue state, having found them, and having Matt Butcher repeatedly drilling into him that "nothing can besmirch the event." Obviously, Matt Butcher denied this.

Of course, within an hour of Aaron being charged with anything to do with this, an expensive solicitor, paid for by the Crawford-Dunne family appeared, and within a few more hours, Aaron had been released on bail, and any hope of getting him on any kind of hindering charge looked increasingly unlikely.

Declan knew that by the time he got to court, all charges would have miraculously disappeared, likely through some higher-up conversation between Lords and Chiefs of Police. After all, Aaron might have moved the bodies, but he also rediscovered several long forgotten and stolen items of the Crawford-Dunne family, with a good idea of where others could be found. Declan was amused that already Chivalry Fitzwarren had made offers for items he hadn't yet seen, including the now complete set of duelling pistols.

As for Georgia Wingate, she was claiming some kind of post-traumatic stress disorder brought on by a mixture of grief, and the learning of who truly killed the woman she loved. Again, Georgia's defence was quite good, and provided by yet another expensive solicitor, this time, however, at her own expense, paid for probably with a variety of long-held cryptocurrency coins. As far as Georgia was concerned, grief and anger, and more than a little whisky, had been to blame for her reckless bet about beating people in a duel, something she never expected to continue with. She didn't know Aaron would have convinced Adam Harris and Benedict Dee to take on such a bet, nor was she aware that once they took this, they would then try to kill each other. All she was really guilty of was deciding to and almost attempting to murder Susan Cowell, but this again was quelled on two aspects. The first, that Susan was now accused of murdering Bridget Farnsworth, which altered the narrative, and second, that Declan had stopped this happening in the first place when he arrived in the middle of a battlefield on the back of a flashing motorcycle.

As far as the case was concerned, Georgia had stepped down from playing Boudicca, had accidentally picked up Rolf's spear, and was likely going to return it at the end of the event. Declan knew that Georgia Wingate could return to her normal life; in fact, she'd be a little happier knowing that her late girlfriend's murderer was now being punished for the act.

Unfortunately, the unsung hero here was Nicholas Stephens, whose work in finding out the truth of a terrible accident three years earlier may have caused his death, but had unravelled everything following it.

Susan Cowell and Rolf, her brother, were both arrested and charged as accessories to the theft of Pennington Hall's weaponry, a horde of stolen items that was easily in the hundreds of thousands of pounds, possibly even millions if you listened to Chivalry Fitzwarren. But with the confessions on the battlefield, and that both siblings seemed confident in throwing each other under the bus once they were arrested, Declan now knew that during the argument with Henry Crawford-Dunne, it was Rolf's violent actions pushing him that had caused the heart attack, while Susan had stood to the side convincing Adam Harris to help them steal the items.

It had also been *Susan,* passing the dandy duellist priceless antiques to Benedict Dee, who had convinced him to side with them.

Susan, who had arranged for the murder of Bridget; she had known there was nothing to gain from the will and had decided that the only way that Matt could keep the landholding would be through life insurance. This might be contested, but this had been a gift. Only if the will had stated that he no longer owned such a thing could they have changed this.

Susan, who'd convinced Rolf to swap the spear.

Susan, who'd convinced Adam Harris to nudge Stephen. He hadn't known why at the time. He thought it was purely to anger him. Or maybe he did know. Nobody could answer that, without a seance, as Adam Harris and Nicholas Stephens were both dead.

Doctor Marcos had examined the motorcycle and found bark that matched the tree branch that had skewered Nicholas Stephens, and with a burner phone discovered within her belongings that matched the text message conversation which Stephens had had before his death, Susan was pretty much damned as the murderer.

She'd also arranged the tracking USB that had been

placed on him, sent by courier, purely so they could keep an eye on him. She hadn't been aware that he was working with DCI Warren. She wasn't aware he was even looking to wear a wire and record her. All she knew, is that *he* knew, and that meant he had to be stopped.

It was *always* Susan. Whether Rolf was involved in this was a matter for the courts. Either way, the pair of them would not be re-enacting for a very long time.

Georgia Wingate wouldn't be re-enacting either.

In the end, she had decided that this was her last time standing with Boudicca and the Iceni, and Declan understood why such a thing would be so traumatic for her. Finally, she had closure for the death of Bridget.

Of everybody brought in, and apart from the now dead Nicolas, Matt Butcher was the only person who was blameless. Even though he had had the affair, the only thing that he could be charged with was bad judgement by dating and sleeping with Susan Cowell. He hadn't been aware, from what they could work out, of the murder. He hadn't been there when the theft had happened. And he had actively told both Benedict and Adam not to take the bet when Georgia had given the drunken challenge. He was released the following morning, clear of all charges, and by the end of the day was once more running the gladiator arena in Finsbury Circus for the rest of the festival. He had told Declan that he had nothing else now. Even the landholding that he had, his woodland retreat, would likely now be taken from him in the upcoming court case, as there was every chance that Susan's actions in murdering his wife could be seen as suggested by Butcher.

Declan felt sorry for Butcher. His relationship had been unhappy, as evidenced because both people in it had moved on. But at the same time, Declan was aware that Butcher had buried his head in the sand for too long.

Maybe some time without the distractions would do him good.

WITH THE FESTIVAL NOW ENDING, DECLAN AND THE OTHERS turned to more important matters, in particular, Monroe's upcoming wedding. It seemed that somebody high up in Westminster had deemed it proper to annul the wedding, by going to the Archbishop of Canterbury himself and pretty much demanding it.

Declan was amused by this. He didn't know if Emilia Wintergreen had begged the favour of Charles Baker, or whether Baker himself had done this purely to ensure that Monroe owed him in the future; after all, next year was an election year and there was every chance that Charles Baker would need as many friends as he could get. With the wedding now rearranged for a week's time, they had agreed to hold one more set of stag and hen nights, although Doctor Marcos had been, by unanimous decision, banned from having any lecture series as part of it.

And so, Declan found himself once more in a bar with a variety of DCIs, DIs, detective superintendents, gangland bosses, and MPs, among others, wishing Monroe a pleasant wedding.

The only problem was that someone was missing.

Monroe's best man, Derek Sutton, hadn't appeared.

Monroe assumed that Derek had returned to Scotland. Or, more worryingly, that Derek had been arrested. That was more plausible, but there was no information on *Holmes2* to suggest such a thing. Derek himself had constantly claimed he was on the straight and narrow. Though, they still had a week before the wedding itself, so there was plenty of time for Derek Sutton to come out of whatever drunken stupor he was in and perform his best man's duties.

Declan smiled as he turned to Anjli, standing there beside him in a fedora hat and fake moustache.

'Are you glad you were invited this time?' he asked.

Anjli grinned.

'I've learnt more secrets from several DCIs than I've ever had,' she said. 'Is this what men always do when they hang out together? You're worse gossips than the women.'

'What happens in man club stays in man club,' Declan shrugged. 'Unless you're wearing a fake moustache and a hat, of course.'

Anjli squeezed his arm.

'At what point can we leave without causing a problem?' she asked.

Declan looked at her. She winked at him.

'I quite like wearing the suit,' she smiled.

'Maybe we should have an Irish goodbye,' Declan said, nodding towards the door and grabbing his jacket as he did so. And with that, the two of them left, sliding out of the back door of the pub, heading back to Hurley and their bed.

The moment didn't last long, though, as they'd only reached the door to the street when Declan received a text.

Looking down at it, he felt the ground disappear from under him.

From: Tom Marlowe

You were right. The DNA doesn't match. Watch your back.

Declan showed the text to Anjli and looked around the London street, feeling as if he was being watched.

Karl Schnitter, the Red Reaper, *was* alive. Declan had been right when he found the secret hideaway and the potentially missing items in Hurley.

But what that meant for Declan, he had no idea.

DEREK SUTTON HADN'T MISSED THE STAG NIGHT BECAUSE HE was drunk, nor had he missed it because he was arrested. Derek Sutton missed it because he was currently tied to a chair in the basement of what looked to be an old Victorian house.

The figure standing in front of him, tall, probably male, and wearing a mask to hide their identity, stood watching him.

'I don't know what this is about,' Derek said. 'And usually, someone like you doing this to me, I would tear your face off. But you're wearing a freaky mask, and that makes me think you're not one of the usual suspects. So how about you tell me what I've done here, we sort this out and we move on, yeah?'

The masked figure stared at him, idly flicking what looked to be a playing card, finger to finger. They leant closer and through the mask, Derek could almost smell the breath as they breathed in.

'You have been guilty of many things,' they said, the voice altered by some kind of voice changer, making a mixture of both male and female. 'You did time for something that wasn't yours and you gained money for it. But we both know that you are guilty. And unfortunately, this means that you must be punished.'

They reached into their pocket and pulled out a coin, rolling it over their fingers, staring down at Derek.

'You know what this is?' they asked, not waiting for an answer as they explained. 'This is a solid silver East-German Mark.' They twirled it in their fingers. 'See? A number one is on this side, that is heads, while on the other side is a compass and a hammer, tails. I have had this for many years now. I lost it, but it always comes back.'

'Aye? It's a nice coin,' Derek frowned. This felt familiar, like he knew the man. 'So what's your deal, then? Maybe we could discuss it, like?'

'They thought I wouldn't be back,' the figure said. 'They thought I couldn't reappear. Lost. Believed dead. But I am back, Mister Sutton. I'm back to fulfil a debt. To explain to Declan Walsh and his friends at the Last Chance Saloon that there is no escape from the Reaper.'

They placed the playing card down and with a lurch of horror, Derek Sutton realised it was not a playing card but a joker, specially made with the figure in the middle of a red-robed man holding a scythe.

An *Ampelmann*.

'I won't kill youmyself,' the figure, now revealed to be the Red Reaper said soothingly. 'For that would be murder. You will do it for me, for that is the way it has always been – and if you don't, your friends, your family, your daughter in Scotland, they will all die painfully and slowly, as I skin them alive.'

The Red Reaper held up the coin.

'This used to be a fake,' they said. 'A cheater's coin. One that was double-sided. No way for you to win.'

The Red Reaper flipped it over to show that this was indeed a legitimate East German mark.

'But I believe differently now,' they said. 'As my eyes have been opened. And so, Mister Sutton, I will flip it. If it lands heads, I will take a very sharp blade and slash my wrists open, right here, in front of you. If it shows tails, however, you will take the blade and do the same, okay?'

'No, that ain't okay,' Derek said. 'I haven't done anything to you—'

'But your friends have,' the Red Reaper cooed gently. 'A new game then. Heads, I send a message to them. Tails, you send the message. Do you understand?'

'What's the message?'

'Same as it always is, Mister Sutton, pain and death.'

'Fine, just flip your goddamn coin, you lunatic,' Derek said. 'I ain't scared of nobody.'

'Good,' the Red Reaper replied, flicking the coin into the air, watching it lazily flip before landing on the back of their hand.

'Let's play a game.'

DCI Walsh and the team of the *Last Chance Saloon* will return in their next thriller

Order Now at Amazon:

www.mybook.to/harvestforthereaper

ACKNOWLEDGEMENTS

When you write a series of books, you find that there are a ton of people out there who help you, sometimes without even realising, and so I wanted to say thanks.

There are people I need to thank, and they know who they are, including my brother Chris Lee, Jacqueline Beard MBE, who has copyedited all my books since the very beginning, and editor Sian Phillips, all of whom have made my books way better than they have every right to be.

Also, I couldn't have done this without my growing army of ARC and beta readers, who not only show me where I falter, but also raise awareness of me in the social media world, ensuring that other people learn of my books.

But mainly, I tip my hat and thank you. *The reader.* Who once took a chance on an unknown author in a pile of Kindle books, and thought you'd give them a go, and who has carried on this far with them, as well as the spin off books I now release.

I write Declan Walsh for you. He (and his team) solves crimes for you. And with luck, he'll keep on solving them for a very long time.

Jack Gatland / Tony Lee,
London, November, 2023

ABOUT THE AUTHOR

Jack Gatland is the pen name of *#1 New York Times Bestselling Author* Tony Lee, who has been writing in all media for thirty-five years, including comics, graphic novels, middle grade books, audio drama, TV and film for *DC Comics, Marvel, BBC, ITV, Random House, Penguin USA, Hachette* and a ton of other publishers and broadcasters.

These have included licences such as *Doctor Who, Spider Man, X-Men, Star Trek, Battlestar Galactica, MacGyver,* BBC's *Doctors, Wallace and Gromit* and *Shrek*, as well as work created with musicians such as *Ozzy Osbourne, Joe Satriani, Beartooth, Pantera, Megadeth, Iron Maiden* and *Bruce Dickinson.*

As Tony, he's toured the world talking to reluctant readers with his 'Change The Channel' school tours, and lectures on screenwriting, story craft and comic scripting for *Raindance* in London and *20Books* globally.

An introvert West Londoner by heart, he lives with his wife Tracy and dog Fosco, just outside London.

Locations In The Book

The locations and items I use in my books are real, if altered slightly for dramatic intent. However this time, many of the locations are completely fictitious, meaning we can't really look into their history, apart from...

The London Wall does indeed still exist in parts throughout London, and the tour that starts through Moorgate is pretty accurate, with the pub, Livery hall and ruined gatehouse all in the correct locations. You can also find pieces of the wall around Tower Hill, and at the back of the car park of the Leonardo Hotel, on Cooper's Row.

Finsbury Circus Gardens does exist, but to my knowledge has never been a gladiator arena, although the line about Guildhall is correct - if you visit their art gallery and go downstairs, you can actually see a basement space they've created to show the Roman ruins of the amphitheatre they found while rebuilding.

Finsbury Circus Gardens is the largest public open space in the Square Mile. A Grade II listed garden, it's all that remains of Moor Fields, London's first public park, dating from 1607. The present garden was originally laid out in 1815 to a design by George Dance the Younger. It's well known for its mature London plane trees and fine Japanese Pagoda tree - the only one in the City.

Pickering Place, in Mayfair exists; the tiny courtyard has a wealth of history attached to it. Not only was it home to the Texan Republic's embassy until Texas joined the United

States in 1845, it is also the last place in London where a duel was fought. The courtyard is the covered remains of a garden that existed when houses were first built here in the mid-1660s when the Earl of St Albans secured a lease from King Charles II.

In 1731, some of the nearby houses and tenements were demolished, and the square was named Pickering Court, after William Pickering – a coffee merchant and son-in-law of Widow Bourne, founder of Berry Bros & Rudd Ltd wine merchants, whose shop still operates on the premises, and who are said to be the oldest wine merchants in London.

The Lyttelton Arms Pub in Camden exists. Once the **The Southampton Arms**, it was renamed in tribute to jazz trumpeter and 'I'm Sorry I Haven't A Clue' radio host Humphrey Lyttelton. The Radio Four show conferred cult status on Mornington Crescent, the tube station across the road, with its game of the same name, defined only by its lack of any rules.

In it's Southampton Arms incarnation, it was one of the centres of conflicts between the gangs who tried to control race course betting, including the Clerkenwell Sabini Brothers and Camden's George Sage.

The following report from the St. Pancras Gazette on the 6th of October 1922 illustrates one of the incidents:

"*RACING MEN'S FEUDS – At Marylebone on Tuesday, Alfred White, Joseph Sabini, George West, Simon Nyberg, Paul Boffa, and Thomas Mack made their eighth appearance on the charges of shooting George Sage and Frederick Gilbert with intent to murder, at Mornington-crescent, Camden Town, on August 19, having loaded revolvers on their possession with intent to endanger life, and riotously assembling.*

Helen Sage, wife of one of the prosecutors, said she was talking to her husband outside the Southampton Arms at Camden Town when several taxicabs drove up and a number of men alighted. She then heard a shot, but could not say who fired, as it was dark. The witness admitted that she told the police that West and White fired the shots, but now declared that this statement was untrue."

Finally, **Pennington Hall** never existed, but was based loosely on a variation of Stately Homes and Manors in England. I took the name from *"Pennington's,"* a menswear shop I worked as a Saturday assistant in my teens, during the eighties.

If you're interested in seeing what the *real* locations look like, I post 'behind the scenes' location images on my Instagram feed. This will continue through all the books, after leaving a suitable amount of time to avoid spoilers, and I suggest you follow it.

In fact, feel free to follow me on all my social media by clicking on the links below. Over time these can be places where we can engage, discuss Declan and put the world to rights.

www.jackgatland.com
www.hoodemanmedia.com

Visit Jack's Reader's Group Page
(Mainly for fans to discuss his books):
https://www.facebook.com/groups/jackgatland

Subscribe to Jack's Readers List:
https://bit.ly/jackgatlandVIP

www.facebook.com/jackgatlandbooks
www.twitter.com/jackgatlandbook
ww.instagram.com/jackgatland

Want more books by Jack Gatland? Turn the page...

THE THEFT OF A **PRICELESS** PAINTING...
A GANGSTER WITH A **CRIPPLING DEBT**...
A **BODY COUNT** RISING BY THE HOUR...

AND ELLIE RECKLESS IS CAUGHT IN THE MIDDLE.

JACK GATLAND

PAINT
— THE —
DEAD

A 'COP FOR CRIMINALS' ELLIE RECKLESS NOVEL

A NEW PROCEDURAL CRIME SERIES WITH
A TWIST - FROM THE CREATOR OF THE
BESTSELLING 'DI DECLAN WALSH' SERIES

AVAILABLE ON AMAZON / KINDLE UNLIMITED

THEY TRIED TO KILL HIM...
NOW HE'S OUT FOR **REVENGE.**

NEW YORK TIMES #1 BESTSELLER **TONY LEE** WRITING AS

JACK GATLAND

THE MURDER OF AN **MI5 AGENT**...
A BURNED SPY **ON THE RUN** FROM HIS OWN PEOPLE...
AN ENEMY OUT TO **STOP HIM** AT ANY COST...
AND A **PRESIDENT** ABOUT TO BE **ASSASSINATED**...

SLEEPING SOLDIERS

A **TOM MARLOWE** THRILLER

BOOK 1 IN A NEW SERIES OF THRILLERS IN THE STYLE OF
JASON BOURNE, JOHN MILTON OR **BURN NOTICE,** AND
SPINNING OUT OF THE **DECLAN WALSH** SERIES OF BOOKS

AVAILABLE ON AMAZON / KINDLE UNLIMITED

EIGHT PEOPLE. EIGHT SECRETS.
ONE SNIPER.

THE
B⊕ARD
ROOM

HOW FAR WOULD YOU GO TO GAIN JUSTICE?

"★★★★★ AN EXCELLENT 'INDIANA JONES' STYLE FAST PACED
CHARGE AROUND ENGLAND THAT WAS RIVETING AND CAPTIVATING."

"★★★★★ AN ACTION-PACKED YARN... I REALLY ENJOYED
THIS AND LOOK FORWARD TO THE NEXT BOOK IN THE SERIES."

JACK GATLAND
THE
LIONHEART
CURSE

HUNT THE GREATEST TREASURES
PAY THE GREATEST PRICE

BOOK 1 IN A NEW SERIES OF ADVENTURES
IN THE STYLE OF 'THE DA VINCI CODE'
FROM THE CREATOR OF DECLAN WALSH

AVAILABLE ON AMAZON / KINDLEUNLIMITED

Printed in Great Britain
by Amazon